LEGEND OF A MUSICAL CITY

LEGEND
OF A
MUSICAL CITY

MAX GRAF

PHILOSOPHICAL LIBRARY
New York

Printed in the United States of America
By F. Hubner & Co., Inc., Printers
New York, N. Y.

13872

TO POLLY

TABLE OF CONTENTS

LEGEND OF A MUSICAL CITY

1

The Musical Centre of the World

The March into Vienna

On March 13, 1938, the soldiers of the German Reich, in full panoply of war, marched into peaceful Vienna. Through its ancient streets pounded the tread of infantry and the heavy clanking of cannon, tanks and Panzer trucks. The eyes of the young soldiers, beneath their steel helmet brims, stared straight ahead. They turned neither right nor left; neither toward the palaces nor the old baroque churches, nor upward toward the golden spire of St. Stephen's Cathedral. Gazing into the distance, the eyes of these marching men were cold, unemotional and earnest, and in their depths lay war.

Aeroplanes cruised over houses, towers and church domes like grey birds of prey. Few Viennese were in the streets. Inside the houses, families were just sitting down to supper. Through closed windows, the unified sound of marching feet and clanging noise penetrated the rooms, chilling the hearts of all who heard with gloom and apprehension. Hours passed before the march of the German soldiers finally ceased, and the drone of aeroplanes persisted far into the night.

In the streets, no rejoicing greeted the victorious army. Vienna, which usually took such great delight in festive celebrations, was silent. There were no smiling strollers to be seen, no lovers embracing in shadowy doorways or sitting on the benches of the parks and promenades. This was no time for love. And from the taverns came no revelers, faces flushed with wine, singing songs of Vienna and its lovely women. The night seemed not only darker, but more oppressive.

In that hour, when a brutal hand grasped the city by the scruff of its neck, there was more involved than war. All European culture was threatened. In Vienna, which found itself transformed overnight into a typical German "big town," all the independent spirit, the joy of living, the freedom, the natural intelligence, were harshly forced under the yoke; while a national fanaticism, imported from Germany, murderously stormed through this city which had never been fanatical, but always humane, gay and friendly. What could Vienna mean to the world without its famous joy of living, which had survived so many troublous times, without its culture, nourished from so many different sources, without its sensuality—Vienna, the "Falstaff of German cities," as it was once termed by one of its ironic poets? A legendary city of pleasure, it was quickly being transformed into a prison like those erected throughout Europe in the wake of soldiers in field grey uniforms. What could it mean for the world which loved this city as one loves a beautiful, smiling woman?

For the world at large, Vienna was, above all, a city of music, or better, *the* city of music; in fact, the only city in the world which would have been unthinkable without music. One could no more imagine Vienna without it than Rome without St. Peter's and the Vatican, Paris without its boulevards, or New York without Wall Street and skyscrapers. Vienna was the city where great composers had lived. It was the city of Haydn, Mozart, Beethoven and Schubert; of Brahms and Bruckner, Gustav Mahler and Arnold Schoenberg. From it had emanated the Strauss waltzes which flowed around the

4

world, everywhere preaching the gospel of life's enjoyment in three-quarter time. From Vienna, too, came the operettas of Lehar, Oscar Strauss and Fall. The city was as full of music as a vineyard with grapes. Not only concert halls and theatres vibrated with sound, but the air itself. As Paris was the city of the mind, Rome the center of the Catholic world, London the capital of the greatest empire of modern times, so was Vienna the acknowledged music capital of the world. Musicians from all corners of the globe came there to study. Virtuosi came, too, because success in Vienna was a prerequisite of being "world-famous." The Vienna State Opera, the Vienna Philharmonic Orchestra, the Vienna Conservatory were internationally recognized. Every tourist visited the houses where the great classics had lived just as, in Rome, he would visit St. Peter's and Michael Angelo's statue of Moses. Every musician who came to Vienna visited the graves of the classic musicians in the same spirit as a pious Catholic makes a pilgrimage to the tombs of the saints in Rome. Everything of greatness and of value which had been accomplished in Vienna—the famous medical school, the Art Academy, the new living quarters for workers—was dwarfed beside its place in music.

In the course of centuries, Vienna had become a kind of fairy-tale city. And, as in all fairy-tales, life there was easier, more brilliant and more exciting than anywhere else. Everywhere there was song and sound. The fairy-tale omits to say, of course, that there, as in all modern metropolises, poverty and misery stalked through the streets, in its outskirts, and that, despite the fabled gaiety, hard and earnest work was done. The tale does not speak of the political battles which took place there, nor of the colossal rise of the workingman to political rights, to education, culture, and finally, to political might. According to the saga of Vienna, there was only loving, dancing, singing, drinking and music-making. This legend has been propagated primarily by the motion picture which, for the masses of our time, is the biggest story-teller of them all. Everyone has seen films whose scenes were laid in Vienna. In such pictures, certain connoisseurs of mass taste depicted the fairy-tale Vienna. There were always poor but decent girls who fell in love with dashing officers, nobles and grand dukes. Lovers sat in Prater inns under chestnut trees, and everywhere there was music. Orchestras played waltzes, peasants sang Viennese songs. There were kisses and embraces during the music. Although this type of Viennese film belongs to the most mendacious products of fabrication, it is none the less characteristic that in every case Vienna and music are inseparable.

On that sad March day which was the beginning of a great world catastrophe, the city of music was struck dumb. As in Haydn's "Farewell" Symphony, the musicians packed up their music and their instruments, and the candles burned down in the music stands. A great epoch of music came to an end on this day.

Ten generations had labored at the development of Vienna into a great music capital. The long process had begun at the end of the 17th century, when Vienna had achieved the rank of a European city noted for music. From that time on, the graph of its development rose higher and higher in an unbroken ascent. Its peak was reached at the time when the classic musicians lived in Vienna, and on this marvelous construction, the powerful towers of the Haydn symphony, the Mozart Opera, the Beethoven Music of Humanity, and the Schubert song stood in all their glory. Then the graph descends to points which are, nevertheless, still high and strong—Brahms and Bruckner. Finally came the great demolisher of the architecture of classic music, Arnold Schoenberg. There ended a unique and great development such as the world had seen only twice before: first, when Greek art rose to the brilliance of the Periclean Age, to Phidias, to the tragic poets, to Plato, Aristotle, to the divine laughter of Aristophanes, and to the mighty marble pillars which looked down from the Acropolis to the blue sea. And a second time, when the painting of the Renaissance had risen to Raphael, Michael Angelo and Titian. Vienna's development was a similar one, showing a steady growth of artistic fantasy, an increasingly large creative scope, the work of generations, a continuously richer unfolding of the powers of intellect. It was like a symphony, which flowed on to more and more powerful crescendos, to magnificent climaxes, and then, in 1938, died away with a dreary and mournful sound.

For almost three centuries there was great music in Vienna. While Venice, Rome, Naples, Paris, Dresden, Munich, Leipzig and Berlin existed simultaneously as musical centers, they could offer no comparison in the extent and length of their development. In their cases, the superb picture of a clear-cut epoch of history to be seen in Vienna, was lacking, as well as the close bond between music and life which characterized the city. Music had traversed its length and breadth; the Emperor's castle, the nobles' palaces, the townspeople's houses, the city proper and the suburbs, the squares and gardens, the

7

churches, and the winehouses on the fringe of the Vienna woods. Each new generation which sprang up in Vienna wished to outdo the old one which had just been lowered into the grave, in the cultivation of music. Children were brought up as musicians and music lovers. Thus it was possible that even the rather foolish and superficial aristocrats of the 18th century comprised a most sensitive musical public who understood and loved Haydn, Mozart, and even Beethoven. One of the most stupid rulers of Austria, Francis I, used to sit, on summer evenings, in his castle on the Danube, playing violin in a string quartet. In the period of the most narrow-minded reaction after the Napoleonic Wars, during which the intellectual life of Vienna was suppressed and the greatest Austrian poet, Grillparzer, locked his finest works in his desk because he did not wish them to undergo police censoring, the elderly Beethoven, Schubert, Lanner and Strauss the Father, uninhibited by censor or police, kept on writing, and the city was full of music. Here music was not taken as occasional entertainment. It belonged to the people, like the homes in which they lived and died, like the clothes they wore, like the people whom they loved, and like the happy and unhappy hours they experienced.

Upon the German occupation, all this came to a dead end, just as did the chatter at the cafés on the Parisian boulevards, the gossip in the Brussels restaurants, the pilgrimages to Rome, the sensuous gypsy music in Budapest, the elegant frivolity in Warsaw, a short time later. Europe was becoming a battleground, a police barracks and a dreary prison. Disturbances raged everywhere. Death rained out of the air. A new age, a new social order, a new world history were being born amid a thousand pains, cries of anguish and streams of blood. The artistic construction of Viennese musical life was shattered like the other priceless treasures which belonged to the greatness of European culture. An old and noble epoch of Vienna's music became a pile of débris.

As a world music capital, Vienna was an artistic masterpiece. How many elements had to be assembled before such a city stood, and had grown into music! The people who lived in Vienna, the landscape surrounding it, the history which unrolled there, the social order of its society—all these factors combined to make it what it was. The city's geographical position and the temperament of its population had their part in this development, from the baroque period of pompous clothes, wavy perruques and luxurious display until the modern times of electric street-lighting and the automobile, which brought this combination of nature and history to a completion. The inherent force which guided Vienna to its unique musical destiny was that which we call talent or genius. And during three hundred years this talent was equally original, equally strong and equally creative. When one considers the comparative brevity of the Elizabethan Age in England, one comprehends the extent of Vienna's creative talent which produced great music of all kinds for such a long time without becoming exhausted.

It required three centuries to make Vienna a musical city. One single day sufficed to destroy this historical edifice.

Houses of Music

As from the pages of an old chronicle, from its buildings one can read the history which shaped Vienna into a great musical city. Although it was since the beginning of the second half of the 19th century that Vienna developed into a modern city, there are still parts of it which either have not changed at all, or changed only unessentially. Right next to fashionable streets with modern houses and the noisy traffic of the new era, there are silent old streets which are so narrow that they are dark and shadowy. Many of these streets, where houses dating from the middle ages still stand, are very crooked. The old houses have low doors, and small, lightless courtyards. There are palaces whose pillars support balconies and mythological figures carved out of sandstone, over the heavy cornices. Through these same dim alleys went Haydn, Mozart and Beethoven, and at night when all is still, one imagines he can still hear their echoing steps.

Thus the past is vividly alive in Vienna. Its musical history is bound to the present and does not lie dead in books. Walking through these streets, one realizes that here dwell contemporary musicians who are grandsons of the classical musicians of old.

Starting a musical stroll at St. Stephen's Cathedral, from whose open "Giant Door" comes the sound of the old organ, one remembers, perhaps that in its choir Haydn and Schubert sang as boys; and that on a stormy winter's day, at the south door, Mozart's shabby coffin was blessed. I saw Anton Bruckner seated at the organ there, his short legs treading the pedal. On the manual, his bony fingers improvised variations on the Austrian national hymn, and his clear-cut, patriarchal face shone when the sound of the organ streamed forth, growing in strength, finally rising to a brilliant Gloria. Ever since the 16th century, when the famous Paul Hoffheymer played his Te Deum on the organ while Emperor Maximilian knelt praying, great musicians were at home in St. Stephen's.

A few steps from the cathedral, at the head of a narrow, dark street stands a house from the time of Charles VI, where Mozart composed the music for "The Marriage of Figaro," and not far away is the "Deutsches Haus" where he lived when he came to Vienna as a member of the suite of the Archbishop of Salzburg. In this massive building, Mozart sat at the servants' table with the Archbishop's lackeys, cook and baker. Here he came for orders from his strict master as to in what noble's palace he was to play piano. Here, too, the Archbishop's chamberlain, Count Arco, showed him the door with a kick, when madly in love and furious, he requested his release from service. Through the narrow Wollzeile ("Wool Row"), which runs eastward from St. Stephen's, Mozart's coffin was carried to St. Mark's cemetery. Neither his ailing wife nor his friends followed his coffin which was hurriedly borne to the cemetery and, during a snowstorm, lowered into a mass grave, where it disappeared. Also, the house where, with the pallid hand of a dying man, Mozart wrote the score of his "Requiem" and died, still stands in a street which time has scarcely changed. A "Haydn House" is in the neighborhood. Here Haydn, already old, composed the pious prayer of the Austrian National Hymn.

Not far from the cathedral is a little square where the bustle of the city traffic never penetrates. Here all is as still and peaceful as on an isolated island. Here is old Vienna, the Vienna of the 18th century, preserved as if through enchantment. Three buildings enclose the square. One is a baroque church from the time of the Thirty Years' War, in magnificent Jesuit style. From the roof, colored frescoes gleam. High red porphyry pillars frame the chapels, and marble statues of the saints adorn the altars. The second house is a low, broad one which, at one time, was a Jesuit cloister. The silent corridors are vaulted, and one's step echoes on the stair. In this building, Franz Schubert spent four years as a young student in the City School. Here the boy with the round Viennese face and blond hair played violin in the student orchestra. Here, too, he wrote down his first compositions. At that time, the clear laughter of boys rang out in the dusky halls, and on the stairs, Schubert and his friends used to play hide-and-seek. The third house was built during the reign of Empress Maria Theresia as a university. In it is a state-room with frescoes by an Italian painter, illuminated by concealed lights, and there, on the 27th of March, 1808, occurred the performance of Haydn's "Creation" at which the old composer made his last public appearance. The carriage of Prince Esterhazy brought him to the building. The Rector of the University and several musicians, Beethoven among them, assisted the old gentleman from the carriage. Trumpets and trombones sounded a fanfare as Haydn was escorted to the concert hall, and the ladies of the aristocracy wrapped him in their shawls so that he would not feel cold. After the first half of the concert,

12

the composer, who was deeply moved by his work and the premonition of his death, was again taken to the carriage. Only a few years after, in the same hall, a no less famous Beethoven concert took place, when his Seventh Symphony and his musical battle picture, "Wellington's Victory," were played for the first time. The most prominent musicians in Vienna played in the orchestra. Court Conductor Salieri beat the time for the cannonade, Hummel played the timpani, young Meyerbeer, Spohr, Mayseder, Dragonetti, Moscheles, Romberg sat at the music stands. At the piano was the deaf composer, shouting without being able to hear, springing up at the fortissimi, bending low during the soft passages, and shaking his leonine grey head. That was on the 8th and 12th of December, 1813. Thirty-five years later in the same room, fiery students made freedom speeches, harbingers of the Vienna Revolution of 1848. Across the University Square stormed the Viennese youth, wearing black, red and gold bands across their chest, crying "Hoch!" for freedom. Then for another hundred years all was quiet in the old square where time seemed to stand still.

If one returns again to the noisy, traffic-cluttered neighborhood of St. Stephen's, and follows the stream of promenaders who chatter, laugh and flirt along the Graben, one passes the house where Mozart composed "The Abduction from the Seraglio"—music of springtime and a first great love. Nearby is a quiet street of nobles' palaces. The largest of these, massive and broad, is that of the Esterhazy princes. When Haydn came from Eisenstadt as conductor for this wealthy noble family, he lived here. At that time he wore the uniform of a house-servant of the Prince—a light blue frock-coat with

13

silver lace and buttons, white neck-band, blue vest, white stockings, dagger, wig and buckled shoes. At the palace door Prince Esterhazy's soldiers kept watch, and Haydn used to doff his three-cornered hat when he passed an officer. Then from his pocket he would pull the silver snuff box the Prince had given him, take a pinch, and think of the theme for a new string quartet which had just occurred to him.

Palaces of other nobles are nearby, because this is the vicinity of the Imperial Castle, and the aristocracy built their own dwellings around it, with heavy doors, broad steps, decorative pieces and frescoes, with forged iron lanterns hanging in entrances broad enough to admit great, gold-ornamented carriages. The Palace of Prince Lobkowitz, the rich Bohemian nobleman, contained a magnificent music salon. High pilasters of grey marble supported a ceiling of colored paintings. Here, in 1807, Beethoven gave two concerts, the first presenting the Fourth Symphony, the G Major Piano Concerto and the Coriolanus Overture; the second including his first three symphonies, and arias from his opera, "Fidelio." The aristocratic audience sat on richly embroidered chairs, while lackeys stood against the marble walls holding candles.

Before arriving at the square in front of the Imperial Palace, one passes a stately town house which attracts the eye because of its air of quiet distinction. Next to the grey house is a church, on whose roof stands a statue of St. Michael with drawn sword. Here the courtiers of the Emperor lie buried. In an attic of the town house Haydn lived, above the apartment of the court-poet, Metastasio. Metastasio permitted the young musician to instruct his ten-year-old protegée, Marianne Martinez, in piano. In return for this privilege, Haydn was

14

allowed to clean the poet's boots and clothes.

From his attic room, Haydn could see the Imperial Palace and the little theatre which snuggled against it like a baby chicken at the breast of a mother hen. Into this theatre, Gluck used to go, when he was conductor there—very dignified, wearing embroidered silk clothes, sword at his side, and a costly walking stick in his hand. Here his "Orpheus" was performed for the first time, as well as his "Alceste," which latter work the Viennese found a sad and boring "Requiem." Mozart's "Abduction from the Seraglio," the "Marriage of Figaro" and "Cosi fan Tutte" also had their premières in this theatre.

On fast days and days of mourning decreed by the Catholic Church, the pious Hapsburgs permitted no operas to be given in the theatre. On such days the emperors prayed in the court chapel, and on Maundy Thursdays, they washed the feet of twelve poor men; while on Good Fridays they fasted. The only theatrical events allowed on such occasions were performances in the court theatre, but in the pauses between two parts of an oratorio, virtuosi were heard. In 1798, Haydn conducted his new military symphony in this theatre. Time and time again Mozart sat there at the piano, and he gave most of his subscription concerts there. Between the two sections of a Dittersdorf oratorio, he played a new piano concerto (1783) with cadenzas between themes in which his whole heart sang out. Emperor Josef II often came to his box on the left side of the stage and, as connoisseur, observed the fingers of the slight, pale Mozart tenderly flying over the keys. Beethoven, too, played here. During the intermission of an Italian oratorio, he played his B Major Piano

Concerto in 1795. He played it once more in the same year when Mozart's widow sponsored a performance of her husband's opera "Titus"; and in the intermission, he played Mozart's D minor Piano Concerto, whose elegiac tenderness he loved especially. Where in the world was there a theatre like this, where Gluck, Haydn, Mozart and Beethoven passed regularly in and out?

When I went to high school in Vienna, this theatre, replete with so much glory, was still standing. At that time, it was the most famous theatre in the world, with which only the Comédie Française in Paris could compare in splendor and tradition. Every evening, the greatest German actors played before the nobility and the wealthy citizens of Vienna in the small hall. Everyone present knew everyone else, and Emperor Franz Josef, who sat in the same box where Empress Maria Theresia and Josef II had sat before him, looked down over the society of his residence-city. At this theatre, Franz Josef used to call for his friend of long years' standing—the actress Katherina Schratt, whose Viennese laughter rippled through the comedies like silver bells. Here, too, it was that Crown Prince Rudolph met the dark-eyed Maria Vecera, with whom he went to his death.

We young people used to stand in the gallery, kept in order by an ancient Sergeant, and clap till our hands were sore when Sonnenthal recited the Ring parable with the pathos of a rabbi, when Wolter emitted her famous tragic scream, or Baumeister, strong and simple, played his Judge of Zalamea and the entire audience wept. For us, it was a deep personal grief when the little theatre was demolished and the magnificent new Burgtheater was built on the Ring.

16

In the Imperial Palace itself was a second theatre, the "Redoutensaaltheater," which was built in 1706 for Italian operas, but which was also used for the Austrian court balls. Mozart liked very much to attend the public masked balls which were held here. Dressed in the colored costume of a harlequin, he danced and joked, and enjoyed enormously squeezing the respective waists of his masked partners. Haydn, Mozart and Beethoven composed dance music for the Redoutensaal balls. Concert performances, too, belonged to the history of this theatre, and the names of all three classicists are linked to it. Haydn presented a student recital here, in 1795, which is especially noteworthy because his young pupil, Beethoven, played a piano concerto. As a famous composer, Beethoven returned to the Redoutensaal in 1814. Then he conducted his great battle picture, "The Battle of Victoria," and sections of "The Ruins of Athens." A short time later, his Eighth Symphony had its première here.

In Vienna and its environs, there are no less than twenty-eight houses in which Beethoven lived. Most of them are quite unchanged. Among the most imposing of these is the beautiful Pasqualatti House, its door decorated with coats-of-arms, which stands on a remnant of the old city fortifications. From his window, Beethoven could see the Vienna Woods. The house in the Döblinger Hauptstrasse, where the tempests of the "Eroica" first thundered, was, in his time, still surrounded by vineyards and stood in a rural neighborhood. In no Beethoven house is one so near the spirit of the immortal as in the small, low house on the Probusgasse in Heiligenstadt. It looks today as it did when Beethoven left it. Through the house door, one enters a small court where a flight of stairs leads to the modest rooms where Beethoven spent a summer. The windows of these rooms open upon a garden. Here, when the leaves of the garden trees were already beginning to fall from the branches, in 1802, he wrote the stirring "Heiligenstadt Testament" when he gave up hope of being cured of his deafness. The exalted, sorrowful voice of his great Adagios was in this room and in his soul when he wrote those lines. Nearby are three other houses where Beethoven spent summers. All stand in rural surroundings, far away from the city traffic. From all of them, it is not far to the vineyards, fields and the border of the woods where the composer used to rest and write notes in his sketch book. In Baden bei Wien and in Moedling are the old houses with ample courtyards and thick walls where the gigantic labors of the Ninth Symphony and the Missa Solemnis were undertaken.

Thus one can almost revive Beethoven's entire life in these walks through Vienna. But there is also an entire Schubert quarter, an idyll in the great city. Schubert was at home in the suburbs, with simple modest people who lived in small houses. The house where Schubert was born still stands—an insignificant looking building, five windows broad. In its small courtyard, he played as a boy, and in the little garden adjoining, he first saw the flowers blooming and the trees adorned with green leaves. From here, one can see the baroque tower of the church where he was baptized, and where he often sang in the choir or played the organ. Here, too, he first fell in love with the beautiful daughter of a Viennese manufacturer, for she was also a member of the choir. Nearby is the school house where Schubert taught the suburban children reading and writing while his first master

18

songs, "Gretchen am Spinnrad" and the "Erlkönig" ran through his brain. Between the house where he was born and a large house in the Kettenbrueckengasse which belonged to his brother and in which Schubert died, his entire life was lived. The houses where he visited friends, the taverns where he drank wine, are all still standing in Vienna, and should Schubert return today, he could find his way about without any difficulty whatsoever. Vienna, large, modern city that it is, is still a Schubert town. It goes without saying that the people christened that most beautiful of all graceful Biedermeier houses still standing in Vienna: the "Dreimaederlhaus." Schubert continues to inspire the imagination of the Viennese folk. He himself belongs to these simple people, and he has not become a historic figure but remained a living man— the stocky, good-natured school-master who spoke the dialect of the folk.

With the exception of most of the Schubert houses and those where Beethoven summered, all the houses of musical memory in question, are in the narrow confines of the old fortress-city, the "City of Vienna." But the suburbs, too, hold memories of musicians of bygone days. There is the little house, for instance, which belonged to Haydn as an old man, and where his aged, trembling fingers played the piano. He died in this house. French soldiers kept watch at the door, and presented arms when his oaken coffin was carried out to the nearby cemetery. In a town house on the main thoroughfare of Vienna, an inscription recalls that Gluck once had owned it, and also died there. One may wander as far as one will, even to the mountains which enclose Vienna, but one encounters reminders of the musical great at every turn.

In the little rococo theatre of the Castle of Schoenbrunn Gluck conducted. In one of its halls, the child-prodigy Mozart first played before the Empress and the Princesses, and then sat himself down on one Princess's lap. In the Schoenbrunn garden, Haydn romped widly as a boy, much to the annoyance of the Empress, who saw to it that he was properly spanked.

However, it is not only classical music history's mementos that the music lover encounters in his Vienna rambles. In Hietzing, on the bank of the River Wien, stands a yellow country house with a tower, where Richard Wagner worked on the composition of his "Meistersinger von Nürnberg." In the shadow of Salmannsdorf Mountain, on a steep, rocky path, is an ivy-covered cottage where Johann Strauss, as a boy, wrote his first wonderful waltzes. The "Beautiful Blue Danube" was composed in the garden of a house in the Praterstrasse which is still standing today; and the liveliest of all operettas, "Die Fledermaus," in a Hietzing villa. There too, is the house where Bruckner wrote most of his symphonies, as well as the little gardener's house in the Belvedere, where he died. The house where Brahms lived and died stands in a shady street near the green cupola of the Karlskirche.

*   *   *   *   *

Only recently the old "Freihaus" was torn down. This had been a city within a city, a large edifice which was erected by Count Starhemberg in the 17th century. In one of its courts

The Saint Stephens Cathedral

Guesthouse of the Monastery Heiligenkreuz in the City of Vienna

was a garden which, in the course of time, became very dilapidated. Here stood the little wooden pavilion where Mozart composed "The Magic Flute," a bottle of champagne lying with his notes on a table nearby. (This pavilion can now be seen in Salzburg.) In another court was the small theatre where "The Magic Flute" had its première. This theatre was ideally suited to the suburbs, a rude barn with two galleries. One paid seventeen kreuzer for parterre seats, seven kreuzer for those in the gallery. On both sides of the stage were painted figures: a knight with a sword and a lady with a mask. In such humble surroundings one of the greatest masterpieces of all music had its first performance. Mozart, already ill and pallid, sat at the conductor's desk and laughed at the jokes on the stage.

I often passed through the three courtyards of the "Freihaus," near the spot where the theatre had stood, and where later there was a garage (the "Mozart" Garage, of course). At night, if one's head were agreeably glowing with wine, one could detect a ghostly ringing in the air in this neighborhood. The tender sound would become more distinct and form itself into a jolly, folk-like melody with the words: "Ein Maedchen oder Weibchen wuenscht Papageno sich" ("A sweetheart or a wife is Papageno's plea"). The Freihaus was the real Mozart section of Vienna.

A short time after the première of "The Magic Flute," Mozart died in poverty. However, Schickaneder, the impressario who had produced the opera, was a rich man, and partly from the profits of this production, built a large new theatre on the River Wien. This Theater-an-der-Wien holds many cherished Beethoven memories. For a long time the composer lived in this theatre, working on his opera "Fidelio." In November, 1805, it was performed for the first time. French officers sat in the parterre seats, because Vienna was occupied at that time by Napoleon's army. The court and the high society had fled Vienna. The atmosphere in the theatre that evening was bad, and Beethoven's opera was a fiasco.

Two years previously, in this lovely theatre hall, Beethoven had presented his first and second symphonies, and the oratorio, "Christ on the Mount of Olives." The "Eroica," too, was performed here, in 1805, for the first time publicly, and a shoemaker's apprentice shouted from the gallery: "I'd give a kreuzer if it'd only stop!" Three years later Beethoven presented his fifth and sixth symphonies, and parts of his Mass in C and his Choral Fantasy in the same hall. At this performance he himself played his Piano Concerto in G, and improvised. His Violin Concerto also had its première here.

Another theatre which, like the Theater-an-der-Wien, still stands in Vienna, was festively opened with Beethoven's music. The overture, "Zur Weihe des Hauses" (For the Dedication of the House) was composed for the opening of the Josefstaedter Theater.

Vienna's churches, too, contain brilliant chapters of musical history. As mentioned before, the St. Stephen's Cathedral is the Haydn Church, the Lichtenthaler Church, the Schubert Church. For the Waisenhaus Church in the Third District, young Mozart composed a mass and conducted its performance there. The Court Chapel, where Anton Bruckner was organist, is the real Bruckner Church. This small Gothic chapel is directly in the Imperial Castle. Here I often saw Franz Josef, Sundays, praying in his box, right above the altar.

In the two galleries, sat the members of the Austrian nobility, raised above the people who stood in the chapel nave. In the third gallery was the organ, presided over by Bruckner, and the orchestra and chorus which played under the baton of the broad-shouldered and dignified Hans Richter. Before Mass began, the musicians assembled in the court of the chapel. Here came the "Saengerknaben" (Boys' Choir) in their embroidered uniforms, small swords at their waists; and the opera singers who were soloists.

One ends the musical walk through Vienna at the cemetery where the great musicians are buried. Here Haydn, Mozart, Beethoven, Schubert, Johann Strauss, Brahms, Hugo Wolf and many others have their homes below the earth. These homes, too, belong to Vienna, just as those others where they dwelled in their lifetimes.

While no one accompanied Mozart's coffin to the cemetery, all Vienna was present when Beethoven's was borne to the Waehringer Cemetery. The magnificent funeral of a great musician was a great spectacle for the Viennese, and many a composer who, during his lifetime, was fought, obstructed and ridiculed by the people, would be carried to his grave amid the most extravagant pomp. I was present when Bruckner's coffin was blessed at the Karlskirche, before, according to his last wish, it was taken to St. Florian to be interred beneath the great organ. From the choir sounded the mournful music of Bruckner's Seventh Symphony. Beside the flower-decked coffin the dark-robed priests were praying, while the university students, whom Bruckner so loved, stood at attention with drawn swords. Near the coffin stood a short peasant who kept looking anxiously about him. This was Bruckner's brother who may well have been amazed at the enormous crowd gathered for the funeral. He resembled Bruckner, but his face was merely that of a peasant while the composer's had radiated a kind of holiness.

A sad burial was that of Gustav Mahler in the Grinzing Cemetery, because only a few loyal members of his circle of friends were convinced of his greatness as a composer; and these followed his coffin like the adherents of a new religion who had lost their Messiah.

In any case, all Vienna was present at Johann Strauss's funeral, and the cemetery was crowded with people, of whom even the most humble knew the Strauss melodies by heart. The Mayor of Vienna made the eulogy. For, after all, Strauss's music was the true folk-music of Vienna, and he was the musical potentate of Austria whose kingdom and reign lasted longer than Emperor Franz Josef's.

Thus music in Vienna was not an isolated province where only musicologists and historians went to dig for treasure. It was no dead memory, but an ever active power, belonging to the intellect, to the way of life and the atmosphere of the city. And if one should destroy every building in Vienna, the earth would still be there over which so many great musicians passed; and the air of which they breathed.

Landscape and People

Like Vienna's streets, so its surrounding landscape is rich in memories of its great musicians. This same vivid landscape which holds incomparable charm for visitors today was often the source of inspiration for the glorious works of the past. At the Schreiber brook, which flows down from the Kahlenberg through the vineyards, Beethoven discovered his Pastoral Symphony. The brook ripples and rustles on today just as it did in Beethoven's time, and the birds sing in the trees along its banks.

The real poet of the Viennese landscape was Schubert. There is no music which is so close to nature as his. It sounds like nature, with its fragrance of blooming lilacs. Natural, too, is the line of his melody. His great C Major Symphony was already understood and described by Robert Schumann as a hymn to the Viennese landscape. It was Schumann, too, who rediscovered in this music the cathedral of St. Stephen, the Danube, and the Vienna woods.

Not far from the brook where Beethoven heard his pastoral music is the charming village of Grinzing. Here the Viennese sit every fine evening in the gardens and courtyards of the many wine-houses, drinking the wine which is so famous and "Maulfreundlich" (friendly to the mouth), as the Viennese say, when they first smell the earthy fragrance which rises from the glass and disappears on the tongue. Here Schubert often sat with his friends, played waltzes on out-of-tune pianos, or thought out such music as the last movement of the

G Major string quartet, which has all the exciting flavor of Grinzing wine. In an inn garden here, Schubert wrote his song "Hark, hark the lark," on the back of a menu.

The moonlight passages of Arnold Schoenberg's "Verklaerte Nacht" grew out of the Viennese landscape. And Richard Wagner, in the surroundings of the Vienna woods, composed the poetic end of the second act of "Meistersinger," with the moon rising in the silent night, casting its silver threads over the housetops.

From the heights of the Kahlenberg one has the finest view of the great city, encircling the St. Stephen's Cathedral as a wheel its axle. The broad stream of the Danube winds like a silver ribbon through the Viennese plains, which extend as far as the Hungarian mountains, dimly visible in a misty haze. To the south, the mighty Alps appear on the horizon; and in the west lie forests. All and north along the forests' borders, grapes flourish on the clay-like soil which once the Roman soldiers transplanted from Italy when they established their camp on the Danube.

Every one of the classical musicians has looked down on Vienna from the Kahlenberg. Mozart, inspired by the Kahlenberg, wrote the merry "Magic Flute" duet between Papageno and Papagena, happy and guileless as the tender cooing of love birds. Beethoven stood here, serious, moved, and, as always, religiously impressed by nature, and here he wrote down the wonderful words: "O God, what magnificence in such forest places. On the heights there, is peace—peace in which to serve Him."

From time immemorial, on these wide plains, many races have mingled. Here the roads of Europe meet. To the north, there are Slavic people whose melancholy and tender music is that of a people who have long lived under oppression, full of plaintive desire. From this Slavic north, from Silesia, Franz Schubert's grandfather emigrated to Vienna. In Schubert's music one often hears an echo of Slavic minor harmony, as well as in that of Dvorak and Smetana.

Where the Danube flows to the east and the plain disappears in mist, is Hungary, and farther on, Turkey and the Orient. From the Hungarians comes the gypsy music—sobbing clarinets, passionate violins, crashing cymbals, melancholy preludes and twirling dances with the rattle of spurs, for the Hungarians are a nation of horsemen. In the music of all the classicists, one hears the sound of this intoxicating music. In his musical library, Haydn had a large collection of gypsy music; and in his string quartet, Opus 20, Number 4 (Allegretto alla Zingarese), in his G Major Piano Trio (Rondo alla Ongarese), and elsewhere he has either used the original or imitated Hungarian music.

Beethoven wrote Hungarian music in his "King Stephen Overture"; and Schubert captured the sound which blew over the Viennese plains from the east in his "Divertissement à la Hongrois." For years, including the period of Brahms, who wrote his famous Hungarian dances and made the clarinet sob like an instrument in a gypsy band in his Clarinet Quintet, Hungarian music has been an important influence on much of the music Vienna produced.

The Orient, too, lent its colorful sounds to Viennese music. Turkish merchants, wearing turbans and silk robes, were no unusual sights in Vienna even during Mozart's time. When he wrote his opera, "The Abduction from the Seraglio" where, right at the beginning, Turkish cymbals, drums and triangles conjure up the fairy-tale atmosphere of the Orient, one hundred years had already passed since Sultan Soliman's Turkish army had pitched its tents around Vienna. As the army withdrew, the first coffee house was opened in Vienna, and coffee was served in the Turkish way, brewed heavy and fragrant. Since that time Vienna remained an oriental coffee-house city, where one dreamed, planned and did business while having coffee. Tobacco, too, came from Turkey, and still in the time of Franz Josef, one saw in all stores where tobacco was sold, the picture of a Turk with a long pipe in his hand, puffing forth clouds of smoke. Vienna was near the Orient, and Count Metternich liked to have it said that the Orient began right outside the eastern city limits. Therefore it is no wonder that Mozart and Beethoven wrote Turkish Marches, and that Goldmark became one of the masters of modern oriental painting in music.

In the south, the Alpine roads lead from the Vienna plain to Italy; from the beeches, oaks and firs of Vienna to cypresses and pines. Along these roads for centuries came Italian musicians, bringing their music to Vienna. The Viennese enjoyed the beauty and sensuality of the Italian music. They loved the music of the blue sea, the sounds and harmonies of the fishermen's barks, the melodies which the Venetian gondoliers sang when they rowed their black boats through the canals and under the marble bridges of Venice. Until the year 1859, Milan and Lombardy belonged to Austria. In 1866, only, it lost Venice. On the large piazzas of Milan, Verona and Venice, the Austrian officers used to promenade in the evening before attending performances at the opera. The Milan Scala was, until 1859, an Austrian opera house. As a matter of fact, for a certain time, the State Opera of Vienna, the Scala of Milan, and the San Carlo Theatre of Naples were all under the management of one director, the clever, stocky Barbaja, who organized opera theatres, gambling houses, coffee houses with the same enthusiasm and business acumen. Viennese soldiers returned from service in Italy, whistling Italian opera melodies. From Italy, too, Viennese officers imported the greeting "Ciao." Though it sounded Chinese, it was a contraction of the Italian word "schiavo" ("servant"). From Italy the soldiers brought the Virginia cigar which has become the "people's cigar" of Austria. Austrian military bands brought back Italian music to all the towns of Austria. When Richard Wagner, after the love catastrophe with Mathilde Wesendonck, went to the then Austrian Venice, and walked, evenings, on St. Mark's Square he heard a military band there whose playing he praised highly. Thus, Italian music, even in comparatively recent times, crossed over the Alps to Vienna.

The characteristic music of all these other nations mingled with Viennese music and left its traces. The softness, the melancholy, the folk-song-like human quality of Slavic music took away the German hardness from Viennese music. The voluptuous richness of Hungarian music lent it sparkle; and the Italian melodies augmented the quality of its sound. The basis of Viennese music, however, was German, for even in ancient times, in Vienna, German blood had mingled with that of the Celts and Romanic peoples.

The Bavarian peasants who settled in Austria and changed dense woods into thriving farmland, must surely have had musical talent. Mediaeval folk-songs from Austria, as they were sung in village inns and on the "dance meadows," have a decided power. With the Babenberger Dukes, who built their castles in Vienna, the agile, clever Franks entered the country and soon after started to fiddle and sing on the Babenberger estates. The greatest German poet of the middle ages, Walther von der Vogelweide, told all Germany that in Austria, he had learned "singen und sagen" ("singing and saying"). But its great period as a land of music did not commence for Austria, until, in the 17th century, the Italian musicians came to Vienna; when the Emperors and high society of Vienna spoke and sang Italian, and the city was like an Italian town. Vienna did not become the musical capital of the world as a national city, but as a supernational one. Supernational, too, were the Catholic ideas which waved their battle-flags in Vienna during the time of the Turkish Wars and the Counter-Reformation. Supernational, also, was the idea of the Austrian Empire which comprised peoples of different blood and language; supernational the broadening of the intellectual horizon of the time. A Frenchman of Italian ancestry, Prince Eugene, led the Austrian armies, and Austrian viceroys resided in Brussels and Naples. In the 17th century it was Catholicism which had made Vienna Europe's capital, and had given its music the rich background formed from the unification of French, German and Italian elements. During the 18th century, the great humanistic idea stepped into the place of the religious one. Mozart's "Magic Flute" and Beethoven's "Fidelio" and Ninth Symphony are perfect expressions of this humanism which originated in the musical city Vienna. Thus arose the music capital of the world which has been invaded by German nationalism.

When one stands on the Kahlenberg, one comprehends all this at a glance. One sees the plain with its roads leading into the distance, the great river which is a broad bridge on which the cultures of Asia and Europe meet. One sees St. Stephen's with its golden cross shining over a land which, for centuries, has been accustomed to kneel in prayer under its high, Gothic arches. One visualizes the Roman soldiers and merchants coming from Italy, on the south; the armies of Prince Eugene marching in the east; from the west, merchants from Ulm and Augsburg carrying goods from the Orient on their carts; from the north, Czech businessmen and Slovakian toy-merchants, and on the Danube, ships carrying Turkish carpets and tobacco being pulled against the current by strong horses. One can picture the musicians who came from all sides: Italian opera singers, Hungarian cymbal-players, gypsies with contra-basses on their backs and violins in hand, Czech clarinet players and other orchestral musicians. All this colorful, bright, exotic and sensual band emigrated to Vienna, the capital of a great empire in whose army four languages were spoken, and their music mingled there with German music in the way spices mingle with the taste of a roast. It was this process, which continued through centuries, which brought Viennese music to its unique and unparalleled glory.

Such mixtures and minglings occurred elsewhere in Europe besides in Vienna. In the 17th century, in Munich, Dresden and Hannover, Italian and German music came together. Everywhere there were Italian court composers, court poets, singers and instrumentalists. In Berlin, later the capital of German nationalism, Frederick the Great, in the 18th century, sat in the new opera house, listened to Italian operas which were written by German composers, and gave his orders in French. A German composer, Gluck, and an Italian composer, Piccini, wrote operas for Paris. In London, during the time of Haydn, musicians from all over Europe streamed together during the "season" just as they did, a century later, in New York. From many sides Europe aimed at one goal—a European music which should summarize the best in the music of all nations—a music transcending the national, the music of a unified culture and education. What so many European towns had attempted, however, succeeded only in Vienna. Perhaps this success was due to the fact that, geographically, Vienna lay in the center of the map of Europe. Moreover, in the 17th century, Vienna became the political capital of Europe, for the all-powerful Hapsburgs resided there.

During the time of Emperor Franz Josef, Vienna was still the center of all European nations. The aristocracy came there from their castles in Bohemia, Poland, Hungary, Croatia and Italy. The Emperor's officials came from all parts of Germany and Austria. The Minister-Premier of long years' standing, Count Taaffe, was a descendant of an Irish family, while his aides were mainly Hungarians and Poles.

Even today in humble suburban homes, where the past is preserved like the scent of lavender in old chests, Viennese mothers sing their babies to sleep with a song which begins with the enigmatic words: "Heidi Puppeja." They are nothing else than the Greek words "Aeide Bubaion" ("Sleep, my little boy"). But how did Greek words travel to Vienna and fit themselves into a lullaby? History gives the answer. In the early middle ages, Austrian rulers married princesses of the

Greek Imperial Court in Constantinople, and with these princesses, Greek priests, scholars and courtiers came to the court of the Viennese Babenbergers. Greek nurses sang the children of the Dukes to sleep. And from the ducal castle, the lullabies stole into the more humble Viennese houses where small children lay waiting for sleep. Thus a Greek song came to cling to Viennese soil like gossamer, whose threads are borne from a distance by the wind and remain clinging to the branches of a tree or shrub in the harvest-field.

Marvelous was Vienna's talent to change all men and music from the four corners of the globe into its own possession. Immigrants, after a short time, became genuine Viennese, just as if they had drunk some sort of magic potion to effect the transformation. Their temperament, their thoughts, feelings, lives and loves, all become Viennese. They spoke the Viennese dialect and made Viennese music.

No one has even been a greater glorifier of "Viennadom" than Johann Strauss. What the world knows of Vienna, it knows mainly from his waltzes. They contained all of Vienna—the gaiety, the laughter, the love, the beautiful women, wine and song, the landscape, woods and streams. And did not the music of "Fledermaus" exactly depict the chatter of the Viennese salon, the elegance of the men, the amiability of its ladies, the hilarity of champagne's intoxication? In the Strauss polkas lay the babble, the merry, mocking wit of Vienna. In the Strauss marches, one saw the typical Viennese soldier, his hat cocked over one eye, Virginia cigar in the corner of his mouth. All this was Vienna in its Sunday best—not the everyday Vienna, but Vienna in a festive mood. This was the ideal picture of Vienna, the dream, the fairy-tale.

33

And yet this musician who invented the fairy-tale which the whole world believed, was not a complete Viennese. His grandmother had been born in Spain, and had the surprising maiden-name of Roger. Family history recounts that she was the daughter of a Spanish aristocrat who had had to flee his homeland because he had killed a grandee in a duel. She played the Spanish guitar in Vienna, and sang romances to its accompaniment. All the Strausses are a foreign, non-Viennese, southern type. Strauss's brother, Edward, had the jet-black hair of a foreign race, with an ivory complexion. His brother Josef had an olive complexion, dark eyes, and looked like a romantic gypsy. Johann Strauss, too, was dark, and the writer Heinrich Laube, when he saw Strauss for the first time, playing violin at the head of his orchestra, said that he was "black as a Moor, with curly hair, the typical King of the Blackamoors."

There were other glorifiers of Vienna who themselves were foreigners, or who had had foreign ancestors. The greatest Viennese popular actor of Franz Josef's time, who made the people laugh and cry like no one else, was Girardi. As his name shows, he was of Italian descent. The writer who pictured the humble, modest class of Viennese with greatest success was named Vincenz Chiavacci. No other Viennese writer described so vividly the earthy market-women, the bourgeois men, with golden watch-chains across their stomachs, sitting, talking politics at inn tables. No other writer painted this scene so true to life as did this Viennese who, also, had his origin in Italy. The greatest actor of the Burgtheater, whom Emperor Franz Josef elevated to the nobility, and whom Vienna considered its most representative portrayer of men, was Sonnenthal, who came from Hungary.

The most popular song of Franz Josef's time was the "Fiakerlied" ("Song of the Fiacre Driver"). Old and young, rich and poor sang it, but only a Viennese could sing it in the correct dialect. Crown Prince Rudolph had his favorite fiacre-driver, Bratfisch, whistle the song to him before he went, drunken, to his death in Mayerling. And who composed this song, the most Viennese of all songs, in which, even in this age of the automobile, the fiacre-driver lives on, cracks his whip and makes his black horses trot smartly? A Jew from Hungary who had immigrated to Vienna.

The Viennese could never become a nationalist, since in his town, people of many other countries, and of many other languages had gathered. All these people were Viennese like himself. The neighbor who talked with a Czech or Hungarian accent was just as much a Viennese as he who was born there. One did not laugh at his pronunciation and his peculiarities as at a foreigner, but one saw in him a man like oneself. Thus sprang up the spirit of friendliness, companionship and popular humanism which brought Viennese together, caused them to gather in the smoky coffee houses and inns and made them become friends. This spirit found expression, in music of a higher style, in the hilarity of Haydn's symphonies, the humanity of Mozart's melodies, the popular attraction of Schubert's music; and soared to the heights—the truly great heights where one can see the open Heavens, the throne of God and the legions of angels—in the great humanitarian choruses of Beethoven's Ninth Symphony.

Even Johannes Brahms, earnest Protestant and severe musician, who came from North Germany to Vienna, thawed in the sociable, human atmosphere and the serene landscape of this city of mingled races. Here he wrote his most beautiful melodies, and almost became a Viennese in his "Liebeslieder" Waltzes. Like the great masters whose heir he was, Brahms, too, loved the Viennese countryside. Every Sunday he made excursions to the Vienna woods with his friends, wearing the grey-green coat and knickerbockers of the Alpine hunter. I frequently met him at the Hoeldrichs Mill, a rustic restaurant, which stands among beech and pine groves. In front of the building, which had once been a mill, is an old linden tree; and the notes of Schubert's song, "Der Lindenbaum" which are inscribed on the wall of the house, remind one that Schubert is said to have written this song here. Brahms loved to sit in the garden of the inn, under the shadowy trees, drinking coffee. He would beam with delight and contentedness, so pleased was he with his surroundings. The lovely graciousness of the Viennese landscape was in direct contrast to his own severe nature. He had come here from a land of fog where the sea raged and the brown heath stretched for miles on end, and like all northerners, he longed for sunshine and gaiety.

Hugo Wolf, in many of his songs, was inspired by the atmosphere of this landscape. The wonderful Mörike songs were composed in a summer house at the edge of the Pötzleinsdorfer Heath, near Vienna.

The Viennese landscape has something unique which cannot be found in any other town of the world. The surrounding woods are not merely a background but belong to the city and are merged with it. They descend from the hills, swing into the town and finally spread themselves out into the innumerable suburban gardens. The suburbs themselves were once country villages outside the walls and portals of the old fortress town. The magnificent Vienna parks, too, are parts of the Vienna woods which the art of the gardener has ennobled. The "Augarten," which Emperor Josef II, in his humanitarian way, opened to the public, and in which Mozart conducted his morning concerts, is old woodland. The Park of Schoenbrunn, with its clipped hedges, artistic fountains, its graceful Gloriette with its sandstone statues, and the rococo pavilion in the menagerie where Empress Maria Theresia drank tea with the aristocracy, had formerly been the Emperor's hunting grounds. Only the Prater, Vienna's amusement park, was permitted to preserve its original forest character, and the lovers of Vienna are grateful for it.

Vienna's suburbs even today lie in the green. In the inn gardens where the contemporary bourgeois sit over their beer, Strauss and Lanner played their waltzes. The chestnut trees were blooming and scented buds fell from the lindens. It is almost self-understood that the Blue Danube Waltz was composed in just such a garden, at 54 Praterstrasse. The greatest of all Viennese waltzes came into existence in the Viennese landscape which it glorified, under trees, near the Danube.

The Viennese

Vienna is unthinkable without its typical, middle-class citizens. It was they who built the city and lived in its houses. They battled on the walls against the Turks. In the year 1848 they stood at the barricades, workers, artists and students, and fought for a new era. They sat in the workshops and slaved in the factories, frequented the inns and took their wives and children to the Vienna Woods on Sundays. As young men, they wore the uniform of the Emperor's soldiers, and went to Bohemia, to the Balkans, to Italy, where their sovereign was always waging wars. These anonymous Viennese gave the city on the Danube its own characteristic personality, which is recognizable in all the music which was written there.

During the many centuries which passed from the time of Vienna's founding, and its development from a Roman military camp to a dark mediaeval city, and, finally, to a great European capital, the inhabitants showed the same characteristic personality. The "Viennese" was a strong and definite conception. The Viennese, by a greater adaptability, was differentiated from his South German relatives, the Bavarian and the Suabian. He was less heavy-handed, more amiable, more lively. He was not so clumsy in love-affairs, not so ill-mannered in eating. He had good taste and many talents, among which was that of acting. The Viennese played with life a little. He did not take it entirely seriously. He kept a sharp eye out for the weaknesses of his fellow man, whom he delighted in mocking or mimicking. In all Germany, there was no such original Folk Theatre as the 18th century Viennese Folk Theatre. In the small wooden shacks on the Graben, Viennese folk-spirit found its laughing outlet. Here Viennese dialect flourished in all its rudeness, its freshness, and lack of inhibition. He who wished to captivate the people had to speak their dialect. During the time of the Turkish Wars, the great Viennese preacher, Abraham a Santa Clara, although a Suabian by birth, always used Viennese dialect when he spoke from the pulpit of St. Stephen's. Sometimes he spoke as if he had been born in a peasant farm-house near Vienna, or sometimes, even in a pig-sty. When he thundered against the Turks or against the sins of the world, he talked like a native Viennese, sitting at an inn-table after several glasses of potent wine. He made his listeners laugh when he wished to reform them. Paris had its great preachers—its Bossuet, its Père Lacordaire—but they were classical, master orators who spoke the literary language of the universities and salons. For that a Viennese would not stand, for he was essentially a skeptic who considered elevated words "swollen." He wanted to hear his own language which, though not always refined, was gay, natural and witty—the rough language of human common sense.

When, during the 17th century, everywhere in Europe and, of course, in Austria, too, the absolute power of the reigning sovereign developed, and a feudalistic society gathered at the royal courts, the joyous temperament of the Viennese took possession of even this society. The aristocrats who circulated in the courts of the Austrian baroque emperors like planets around the sun, had come from all over Europe, but they learned Viennese dialect. They spoke and lived as

Viennese—that is, they took life as a game which was meant as entertainment. Empress Maria Theresia spoke the dialect like a Viennese bourgeoise, and the Emperor Franz Josef had a slight dialect accent. During his reign, a special kind of Viennese dialect developed among the aristocrats and officers—an elegant, somewhat fatigued and refined Viennese.

Thus a common bond existed between the court and aristocracy on one hand, and the people on the other; a bond created by a common dialect and a common philosophy of life. Externally, the dividing line between "high" and "low" society was not so outspoken in Vienna as it was elsewhere in Europe. In the wine houses and gardens of the "Heurigen," fine society and common people sat side by side, enjoying themselves, singing folk songs like: "Menschen, Menschen san mir alle, Fehler hat ein jeder gnua; S'koennen ja nicht alle gleich sein, S'is schon so von der Natur" (Human, human, we're only human; everyone has faults enough; we can't all be alike—that's how Nature made us.") Archdukes, princes, rich burghers, shoemakers and tailors alike sang such songs. In Vienna, even if nowhere else, in the 19th century there existed a kind of democracy in the taverns which prevailed as long as the effect of the wine. The language of this democracy was the Viennese folk dialect. If Haydn, therefore, in his symphonies, mixed the higher forms of music with popular dance tunes, he was only exemplifying the Viennese spirit.

In Vienna, the joy of music was a part of the general joy of life. Even in mediaeval times, the Viennese wanted to hear music. The town hummed with fiddlers, harpists and singers who made music in fifteenth century rooms and taverns. In the 17th century, a musician became a sort of legendary figure in Vienna, and by rights, he should be included in the city's coat-of-arms. This was Augustin, a bag-piper and folk-singer, who fared from inn to inn, playing, singing. Even to-day the Viennese sing a song which was his favorite: "O du lieber Augustin, alles ist hin." (O my dear Augustin, everything is gone.") And in new Vienna, a monument has been erected in his memory. There he is depicted, blowing his bagpipes, a little shaky on his legs, for the legendary singer loved wine. When, in 1679, the plague broke out in Vienna, he staggered toward home one night and fell in a pit where the corpses of the plague victims were lying. There he slept off his drunkenness, and when he awoke, he climbed out of the pit and gaily and healthily went on living and drinking wine. In the course of time Augustin became a symbol of "Viennesedom," which remained indestructible in the face of any misfortune. This same Augustinian spirit emerges in the song of another Viennese folk-singer of the 19th century: "Allweil lustig, fesch und munter, denn der Wiener geht nicht unter." ("Always jolly, gay and merry, for no Viennese ever goes under.") The Viennese considered himself indestructible even in hard times. He was the born optimist. This quality, along with his sensitiveness and his appreciation of the beauty of Nature, has made him a musician. His unworried, carefree attitude toward life he expressed by singing and playing and dancing, over wine at the inns, at festivals on the village green, on mountain-climbing excursions. One sang or listened to music because one drank, and one drank because one wanted to sing. All this may have been primitive music, even animalistic music, but through the centuries it developed the Viennese into a musician and Vienna into a city of music.

In the 17th and 18th centuries, in no other European city could one experience what one could in Vienna on summer evenings. There is a poem, written by Abraham a Santa Clara toward the end of the 17th century, which describes the "night-music" or serenades in the Vienna streets. It tells how musicians with flutes, kettle-drums, trumpets and lutes serenade in front of the houses of beautiful Viennese women, and how they run away when the police patrol appears.[1]

During the 17th century this serenading became more and more popular, and this led to the composition of masses of "Serenades," "Cassations," "Divertimenti" and "Nocturnes." In the "Vienna Newspaper" on July 16, 1873, the publisher Toricella advertised his "very special night-pieces," in order "to provide the many lovers of night-music with new material for enjoyment." Early in his career, Haydn was connected with this serenade music. Since he had been discharged from his post as choir-boy at St. Stephen's, he needed to earn money, and did so by participating in the serenades, on which occasions he played timpani. This experience aided him in acquiring the folk-like tone of the themes of his symphonies, and the early string quartets he composed are still entitled "Quadri," "Cassatio," "Divertimenti" and "Notturno" from the terminology of the serenade.

Mozart, too, composed such serenade music, among which is the marvelous "Haffner" Serenade. And in Vienna, he

[1] "Ah, lovely Phyllis hear,
Ah, hear our music sighing.
Come let us pass a night
Together sweetly lying."
(Thus closes the poem of the saintly folk-preacher.)

himself was honored by a serenade. In a letter of November 3, 1781, he wrote his father: "At eleven at night I was serenaded by two clarinets, two horns and two bassoons. The six gentlemen who executed it are poor devils, but who nevertheless blow nicely together." Beethoven's "Serenade" and the romantic Schubert Octet are the classic fulfillments of Viennese night-music, and the serenades of Brahms and of Richard Strauss are its last fading notes.

In Emperor Franz Josef's time, in the streets the Viennese could hear music which also was a part of his folk-music. This was military music. Every regiment of the Austrian army had its band, and the people used to swarm in the streets when the first sounds of the deep wind-instruments, then the bright clarinets, could be heard. Most of the crowd marched in front of the band, in step with the beat of the great drum, which was carried on a small wagon, drawn by a pony. The drum-major, who according to an unwritten tradition, always had a long, martial beard, raised and lowered his commander's baton. The drummer artistically tossed his sticks in the air, and just as artistically caught them.

On the stroke of twelve, at the old Imperial Palace, the guard was changed, under the Emperor's window. Then, throughout the city, all life in the streets seemed to come to a standstill, for the people would hear the music of the military band on its way to the palace. Hundreds of Viennese, first boys, then grown-ups, would crowd into the very courtyard of the castle, where music-stands were set up. The concert began while the officers changed watch and the soldiers marched to their posts in the different castle courts. Often one would see the old monarch, from the window of his office, look down at the crowd while the band played for hundreds of his subjects.

There was another man whom I used to see, listening as if electrified, when a military band paraded the streets of Vienna. He was the composer, Gustav Mahler. I used frequently to sit with Mahler, of evenings, on the terrace of a Ringstrasse café. When, in the distance, the "boom-boom" of a military band's drum became audible, he would interrupt the most serious conversation about music and the world, and hurry out to the curb. There, with the wind blowing through his hair, he would stand as if spell-bound, not returning until the last boom of the drum died away. The great role military music played in Mahler's compositions is known to everyone familiar with his symphonies, especially his third. He himself told me that, as a child, he had lived opposite a barracks, and that the military music and signals he heard at that time made a deep impression upon him.

Some military marches belonged to the music of the folk; above all, the famous "Radetzky" March by Johann Strauss's father. To its accompaniment, Viennese soldiers went to Italy in 1848. Marshal Radetzky, with drooping white mustaches, sat, bent forward on his horse, and the soldiers marched to the bloody battle-fields of Novara and Custozza.

The trio of the Radetzky March is a yodel-song of the Austrian mountains which the recruits from Upper Austria used to sing when they were marching to Vienna in 1848. So the mountains, too, made their contribution to Viennese music. The greatest composers like Haydn, Beethoven and Anton Bruckner, did not consider it beneath their dignity to compose military music.

THE VIENNESE

When Goethe, in 1823, was taking the cure at Karlsbad, he heard the band of an Austrian hunter regiment play. He was, as he wrote, "touched." And when Rossini heard Austrian regimental music, he wrote: "There is no artistic enjoyment which may be called democratic to such a high degree as the playing of regimental bands. Everyone may take part without entrance fees and without evening dress." Military bands achieved an inestimable contribution toward the music education of the Viennese. These bands, at their concerts, played in addition to their military marches and waltzes, opera and symphonic music also, in the public parks; and every fine evening, hundreds of Viennese surrounded the concert podium and listened to the music which formed one part of the city's musical life which was accessible to everybody.

The church, too, played an important part in the musical life of the Viennese. On Sundays and holidays, it was their real concert-hall. There was good music in all Vienna's churches. Well-trained choirs sang and orchestras played. So it was since the middle ages, when students of the University of Vienna sang in St. Stephen's Cathedral choir, up to the period of baroque when the Catholic Church employed the most brilliant musical means to win souls for Catholicism. It must be admitted that the church-music of this fanatical battle-period of Catholicism was what determined the musical taste of the Viennese until present times. From that time on, the Viennese have loved brightness and splendor in music; the sensual enchantment of sounds streaming powerfully through 17th century churches, making the Mass a brilliant concert.

The role of Catholicism in the development of Vienna into

a music capital has not, as yet, been sufficiently acknowledged. The Viennese has been a devout Catholic ever since the time the holy Severin preached this faith in the vineyards of Sievering. Under the leadership of the Archbishop of Vienna, Count Kollonitz, the Viennese defended his city against the Turks in order to save the Catholic faith for all Europe. He loved the pomp of the Church, the brightness and color of its processions, and, during pilgrimages, walked ecstatically behind the cross which was borne by the priest.

This Viennese Catholicism is different from Spanish or Italian Catholicism. It was not sombre like that of Spain, nor was it theatrical or operatic like that of Italy. It was a friendly, comfortable Catholicism which gave free play to the Viennese joy of living and its hilarious spirit of life. On the many Catholic holidays which the Viennese celebrated, the festival meal was the most important. On the feast-day of St. Martin, when one said the prayer: "You shall multiply the geese and also the cool wine," the first geese were slaughtered. On this day, too, emissaries came from Pressburg, bringing geese to the emperor. This was an old Austrian court-custom. The cloisters of Vienna, Klosterneuberg, Melk and Gottweih, provided wine for the Viennese. Each of these ancient monasteries had its wine-cellar in Vienna proper where the people went to drink "cloister wine." Here, the behavior was not on a very pious level, and the laughter of Viennese girls rang out in the low-ceilinged rooms. On St. Leopold's Day, hundreds of Viennese went with their wives and children to Klosterneuburg to drink wine in honor of the good saint, who is buried there in the famous altar of Verdun. The monks provided good food and sweet wine, and they did not hesitate to sit down with the Viennese and join the celebration. This was Viennese Catholicism. All the pilgrimages ended up at the inns, after the religious ceremonies. The same held true for funerals. Near every Catholic cemetery, even to-day, in Vienna, there is an "Inn of the Eye of God" where God can look down on the Viennese, who, after a funeral, enjoy life and their drinking. Most of the Viennese went to church on Sundays, and at any hour of the day, one could see hundreds of people from all walks of life kneeling in prayer before the image of the Blessed Virgin Mary in St. Stephen's after lighting their votive candles. Understanding Father-confessors in Vienna's churches forgave the people's sins, and from the pulpits, priests spoke in dialect about God, Heaven and salvation in the faith. One of the great cardinals of Vienna in Franz Josef's time said: "In Vienna, one can appoint anyone and use him as cardinal, even a complete idiot. Just no fanatic." Therefore Catholicism in Vienna wore popular dress.

One has only to listen to the Masses of the classic masters in order to feel that Viennese Catholicism was human and merry. Haydn's masses are full of folk-like melodies, and when he was reproached for composing church music which was too gay, he answered: "Why shouldn't I be gay when I think of dear God?" When Goethe related this story, tears rolled down his cheeks, so moved was he by Haydn's child-like soul. Child-like, pure and melodious, too, are Mozart's masses. The most beautiful piece of church music he ever wrote was the "Ave Verum," composed at Baden-bei-Wien. It sounds like a piece sung by angels who had been Vienna choir boys. Beethoven, in his two masses, wrote great Catholic festival music containing the pathos of the baroque. Bruckner's masses, too, were baroque services.

The masses of Schubert all have their roots in Vienna. In this music, one feels one is looking from the open church door out over the vineyards and woods. The melodies are like folk songs sung by happy young girls. This music has all the splendor of Catholicism, but also Viennese humanness.

Every Sunday, the masses of Haydn and Mozart were performed in the churches. Viennese girls sang in the choirs, and in the pews, the citizens in their Sunday best sat enjoying the sound of fresh young voices. Only in the court chapel and at St. Stephen's was there a boys' choir, for the Viennese preferred the sound of women's voices in church. Here, too, he loved sensuality in the music; and had little understanding for the spiritual charm of Palestrina or the mediaeval tartness of the Netherland mass music. In church, he wanted to hear the sound of instruments, beautiful voices, the roar of the organ, trumpet fanfares praising God above. The Catholic Church, therefore, which so richly maintained the 17th century tradition in Vienna, has been one of the main influences in preserving the musical taste of the baroque among the people.

When one speaks of influences which made a musician out of the Viennese, and a musical city out of Vienna, one must not omit mentioning the most important. Beside the Viennese man stands the Viennese woman, and though music history, which was written by dry pedants, makes no reference to this fact, it is surely because no ancient manuscript reveals specific instances of her influence on Vienna's music and musical taste. And yet this influence was strong. For ages

Vienna has been a town of beautiful women and girls. They are at home not only in the palaces of the aristocrats, but in the small suburban houses, where they appear at their best and most original.

The Viennese woman has given sensual color to the city's life. Her gay, natural laugh—different from the *spirituel* laugh of the Frenchwoman—could be heard in Vienna through the centuries. It was her chatter, kisses and embraces which inspired great music and small music, folk songs and dances. Though there exist no statistics by which one can measure exactly what Viennese music owes to women, there is one instance where a definite relationship between the two can be established.

If there exists a form of music which is a direct expression of sensuality, it is the Viennese waltz. It was the dance of the new romantic period after the Napoleonic Wars, and the contemporaries of the first waltzes were highly shocked at the eroticism of this dance in which a lady clung to her partner, closed her eyes as in a happy dream, and glided off as if the world had disappeared. The new waltz melodies overflowed with longing, desire and tenderness. No composer gave the waltz more passionate warmth than Johann Strauss. When he was composing his seduction waltzes, Strauss was continually surrounded by women, and the titles of many of his waltzes show by which of them he was inspired. There are "Irene" waltzes, "Siren," "Lady Bug" and "La Viennoise" waltzes. Then there are "Wilhelmina" quadrilles, "Martha," "Maria," "Anika," "Sophie" and "Alexandra" quadrilles. On goes the bacchantic train of the waltz from "My Life is Love and Desire" to "Wine, Women and Song."

The great erotic whose love of life and sensuality flamed up so overwhelmingly in the three-quarter time of the waltz, had three wives. The first one, Henriette Treffz, a prima donna at the Kärntnerthor Theatre, he married in 1862. This woman came from low origins. She was the daughter of a Czech laborer, Challupetsky, and all Vienna knew her as the mistress of Baron Tedesko, by whom she had several children. For Strauss, she was apparently the primitive erotic element which gave him his artistic energy. During this marriage, in addition to other music which became world-famous, "Die Fledermaus" was written. After the death of "Jetty," Strauss married Angelica Dietrich who called herself "Lilly." At that time he was fifty-three years old. His wife, who was young, seductive and full of temperament, eloped with a friend of Strauss's, and disappeared from his horizon. Apart from his marriages, not very much is known of the more personal aspects of the composer's life. Like the Pied Piper, the swarthy Strauss, bowing his violin, would lead his orchestra, and each waltz would plead his suit.

In the year 1859, Strauss fell in love with a beautiful lady in St. Petersburg. This was a romantic passion, with Werther tears, melancholia and soul-suffering, which streamed into some of the waltzes Strauss wrote around this time.

In 1883, fifty-eight years old, Strauss married Adele Deutsch, a young Viennese widow. In his soul, feelings of love were still storming ardently. When Johann, or "Jean" as he called himself in this marriage, composed at night, he would interrupt his work frequently to write messages and greetings on slips of paper to his beloved wife, who was in the next room. "How you have made your Jean quite beside himself!

There you are! How excited he becomes! There you are! He would like to laugh, leap, even dance . . . Let's be merry, Adele. On ne vit qu'une fois!" The music of the Cagliostro Waltz, which had just then occurred to Strauss, confirms these happy lines. Another time he wrote her: "It's merry in my soul, gay melodies hum in my head, and my heart overflowing with joy and happiness, is gaily beating the measure." And again: "Sleep sweet, you blue-black-eyed Adele and only wife on earth." Or, on another occasion, "I am wishing you a good-night, peaceful sleep, and a great deal of humor when you awaken. Humor is half the joy of living. To wander merrily through life is my desire." For sixteen years, Johann Strauss lived most happily with Adele. She was the last woman who brought the joy of love to the life-loving composer. On one of the slips of paper he had written her, he swears that he has been "faithful, yes, faithful. I am astonished at myself." Strauss dedicated the "Adele" Waltz to "my beloved wife." After so many Viennese women who loved, are loved, laugh and shine with happiness through his waltzes, he had found *the* woman. Each of the three wives, and the other anonymous women who had, from time to time, enflamed the heart of Johann Strauss—small fires which quickly died and great conflagrations—are all, somehow, still living in Strauss's waltzes.

Viennese women had refined the waltz rhythm, which was originally that of a peasant dance, even by the time of the Schubert waltzes. With Lanner and Strauss, the father, the women lent romantic grace to the waltz; and they gave this rhythm the élan of great passion to be found in the music of Johann Strauss, the son.

But as a woman stood beside Strauss, so did a woman stand beside another composer who wrote in Vienna. In Mozart's "Abduction from the Seraglio," at the beginning of the opera, how tenderly sounded the love-call "Constanza!" This meant a great deal more to Mozart's dark-eyed, frivolous and child-like Constanza, than to the opera-character Constanza. But Constanza was there, too, when he wrote the music for his coquettish Zerlina in "Don Giovanni" and the melodies for his Susanna in "The Marriage of Figaro." She is there, completely, in his Papagena. When Mozart wrote the tender melodies of his Despinetta in "Cosi fan Tutte," he probably was thinking about the lovely Viennese chamber-maids whom the artist, Liotard, so liked to paint, with the little white cap on their heads, and the chocolate-cup in their hands. Mozart loved to put his arms around the waists of such Viennese girls. Laughingly, he used to speak of his "chamber-maiding."

When Beethoven improvised on the piano, he was surrounded by lovely Viennese women who stared, with admiration, at this musician who, according to the testimony of his most intimate friend, "was always in the clutches of love, and that to the highest degree."

When Schubert made Sunday excursions with his friends, the wagon was full of laughing girls. And so it was with all the composers until Brahms, the clumsy, North German, in whom a passion burned which he hid by force behind his silence. How many of his love songs may have been inspired by Viennese women! Of one, however, we are certain—the lovely melody of the "Liebeslieder" Waltzes: "Upon the Danube bank there stands my house; from it my dearest darling looks out." Of all the melodies which Brahms composed in

Beethoven's House in Heiligenstadt

Parc of the Imperial Castle Schonbrunn

Vienna, this is the most tender and most beautiful, and it contains all the grace of the Viennese.

The men and women of Vienna contributed in building the music city. Not only the aristocracy and the court helped, but the bourgeoisie, and the "folk" of Vienna. This folk, the nameless, little people, the many hundreds of thousands who lived a humble life in narrow rooms, prepared the ground which later bore such rich fruits. Without their musical talent and love of music, the music of higher society would have presented a lifeless, artificial picture such as music presented at the court of Frederick the Great in Berlin.

Music filled every corner of Viennese life. From the music of the people came the themes of Haydn symphonies; from their folk-dances came the melodies of the scherzos; from the folk-songs came the Schubert "Lied." Only so long as the music of the Viennese people possessed this vital strength, derived from the folk, was there great Viennese music, and a great musical city, Vienna.

Fame and Traditions

In the year 1540, a man from Suabia came to Vienna. On a wooden ship, he sailed up the Danube which, from Ulm, flows past peasant houses, fields and the mountains of Upper Austria. In all the gardens, the trees were laden with apples and cherries, and off to the south, ranged the mountains of the Salzkammergut. From a promontory, the Benedictine Monastery of Melk overlooked the river. In Wachau, vineyards began to accompany the river on its way, and on one of the mountains, now higher than in the previous country, stood the Goettweih Monastery. Then the hills along the Danube banks grew lower and the land flatter. Only small trees lined the shores, and in their branches the water-birds nested. At last Vienna with its churches and St. Stephen's Cathedral at its centre, came into view. The ship which carried this much-traveled, forty-year old man to Vienna anchored at the foot of a hill where the gate to the city was located.

The way by which this man, Wolfgang Schmelzl, journeyed to Vienna was the ancient one along which, in bygone times, the Nibelungs were drawn to Hungary. Later, on the same highway, Mozart and Beethoven, Bruckner and Brahms, merchants, journalists, artists, came to Vienna, and last of all, Hitler and his armies. This was the road from South Germany to Vienna.

Wolfgang Schmelzl, as a qualified musician, found a place in the Schotten Monastery. He became a schoolmaster and a priest, and wrote plays which were performed in the monas-

54

tery and in the Town Hall. He assembled a song book of Viennese music of those times, for the most part "Quodlibets," in which beloved melodies were shaken and tossed about together like dice in a cup. Like so many others who came there, Schmelzl quickly became a Viennese, and in gratitude to the hospitable city, wrote a poem entitled: "Eulogy to the Praiseworthy, World-famous, Royal City, Vienna" in the year 1548. In it, one may read the oldest praise of Vienna, the musical city: "Ich lob diss Ort fuer alle Land, Hier seid viel Singer, Saytenspiel, Allerley gesellschaft Freuden viel, Mehr Musikos und Instrument, Findt man gwisslich an keinem End."[1]

Thus Vienna rises out of the darkness of history as a city of music, and begins to sound.

Since the time when Wolfgang Schmelzl wrote his Eulogy, the musical fame of Vienna kept growing greater and greater, spreading out over the entire world. Its praises were sung by countless musicians and music-lovers who visited it through the ages. Reichardt, the Berlin Court-Conductor, calls the Vienna of 1793 "the first city for practical music." The composer, Spohr, in 1812, greeted Vienna as "the uncontested capital of the music world." The composer Zelter, a keen and rude thinker, very beautifully described the Vienna of 1819 and the Viennese musical public in a letter to Goethe: "Here people know something about music, and that in contrast to Italy which believes itself to be the beatific church. Here people are really deeply educated. Though they are

---

[1] "I praise this place above all lands,
  Here are many singers, players of strings,
  Everybody enjoys life.
  More music and instruments surely can't be found elsewhere."

pleased by everything, nevertheless the best sticks permanently. They enjoy hearing a mediocre opera which is well cast.
An excellent work, even though it is not so well cast, they
retain."

Of the opinions of more modern musicians, I shall mention,
because it is not so well-known, the one Wagner had of Vienna
when he came there in the revolutionary year 1848 with re-
formatory ideas for the Viennese opera: "Vienna, which on a
beautiful clear Sunday I saw again, has, I must confess, completely enchanted me. I have re-discovered Paris, only a more
beautiful, more lively and German one." In a second letter,
Wagner wrote to his wife: "This Vienna is a glorious city;
here everything with which I come in contact is so warm and
so pleasant! The atmosphere is home-like, yet wonderful.
What surroundings! I had forgotten everything, and now,
for the first time, I am really enchanted." Still more enthusiastic is Wagner's opinion of Vienna in the section of his
autobiography where he tells of the Vienna "Lohengrin" performances in 1861, and of the "uninterrupted, hot-blooded
ovations which I have experienced nowhere except with the
Viennese public." Wagner also speaks here of "the great gifts
of the Viennese public in respect to music,"—high praise,
indeed, from the greatest musician of the 19th century.

In a bad humor, Hans von Bülow sprays poison over Vienna
which, as unwilling praise, appears especially valuable. In a
letter to Raff, he wrote, in 1860, on Vienna: "Moreover, the
Berliners are musically more intelligent than the Viennese,
although all the means here, especially the official, are of the
highest rank in Germany, in any case. Here they have the
best orchestras, the best soloists." And in another letter of

the same year, written to Draesecke, it is again a case of mixing gall and praise: "Orchestra and opera in Vienna magnificent—otherwise pure filth, stupidity and colossal meanness."

There was some sort of enchantment in the musical ground where Vienna stood. Great musicians trod this ground and were held fast by it. Thus one day Beethoven came from the Rhineland to Vienna and never went away again. Brahms came there from the cold north, and never deserted Vienna. For a time it looked as if Richard Strauss, too, would be one of those composers who came only to remain permanently; for in 1919 he became Director of the Vienna Opera, and built a house in Vienna. This house stands in the Botanical Garden, the Director of which was once the famous botanist Jacquin in whose home Mozart composed so much wonderful music; and near the Belvedere Garden where Bruckner spent the last years before his death. But what vicinity in Vienna was not a musician's neighborhood?

In his Vienna home, Richard Strauss worked in his high studio, which was adorned with a costly wooden ceiling he had brought from Italy; among Greek terra cottas and old pictures, writing his notes in a most elegant script. Often I have sat there waiting for him after opera performances which he had conducted. When he came home, stimulated and red in the face, after the opera, I have often heard him exclaim enthusiastically: "One can do such things only in Vienna!"

There were but a few musicians in recent times who either could not find a footing in Vienna or were pushed aside by it. Among these was Robert Schumann, who came to Vienna during the Revolution of 1848 and went away again, because he found there no interest for his music which, at that time, was considered revolutionary. Lortzing, too, one of the great masters of German Comic Opera, was not held fast by Viennese soil.

Lortzing was active only three years in Vienna as Conductor of the Theatre-an-der-Wien. He had rejoiced when he received this offer. "Anyone who doesn't go to Vienna is a nobody," he wrote in May, 1845, when Director Pokorny made him the offer to come to Vienna. "How beautiful Vienna is!" he cried out in July, 1846, when he was honored there as conductor. But soon the tone of his letters changed. As soon as March, 1847, it was: "Life in Vienna is quite nice; but theatre conditions are less so—no repertory, no system!" Then in May, 1847, Lortzing wrote that Vienna was "no place" for him, and that "here not a soul speaks to me." In November, 1847, he complains: "I have been here now for fifteen months, but nevertheless, I still cannot feel much at home in the so-called beautiful Vienna . . . Its musical taste is the most spoiled one can find." In 1848, he shouts: "The musical life displeases me. The taste is horrible." Great artists, too, are only human. Human nature colors opinion, and Lortzing was influenced in his because his operas, as he himself communicates, "have not been in the repertoire for half a year." Italian taste predominated in Vienna, or, as Lortzing complained, "Just tootling and more tootling and trilling."

But such phenomena and manifestations were exceptions. In general, through the centuries, Vienna showed an astounding force in attracting and holding musicians fast. Their various nationalities and races joined to create the great tradition which made Vienna's music rich and colorful.

Thus the sound of the famous Viennese violin is unthinkable without the influence of the Hungarian. The great violin teacher Joseph Boehm, who kept educating generation after generation of violinists at the Vienna Conservatory, came to Vienna from Budapest in 1816. He had the whispering, voluptuous sound of gypsy violins in his blood. One of his most famous pupils was Joseph Joachim, who studied under him at the Conservatory, along with H. W. Ernst, Hellmesberger, Gruen and others. Everyone who heard Joachim play the great Beethoven quartets knew that this classical violinist carried the dark sound of Hungarian violins over into his classical greatness. It was this Hungarian-colored violin tone which was passed on by Boehm, Hellmesberger, and Gruen, who later became violin teachers themselves at the Vienna Conservatory. Almost all the violinists of the Vienna Royal Opera Orchestra under Hans Richter and Gustav Mahler were pupils either of Gruen or of Hellmesberger. Fritz Kreisler was the last great pupil of Gruen.

The Viennese violin-tone is like the fragrance exhaled by famous cross-bred roses. The same holds true for all the other forms of Viennese music. They are the result of cross-breeding, like Vienna itself.

When I mentioned this drop of Hungarian perfume the Vienna violin tone gives forth, I have not by far exhausted the history of this sound which the Vienna Philharmonic, the Rosé Quartet, Joachim and Fritz Kreisler made world-famous.

Joseph Boehm was not only a violin teacher, but also the leader of a string quartet, about which the Leipzig Musikzeitung of 1821 delightedly exclaimed: "So must one hear Beethoven's and Mozart's quartets played!" Also members of this quartet were Weiss and Linke, who had played in the famous Rasumoffsky Quartet which Count Rasumoffsky had engaged, and who first played in his great palace Beethoven's last quartets. Weiss and Linke had often seen Beethoven at rehearsals, and had heard his thunderous voice cry out: "Does he believe that I give a thought to his miserable violin when the spirit overcomes me?"

When members of the Schuppanzig Quartet, in 1816, gave a farewell concert which consisted entirely of Beethoven's works, the composer was present, and the newspapers announced: "Beethoven attended and seemed very much pleased." The Schuppanzig Quartet was the authentic Beethoven quartet.

When Weiss and Linke later played with Boehm, the concerts took place under the trees of the Prater, in a coffee house, at eight o'clock in the morning, so early did the Viennese arise to hear music. And the spirit of Beethoven was among them. Thus, the sound of these violins became Beethoven's sound, which was always preserved in Vienna wherever violins played.

The sensual Viennese violin sound which streamed out of the orchestra had still another effect. In the center of the Viennese Opera Orchestra, great conductors—Hans Richter, Arthur Nikisch, Franz Schalk, and last, Arthur Bodansky— sat as musicians, and all of them with the exception of Hans Richter, who played horn, were violinists who had retained in their ears the sound of this warm, streaming violin-tone. Later, when they stood at the conductor's desk, they carried something of this sound over into their orchestral visions. The full-bodied sound of Hans Richter's orchestra, the romantic, luxuriant tone of Nikisch's, was inspired by that of the Viennese violins.

Thus, in the course of centuries, a great musical city arose in the center of the Danube lands, a city where old traditions were piled up like the ancient crowns and swords, the jewel-adorned glasses and ornate gold plate, the silken mantles and tapestries in the Treasure Chamber of the Viennese Court. These traditions worked so long as living forces in Vienna that they were no more memory and history, but the present. There was no musician in Vienna who could escape them. Great musicians had created this tradition and each new generation of musicians carried it on. Even revolutionaries like Arnold Schoenberg and Alban Berg recognized this tradition which they sought to disturb, since their hate was only reversed love. In this Viennese music tradition all the spiritual streams of north, east, south and west met. Haydn's symphonies bound together all the characteristics of northern and southern German music—Austrian folk-music and the strong logic of the developments of Philipp Emmanuel Bach, the forms of the Mannheim Symphony and the rhythms of the folk dances of the Alpine landscape. In his Military Symphony, the Adagio is built upon a French song. His Folk Hymn originates from a Gregorian melody. Hungarian and even Croatian music left their traces upon his music. And everywhere Italian melody is mingled. Along this road Viennese music was fused into world-music. All Europe made music in Vienna. And that made Vienna a great musical city.

2

The Last Chapter of Great
Music in Vienna

On The Ringstrasse

I myself lived through the last chapter of the great musical city Vienna. We who were born in Vienna, and grew up there, had no idea, during the city's brilliant period before the first world war that this epoch was to be the end of the greatest development of history of music known to the world; and still less did we suspect that the Hapsburg Monarchy, of which Vienna was the capital, was destined to decline.

We grew up in a beautiful, large city which had adorned itself with new palaces, new gardens and new avenues. A new Royal Palace, too, rose out of the earth, next to the low, old one which had seen so much history, and before which, as children, we had played among blooming elder trees and proud equestrian statues. From the great, open, pillared hall of the new palace, one could see the marble columns of the new Parliament, which was a Greek temple, stylistically; the iron man on the Gothic Town Hall's tower; the garden of the Town Hall and the fortress; and from there on out to the Kahlenberg. We enjoyed the splendid city which was so elegantly beautiful, and never thought that the light which shone over it could ever be that of a colorful sunset.

We saw the traffic of modern times stream through the streets and watched, amazed, when the first electric lights went on in a shop window, and the first small electric street-car started its way to the Mödling woods. The new time of technical wonders was apparent everywhere in the streets. Big-city life had lively aspects. Well-dressed men and women, chatting and laughing, walked slowly through the new streets. Elegant riders sat on full-blooded horses. Fiacres drove through the streets and when the driver cracked his whip, the horses raised their feet as if in a graceful waltz-step. There were Austrian army officers in colored uniforms and white kid gloves; the Emperor's guards, marching past, in red-braided uniforms, white leather breeches and highly-polished boots, halberds in hand, on their way to the old palace. There were mounted guards, too, with leopard skins and long white helmet-plumes, riding Arabian horses. The great city seemed festive, lively, full of color.

Even the modest citizen had an easy existence. At ten o'clock in the morning, after two hours' work, he would go to his favorite inn and fortify himself for further accomplishments with a glass of fresh beer and a portion of goulash. Evenings, with wife and children, he would saunter in the Prater where in good weather the inns were crowded, where games and entertainments were continuously patronized, and where music sounded from all sides—shrill barrel organs, blaring, brass bands, or waltz violins. Or he might sit in a corner of the tavern he regularly frequented, and talk politics with his cronies. The waiters kept carrying glass after glass of foaming beer, while smoke rose to the roof from numerous meerschaum pipes or long Virginia cigars.

The greatest German poet called the Viennese "Phaecians on whose hearth one always kept turning the skewer." Before 1918 this statement certainly was a true one. The Viennese knew it, and sang: "There is only one Imperial city, there is only one Vienna!"

This beautiful, jovial, well-to-do city which today has

66

become a legendary one, was for us, too, a musical city. We became musicians without knowing why or how. Everywhere we went we encountered music. We sang and fiddled. As a student in high school, I took my violin every evening and went to other homes and played classical string-quartets with minor officials, teachers or business people, just as if that were self-understood. On Sundays, I played Haydn's or Mozart's Masses in church choirs. On excursions we all sang choruses and canons. Or we stood, evenings, in front of restaurant gardens or in the parks and listened to band concerts. Thus we prepared ourselves for the holiday when we went for the first time to the Opera palace on the Ring. From noontime on we stood, boys and girls, in front of the small entrance to the Opera House, which still remained locked, with piano scores in our hands, heatedly debating about music. When the door at last was opened, we would storm excitedly to the box-office, and then up four flights of stairs like competing foot-racers—up the still dimly-lighted passageway to the fourth gallery from where we could look down on the stage. Slowly, after some time, the musicians came into the comfortable orchestra pit. The violinists tuned their instruments and little runs rose on high like butterflies. Wood-winds tried passages, and the low brasses tossed growling, antedeluvian tones into the bustle of the orchestral voices. The sounds kept swelling louder and louder, like the buzzing of a tea-kettle about to boil. Then the lights in the hall were extinguished, the great chandelier went slowly out and one could see only the ghostly glow of the lights over the musicians' desks. When all had become silent and one's heart pounded excitedly, the conductor came, sat at his desk, opened the sorcerer's book and raised his magic wand. This was a festive moment. For then, for the first time, were we taken in to the great Viennese music community which assembled every evening in the new opera house. A new generation of musicians and of music had joined itself to the old. We had become full-fledged citizens of the old music city.

Later on, as critic, I sat in one of the comfortable red-plush orchestra seats. But I never entered the opera hall without throwing a glance toward the gallery. It always was a desirous, longing glance, for nowhere else was the enthusiasm for music and the delight in it more genuine than there where young people crowded and sat in corners, looking down at the stage or at their piano scores. It was also a glance of gratitude, for here I was brought up and educated to the position of opera critic. Like almost all Viennese music-lovers and musicians, I began my musical life in the fourth gallery of the Vienna Opera. The Opera House belonged to my existence. I was young there and became old there; and it was one of the most beautiful moments in my career as critic when, on one of my birthdays, the young people of the fourth gallery presented me with an address which lauded my critical activity with flattering and highly exuberant words. In the Opera of Vienna we were a great musical community. The house was a sort of musical Town Hall of Vienna to which each new generation of Viennese sent its representatives. Thus the Vienna Opera House meant something different, something more significant, in the life of the city than did that of the splendid opera houses elsewhere. It stood in the center of Viennese life, and not on its outside.

When we were growing up, Vienna was still the musical

Courtyard of an old Viennese Commoners House

Staircase in the Winter Palace of Prince Eugene

center of the world. To make this clear, I shall invite the reader to accompany me along the Ringstrasse, Vienna's most festive thoroughfare, on a sunny day in 1890. At this period, between twelve and one every day, Vienna's fashionable society took its promenade on the broad street between the City Park and the new Opera House. Everyone whom one might call "all Vienna" crowded on that small section of the Ringstrasse. Here everyone seemed to know everyone else, greeted, chattered and sauntered along; with the bright laughter of the women as the upper voice over the babble and flirting, over the malicious remarks and anecdotes of the metropolis. Here one met politicians and industrialists, young and old aristocrats who spoke the nasal dialect of the castles, officers among whom the dragoons with golden helmets, and Hungarian hussars with braided coats and tightly fitted breeches were the most elegant; well-known artists, women of whom Vienna spoke, the "wits" who were invited to all the parties and whose latest bits of gossip flew swiftly along the Ring. What was the subject of all this conversation? The last theatre première, the latest excess of the young Archduke, the newest divorce, an interesting guest, a new affair, sometimes politics—which were joked about—always love, which was likewise not taken seriously. One laughed over the greatest vicissitudes of life and was always just as witty, charming, frivolous and superficial as people of every old, overcultivated society are bound to be.

I can still see the distinguished Count Berchtold on a summer's day in 1914, standing in the doorway of a Ringstrasse Hotel. He had just signed the declaration of war on Serbia. Now he stood here, slender, laughing ironically, a gold-tipped cigarette in his well-manicured fingers, watching the crowds and conversing with the passersby. Thus cultivated Ringstrasse society entered the world-war which disrupted it. It had lived laughing and joking, and laughing and joking it died.

On the Ringstrasse bridle-path, one saw distinguished gentlemen and ladies in long black fitted riding habits returning from their morning ride in the Prater. Fiacres passed along the road, or smart English carriages which were driven by the aristocrats themselves. Military music sounded in the distance, and sometimes the old Emperor passed by in an open, low carriage, with his adjutant seated beside him, and his old valet on the coach-seat with the driver. Then the officers would interrupt their jokes, stand straight and stiff as poles on the rim of the Ringstrasse, and salute, while men in civilian clothes removed their hats. Slowly, then, the promenaders started into motion again under the fragrant acacia trees, and went on with their gossip.

This was the Vienna of the 1890 period. In the so-called "Ringstrasse Period," a slightly different picture would have been presented to the reader during a promenade. At first glance, he could recognize Johannes Brahms as one of the strollers. Almost daily, Brahms would come from his nearby dwelling, his bowler hat pushed up over his forehead and his hands crossed behind his back. He was, at that time, rather corpulent, a bourgeois-looking man with a flowing beard whom one might have taken for a professor, had not his blue eyes been genuine artist's eyes, and had not his rocking gait been that of a dreamer.

There was still another famous musician one often met

on the Ringstrasse who looked like a professor. Going unhurriedly on his way to the opera, he was big and broadshouldered, and impressive. This was the famous Wagnerian conductor, Hans Richter, first conductor of the Vienna Opera. When Wagner made him his conductor, Richter was young and had a blond beard like the youthful Wotan. Now his beard was already greying, but the eyes behind their spectacles still preserved their steel-blue glitter.

Brahms and Richter lifted their hats to a small man with heavy, bushy eyebrows, white goatee, and hook-nose which looked like the beak of an old hawk. This was the famous music critic and Wagner-slayer, Eduard Hanslick, who wrote witty and intellectual music criticisms for fashionable Ringstrasse society. Brahms, Richter and Hanslick, though, could not help smiling when, in the distance, they saw a little man approaching who looked strange indeed in these surroundings. He did not wear a smartly-cut town suit, but instead, a wide jacket of heavy material which he had had sent from Upper Austria, where his home was. His trousers fell in countless wrinkles to his small feet, and their bagginess gave his legs an elephantine appearance. His face was that of an old peasant, weathered by air, sun and rain; but it was a peasant face with Roman features and the profile of the Roman Emperor Claudius. The singular appearance of the man became more marked when he lifted the broad-brimmed artist's hat from his bald, round head, and, with a deep bow, bent almost to the ground. This strange man was Anton Bruckner, who, at that time, was still ridiculed and mocked. Now a great bust of him, delineating all the wrinkles of his old face, stands in Vienna's City Park. He is raising the thumb of his right hand as if he wished to explain something, or as if he was just hearing a melody, and wanted to say to the twittering birds who perch on his shoulder: "Be still!"

A younger man was there, also. He had a gloomy fanatical glance, wore a short brown beard, and dressed most of the time in a brown velvet coat. He looked admiringly at Bruckner. This was Hugo Wolf. Nearby was a very short man, almost lost under his artist's hat. His face had a yellow tinge and showed unmistakable Hungarian features, his eyes brown and kindly, a white mustache falling over the sensuous old mouth. It was the famous composer of the opera, "The Queen of Sheba," Carl Goldmark.

There was only one musician who did not go on foot, but drove along the Ringstrasse, comfortably leaning back in his luxurious fiacre. His beard was cut like the Emperor's and dyed black, because this man with the large burning eyes did not want to grow old. He had always been the singer of the Viennese joy of life, of the countryside, of "Wine, Woman and Song," and he wanted always to be the most famous Viennese: Johann Strauss.

Had the guest whom I accompanied along the Ringstrasse come ten years later, still during the reign of Franz Josef, he would have met an unusual man. This man always carried his soft hat in his hand, and walked with a strange, stamping gait, limping with his right leg from time to time. His dark face, framed by long hair, had a sharp profile and eyes which shot out dark looks through his glasses. It was the ascetic face of a mediaeval monk. In this man the nerves pulled tensely and from him a spiritual strength streamed forth. It could be either a good or a bad spirit flashing from the high forehead and the eyes. This was the new Opera Director of the Emperor, Gustav Mahler. Still later, after the first World War, the greatest German musician, Richard Strauss, came to Vienna as Director of the Opera. One could see him on his way there, every day—tall, slender and with a smile that Claude Debussy compared to the smile of a victorious conqueror striding among the huts of an African negro town. It was a new era in which, also, young, audacious musicians were to be seen on the Ringstrasse, much to the horror of the public who saw the palace of classical music practically in flames. Among these were Arnold Schoenberg and Alban Berg.

Thus musical history promenaded on the Ringstrasse between noon and one o'clock. The greatest musicians of the new era were at home there. They had not yet become monuments, but enjoyed, like everyone who lived in Vienna, the beautiful city in which they worked and struggled, and from where their works went forth into the wide world. One encountered the musical great at all kinds of social gatherings, at the opera and concerts, on excursions, in the restaurants and taverns of Vienna. At the "Gause" or "The Red Porcupine"—taverns in the inner city—one could often see Brahms with his friends, a glass of light beer in front of him, and at another table, Anton Bruckner with his pupils, like Franz Schalk or Ferdinand Loewe, both of whom later became famous conductors. Bruckner would eat his beloved roast pork with a mountain of cabbage, and drink his Pilsener beer, just like other mortals, and would look anxiously, from time to time, toward Brahms' table. When Bruckner rose to go, he made the same kind of deep bow which, as organist of the

St. Florian Monastery, he had made to the Archbishop Rudigier of Linz, to Brahms, who laughed mockingly. As one of the Directors of the "Society of Friends of Music," Brahms was Bruckner's superior. The Conservatory where Bruckner was a poorly-paid teacher had been founded by the Society, and was its own school. Thus we see that Brahms and Bruckner were also only human, and had not yet become historical figures.

Great musical history distinguished Franz Josef's entire lifetime in Vienna. When the Emperor was born, Beethoven was still alive and shook his grey forest of hair when he threw his last string quartets at the manuscript paper like a Vulcan tossing forth lava and fire. Only three years, then, had passed since Schubert's death. But when Franz Josef died and, in his coffin, was borne along the Ringstrasse for the last time, throughout the world was a new music which rose from the chaos and the war which was to destroy the Empire of the Hapsburgs. Arnold Schönberg was born in Franz Josef's reign. The whole development of classic to romantic, on to modern music took place under Franz Josef, and the great musicians who promenaded on the Ringstrasse were the leading characters in this development.

The New Vienna

The new Vienna, in which the last chapter of great musical history was set, arose during the reign of Emperor Franz Josef.

This Emperor it was who gave the order to tear down the fortress walls of the city of Vienna. In 1858 the first brick was broken from them. The old city gate where police officials used suspiciously to examine the papers of arriving visitors was demolished. The old Viennese, who had always known their city as a narrow fortress, stood about and watched how the laborers knocked down the thick walls while the dust flew.

Until this time, Vienna, for centuries, had been a small city of high town houses clustered together in dark streets around churches and palaces, with three or four small squares where market booths stood. From the tower of St. Stephen's cathedral in the center of Vienna, the watchman kept his vigil. The city was protected by the old walls and trenches, which the Turks had stormed and broken in.

Evenings the Viennese went walking on the ramparts to take their breath of air. On the "Glacis"—a green meadow beyond the city walls—they watched the soldiers exercising, and looked off in the distance at the outlying districts. Of these, only a few had a citified character, such as "Mariahilf," which is now Vienna's 6th district and the site of numerous silk factories. Here lived the wealthy factory owners, so the people called the suburb the "Diamond Ground." Most of the suburbs were such villages. Here the Viennese noblemen, in the 17th and 18th centuries, had built their summer palaces, with magnificent parks in French style, with ponds where goldfish swam, and sandstone statues lining both sides of the paths. In these gardens they gave their spendthrift summer parties, to which the guests drove in gold adorned carriages, with runners preceding, and lackeys behind the seat.

When the Viennese promenaders looked southward from the ramparts, they saw, surrounded by an enormous garden, the ornate palace of Count Fondi, which later belonged to Prince Schwarzenberg; and beside it the great park with lakes and Egyptian sphinxes, on the brow of a hill where stands Prince Eugene's summer palace. Nearer to the city there was a whole group of palaces—that of Duke Trautson, Master of the Court, that of Marquis Rofrano (whom one knows from "Der Rosenkavalier" as the youthful lover of Maria Theresia), and, farther on, the palace and garden of the princely bishop, Count Schoenborn. The Emperor, too, had a summer palace here—the "Favorita"—summer castle of Emperor Leopold I, Josef I and Charles VI. There was a summer palace in the Augarten, and, most important of all, the castle of Schoenbrunn, in whose large garden Emperor Franz Josef died.

From the woods of the Kahlenberg, a fresh wind blew in the evening. Viennese in high buttoned black coats, with broad ties and wide collars sat with ladies in crinolines and beribboned straw hats in the coffee booths which stood against the rampart walls, and sipped lemonade.

In the 19th century, the fortress city became too small for the many people who came there from all over Europe, and room had to be made for them in a new and larger Vienna. In the classical period, the city had two hundred and fifty thousand inhabitants. When Emperor Franz Josef came to the throne in 1848, it had four hundred and eight thousand. In 1888, the population had risen to seven hundred and seventy-five thousand when room had to be created for it to expand. And when Franz Josef died, the population stood at two million.

In 1865, there were the walls and gates, the trenches and the "Glacis" had been, the new Ringstrasse was laid out—the festival street of new Vienna, fifty-seven meters wide with one path for horsemen and another for pedestrians. Along the Ringstrasse the great new public buildings were erected: the Parliament, where the free word of the new era was spoken by orators of all nations, with Greek temple pillars, marble friezes and bronze statues; the City Hall, with the loggia of a Venetian palace, the two great museums, the new Burg-theater, the ornate Gothic Votive Church, the University with its Renaissance halls, the splendid Stock Exchange, the new Opera House. Archduke Ludwig Victor built his interesting and beautiful Renaissance palace on a corner of the Ring-strasse. Archduke Eugene built a similar town residence nearby. The princes of the new Stock Exchange wealth also built homes on the Ringstrasse, such as the show-place of the banker Tedesco, which was decorated with frescoes by Rahl. There were colored frescoes, too, on the great "Heinrichshof," which the Danish architect, Hansen, had built nearby. Among these new buildings were large and small parks, and when spring came to new Vienna, the fragrance of lilacs floated along the Ringstrasse.

When, in 1876, the Ringstrasse was completed, there was a festival procession the like of which no one had seen since the time of the Renaissance. The greatest Viennese painter had conceived the procession's plan. Austria's trades and arts, drawn in carriages, passed in review before the Emperor's pavilion, just as Hans Makart had sketched it. The small, pale artist was the painter of the new and color-happy Vienna, just as Johann Strauss was its musician. In his palace on the "Wieden," Makart stood in old-fashioned German attire before his easel and let the glowing colors run over the canvas like streams of fire. The most beautiful women of Viennese aristocracy posed nude for him, and one can still see them to-day in his great historical pictures where, naked, they surround Emperor Maximilian during his march into Bruges; or when one of their number, the lovely Princess Liechtenstein, lay on a luxurious couch as Cleopatra. Now the painter rode at the head of the procession, and swept off his feathered hat before the Emperor, who put his hand to his military cap in salute.

In a short time a new metropolis had grown up out of the old fortress town. In 1868, the Danube was brought closer to the city and on its new banks rose warehouses, dock yards and cranes. In 1870, the new water supply system was built, which brought spring water from the Alps directly to all the city's houses. Vienna was the bustling capital of a new time, with free trade, speculation growing more and more. Minds, too, became freer and more active. At the University of Vienna, famous professors taught; students from all nations came there to study. In the School of Applied Arts, Viennese artisans became artists who produced costly glass vessels and leather articles. Writers and artists from many lands came there. In the great Viennese newspapers, one read editorials which resounded throughout Europe, and critiques which were considered authoritative everywhere—all in a clear, intellectual style which, in the feuilletons, also had the light conversational tone of the Viennese salon.

In the new city, a new society had assembled. From the Austrian provinces, which were multi-lingual, men came to Vienna, especially from Bohemia and Moravia, but also from Poland and Hungary. Vienna was still a city of mixed nationalities. From all sections of Austria, urged by the liberal ideas of the time, came Jews who provided a progressive element in business and trades as well as in the intellectual field, and whose women ornamented the new society with an eastern charm. This new society bound itself to the old court aristocracy which still set the tone.

Up to 1914, Vienna was basically an aristocratic city, and behind its democratic forms, the old feudal order of the baroque period was but badly hidden. The court certainly made its compromises with the modern national and social movements, generally at the last moment, when it could not do otherwise—and too late. But Emperor Franz Josef nevertheless felt himself a follower of the old Hapsburgs, who had been a proud race and who knew only ruler and subjects. The social life of Vienna always, as in the 17th century, revolved around the court, like a wheel around its axis; and the new industrial and Stock Exchange men, streaming with wealth, crowded themselves into the court society to receive orders and titles from the Emperor. When they gave parties in their new houses, they invited aristocrats as window-dressing. The young sons of Viennese manufacturers dressed themselves like aristocrats and aped their accent and manner.

A part of the new society was elevated to the rank of nobility. Between the courtly feudal society of Vienna and the "folk," comprised of modest bourgeois and workers, there was still a dividing line which had sprung up in the 18th century, at which time the aristocrats surrounded their palaces with iron chains so as to hold the people at a safe distance away. One can see even to-day, in Vienna, such iron chains hanging on the walls, as decoration, on many of these noble palaces.

The courtly society and newly-rich citizenry which surrounded the Hapsburgs, took possession of new Vienna in which the old order, and that of industry, trade and the stock market mingled. These minglings brought forth complicated mental activities and many break-ups. Here was old and new, history and the present. Here was old baroque Vienna with its court which still lived according to the dictates of the Spanish Ceremonial. Here were the aristocrats who held high posts in military and official circles, the officers who felt themselves personal officers of the Emperor, and here was the Church which sent its confessors to the court and the palaces, and before whose Cardinal of Vienna the Emperor himself knelt. But here were also the modern forms of life of an industrial and a technical age. All these opposite elements which finally destroyed the Hapsburg Empire mingled before 1914 in a general joy of living as in a boiling kettle.

Vienna's new society sat in fiacres which drove out, decked with flowers, on the first of May, along the main allée of the Prater. It occupied the boxes and orchestra of the theatres. It drove out to the fashionable restaurants in Vienna's suburbs—to the "Stelzer" on the border of the Rodaun woods, and to the "Red Barn" where it ordered "milk-cream strudel."

It went to horse races at Freudenau and then on to the fashionable Prater inns where the fresh roasted young geese were served, or cray-fish, or the fragrant "May bowl." This society, which we already encountered on the Ringstrasse, was elegant, sensuous and gay. Its members loved Vienna's life, the wealth, and the women, among whom the girls of the Opera Ballet were especially sought after. They bought villas in the Salzkammergut to which they moved after the big races, and where they could be near the court of the Emperor which was installed in his summer villa at Ischl. When, after the autumn hunts, the court returned to Vienna, the new season could begin with balls and receptions, theatre premières and Prater excursions.

As in every feudal society, in new Vienna the officers played an important role. The old Emperor wore the military uniform, and we used to see him in a marshal's uniform when, bent slightly, the right foot forward and his hand on his sword-hilt, he greeted a deputation or inaugurated a ball. As the Emperor stood, so stood the officers on the Ringstrasse. They copied the Emperor's bearing, the way he held his sword, and his manner of speaking the dialect. The young aristocrats served in the noble Cavalry regiments which accepted no commoners. They built their own caste. Commoner-women had to content themselves with infantry officers. For the Viennese woman, however, an officer counted as the only man. Officers were the best dancers and paid the most ardent court. All spoke the easy Viennese dialect, at court and in the salons. To the theatres and to the streets, to balls and to society, the colored uniforms of the officers lent bright spots which made the whole picture of Viennese life rich and brilliant.

That was the society of new Vienna which, according to old traditions, was a musical public. Opera performances and great concerts belonged to the sensuous, intellectual, happy life in new Vienna, and the music had to correspond to this atmosphere. At the time when the Ringstrasse was opened, Italian opera, the brilliance of Meyerbeer's works, the wit of the French Opéra Comique, waltzes and operettas of Johann Strauss was what the public demanded. Classical music belonged to Vienna and was a heritage of the city, but even in Franz Josef's time, Vienna, in its musical inclinations, was a half-Italian city which, above all, loved melody, lively rhythm and the sensuality of sound. The Viennese—the new Viennese—was not of a profound and earnest temperament, but elegant, gay and formal. He had something of the lightness of a dancer and the motion of a comedian. To this was added the witty, superficial mind of a salon habitué, and the sensuousness of a lover. "My life course is love and desire," announces the title of one of the loveliest Strauss waltzes. This, too, was the prevailing atmosphere of the old city which, also in new times, was an aristocratic one; even when the manifestation of new forces and new social movements increased, working under the brilliant surface, and shaking the ground upon which the Vienna of Emperor Franz Josef stood.

Emperor Franz Josef

Amid all the music which flowed through the palaces, homes, gardens and streets of new Vienna, there was one single man who remained entirely unmoved. This was Emperor Franz Josef who gave his name to the last chapter of Viennese musical history.

At six in the morning, he sat at his desk in the palace, or at Schoenbrunn and signed documents. On the desk stood a box of Virginia cigars. Nearby were the ministers in frockcoats and black cravats, who reported the order of the day.

When Franz Josef entered the Royal Palace as Emperor, he was a youth of eighteen. Now he was an old man with a white beard, and the oldest Viennese could never remember him except as an old man, who traveled through all the provinces of his empire dressed in the uniform of a Field Marshal, or who reviewed military parades, sitting on a brown horse. Wherever he went, mayors, city officials, Catholic priests and rabbis stood, with scrolls in hand, to welcome him. Children in national costumes timidly recited poems, and the old man's friendly blue eyes shone on the speaker. Only in the summer did the Emperor exchange his uniform for the suit of a hunter, when he lived at his country residence at Ischl. On his head he wore a green hunting cap, with a "chamois beard." He wore the grey hunter's coat and short leather trousers which leave the knees bare, when he went hunting in the mountains for woodcock and chamois. At night, he put on an old military coat as night-dress and lay down on an iron army-cot.

He was a lonely old man. During the sixty-eight years that he ruled Austria, there were more unhappy hours for him than joyous ones. His Italian possessions were lost. In the War of 1866, Bismarck's German armies defeated the Austrians. Hungary freed itself from the remaining possessions of the Hapsburgs. The nations of the empire fought for their independence. Emperor Franz Josef had the feeling that he was sitting in an old, decaying house where one dared not move for fear of having the whole thing fall apart. Only unwillingly and hesitatingly did he give the command when the first World War broke out. He had a premonition that the war meant the end of his monarchy.

In the Emperor's own house misfortune pursued him. The Empress traveled about in foreign countries and her romantic spirit was also foreign to this correct and sober man. The Crown Prince was shot on a night of drunkenness. The imperial home was lonely. That music brings solace and that tones can speak with the voice of spirits, the Emperor did not know. He had no connections with music. The singing and organ playing in the court chapel, a court concert on festival occasions, and the daily military concert in the palace court-yard provided all the music which reached the Emperor's ears.

Historians have never ceased debating since the old monarchy was destroyed in 1918, whether the Emperor was a great or a mediocre man. Several wished to see in this Hapsburg a more than average ruler, because of his long political experience, his courtly dignity, his cleverness in forestalling

The Summer Palace of Prince Eugene (The "Belvedere")

The Horse-Ballet "La Contesa dell' Aria e dell' Acqua" (January 24, 1667)

the end of the monarchy. Some saw in him a dry official nature, a zealous worker, a mediocre man who derived a certain routine from long experience. If there is one sure proof that Emperor Franz Josef had an average nature without vision, it lies in the fact that he remained in a city which was full of music without displaying musical interest.

The industrious old official who had virtues but no imagination had no connection with the arts. In his younger years he had taken an interest in the Burgtheater where his dear friend, Katherina Schratt, had played. This simple, sensible Viennese woman was for years the special friend of the Emperor, but he was not very romantic in this respect. When the Emperor left his castle of Schönbrunn and sought his beloved in a nearby villa at Hietzing, she had to receive him at six in the morning in formal salon attire. It was the Hapsburg who called upon her and who remained the Hapsburg even in the drawing-room. The Empress, slender, tall, with a dark crown of hair, had a drop of diseased blood in her veins which drove her to foreign places. She galloped on horseback across the Hungarian plains or climbed in the mountains or voyaged in the south, where, in the hills of Corfu, she had built a marble palace which was like a theatrical setting. Here she walked among laurels and cypresses, past marble statues, gazed nostalgically on the blue sea and had Homer read aloud to her by a small, hunchbacked Greek. The bright laughter of Katherina Schratt, meanwhile, in the Emperor's loneliness, resounded over an abyss which was dry and cold.

When Emperor Franz Josef was older, he seldom went to the Burgtheater. His greatest artistic interest was in paintings. He showed preference for diligently executed still-lifes such as the artist Schoedel painted, with iridescent silk cloths and ivory and glasses which reflected the sunlight. In painting, too, he shunned the imaginative, preferring clever handwork. Each year Franz Josef opened the Art Exhibition, viewed the pictures with interest or politeness and took his leave with words which have become proverbial: "It was very beautiful. I enjoyed it very much." These words were impersonal, because a Hapsburg did not reveal his inner feelings except to the confessor of the Catholic Church, who, during successive Hapsburg reigns, had come to the Imperial Palace, in black monks' robes, prudent and taciturn.

At the Vienna Opera, I seldom saw the Emperor present. He went, naturally, when the Spanish Court Ceremonial prescribed his appearance. It is self-understood that he was present when the new opera house was opened. He went, too, when foreign potentates came to Vienna, and in whose honor festival performances were given. The last time I saw Emperor Franz Josef at the Opera was when he celebrated his seventieth birthday, and the German Emperor Wilhelm, with all the princes of the German Confederation came to Vienna. At that time, Gustav Mahler was the Opera Director, and he conducted the first act of Goldmark's opera, "The Queen of Sheba," which had been newly mounted with great splendor for the occasion. In addition, ballets were presented. The Opera was filled with noble court society. Everywhere were uniforms with many orders and decorations, and white-bosomed shirts. In the boxes glittered the jewels of the ladies, and bosoms and arms gleamed for exhibition. The Emperor sat with his guests in the great Royal Box, from which was suspended the rug embroidered with his initials. Beside him sat Emperor Wilhelm with his turned-up mustache. As the ballet girls made their entrance, Wilhelm slapped his thigh with the palm of his hand. This gesture he repeated at every new scenic effect. It would be interesting to know what the two rulers thought of the little man at the conductor's desk who now directed the opera. Probably they did not spend any thought upon him.

Behind the Royal Box was a room, decorated with frescoes, where the court society ate a buffet supper during intermissions, because the Royal Opera was not only a palace of music, but also a society salon.

If Franz Josef, on less festive occasions, visited the Opera, it was generally at ballet performances. At such times, he would sit in his private box at the left of the stage. His large opera glass lay on the parapet of the box, and from time to time, he raised it to his eyes. He was always alone in his box and gave one the impression that he was an old man who wished to rest.

The Viennese Opera was supported by the Emperor. A high official of the aristocracy—the Lord High Steward—took care of its administrative business, and it was his duty to suggest, when the post was vacant, a new Opera Director to the Emperor. It belonged to the most distinguished tradition of Franz Josef's period that when this position was open, the greatest musician available was sought to fill it. During the forty years I was opera critic in Vienna, only one single time was a so-called "business manager" named Opera Director— Hans Gregor, and, despite his genuine diligence, one found him a foreign element in Vienna. The Royal Opera should belong to musicians, not to routine business. Wilhelm Jahn and Hans Richter, Gustav Mahler, Felix Weingartner, Franz Schalk, Richard Strauss and Clemens Krauss were the names of the Vienna Opera directors of my time—all of them important musicians who created musical traditions or kept good tradition alive.

When the Royal Opera Director was named, he was completely free to carry out his artistic plans. It is understandable that many interested persons who wished favors from the Director sought the assistance of influential court circles, or of Katherina Schratt. The Emperor himself was inaccessible to such intervention. Since Gustav Mahler's unbending character did not fulfil the many wishes of high-standing persons, the way to the Emperor was zealously and frequently sought. But Franz Josef would always say, in such cases, "He is the Opera Director. He must understand it better." Once Mahler decided not to re-engage a very much "protected" singer. A lady of the highest court society, a princess, intervened with the Emperor. Mahler, who had already begun his summer vacation, was ordered to the imperial villa at Ischl. There was nothing for Mahler to do but comply, so from the Woerthersee, where he was composing his Ninth Symphony, he traveled to Ischl and appeared, as officially ordered, on the next forenoon, in frock-coat. The Emperor required him to give a detailed account of why the Swedish singer, Karin, had not been re-engaged. When Mahler had finished, Franz Josef pulled at his collar, embarrassed, and said, "Well, you understand it better."

Mahler delighted in telling the story of how, one day, an opera composed by one of the young archdukes was brought

to him, along with the information that it was the Emperor s
wish that this work be performed. To this Mahler replied, as
he laughingly related: "I am sorry. I cannot fulfil his Majesty's
wishes—only his commands. If the Emperor commanded me
to perform this opera, then I would do so. I would print on
the theatre-posters: 'Upon the command of His Majesty, for
the first time, the opera so-and-so of Archduke Peter Ferdin-
and.' " The opera of the archduke remains unperformed up
to now.

Franz Josef, like many official-minded men, was extremely
correct. He permitted his Opera Directors, whose mainten-
ance he paid, greatest liberty in all things. There was only
one thing which he disliked: that an Opera Director give up
his position of his own free will. This held true for Ministers
as well as Opera Directors. "I will not permit you to throw
your chair before my feet," shouted the Emperor at his Minister, Schaeffle, when the latter wished to resign his post. When
Gustav Mahler resigned as Opera Director, the Lord High
Steward, Prince Montenuovo, did his utmost to dissuade Mahler from his decision, since he realized that the Emperor would
take the news very much amiss. Also, when Felix Weingartner, who was Mahler's successor, resigned as Opera Director
after two years, on grounds of private nature, the Lord High
Steward scarcely dared to inform the Emperor. As Weingartner told me, Mahler's resignation had already angered
Franz Josef considerably, and a second resignation following
so shortly after the first, was bound to make him bitter.

Not only did I see the Emperor seldom at the opera, but
also at the concerts. Once he came to the Grossen Musikvereins
Saal on the occasion of a festival concert in honor of the

fiftieth anniversary of the Philharmonic Concerts (1910). It was then that he heard Beethoven's Ninth Symphony for the first time in his life. It remains unknown what impression the work made on the then eighty-year-old monarch. The last time I saw the Emperor in a concert hall was three years later (1913) when the new "Konzerthaus" was opened. For its dedication, Richard Strauss composed his "Festival Prelude." A gay legion of young girls welcomed the venerable sovereign on the steps of the new building, and he thanked them with a friendly smile of his large blue eyes, which had seen so many different eras.

In the service of this Emperor who was so little touched by his city's music, were three of the best musicians of his time—Johann Strauss, Anton Bruckner, and his Opera Director, Gustav Mahler.

Johann Strauss was Franz Josef's Court Ball Music Director, beginning in 1864, in which year Strauss had composed "The Blue Danube." At the great court balls, Strauss, in a red frock-coat, conducted his orchestra. First he would rest his violin on his hip while he turned it, and then beat the time for the introduction with his bow. When the aristocratic society had set itself in motion—old and young, archdukes and princesses—he would begin to play his magic violin and everyone responded to the beat and the melody of the dark-eyed man on the podium. Many Strauss waltzes were composed for festive court occasions. For the Emperor's wedding, Strauss wrote his "Myrtle Sounds"; for the wedding of the Crown Prince, his "Myrtle Blossoms"; and on the occasion of "the Happy Return of the Emperor," his "Salvo of Joy." For the old Emperor he wrote his "Emperor's Jubilee Waltz" and his "Emperor Waltz." In the "Myrtle Sounds," even the Austrian folk-hymn danced to waltz time.

The Spanish Court Ceremonial put an end to the activity of the world-famous musician, since it proved stronger than the Emperor, even if not stronger than Strauss's music. In order to marry for the third time, Strauss became a Protestant, but Protestants were not permitted to hold positions at the Catholic Austrian Court which had fought Protestantism for so long. Therefore, Strauss had to give up conducting waltzes at court festivals, and hung his beautiful red frock-coat in the closet. At that time, he was fifty-eight years old and the most famous musician in the world. But the Spanish Ceremonial was three hundred years old.

Franz Josef played an especially beautiful rôle in the life of Anton Bruckner, who was his court organist. The Emperor provided funds for the publication of the Third and Eighth Symphonies of Bruckner. Since the composer was growing old, Franz Josef gave him a house in the Belvedere Garden. In gratitude for this, Bruckner dedicated his Eighth Symphony "to Emperor Franz Josef."

It must have been a singular scene when the seventy-nine year old Bruckner went for an audience with the old emperor, to thank him for the kindness he had shown his court organist. Bruckner had to put on his frock-coat which scarcely fitted his broad, short figure, when he went to the Imperial Palace. Franz Josef held such audiences one day each week. In the great anteroom of the palace were assembled the high ranking officers who had received honors, priests who had to introduce themselves to the Emperor, or to thank him for a donation, industrial magnates who had been raised to the peerage or who had received a court title, and male and female peasants from the provinces, dressed in colored national costumes, who had some favor to beg of the Emperor. (Baron Prilesky, the court official who arranged these audiences, told me that Franz Josef was highly irritated if too few people sought an audience.) In the baroque hall stood the Emperor's guards in red coats, embroidered with gold thread, flowing white plumes in their helmets, swords in hand.

Bruckner made a deep, clumsy bow before each one of these guards. Finally the door opened to the room where Franz Josef stood at his desk on which the papers lay with the names of the people who had come for an audience. The Emperor, with cordiality, came toward Bruckner, who stammered a few words of thanks. The Emperor asked Bruckner if he had any further wish, and the composer replied: "Please, Your Majesty, can you not put in a little word with Councilor Hanslick so that he will criticize me better?" Bruckner himself told us this story. But I do not know whether the Emperor was able to fulfil this wish. The critic was never so kindly disposed to Bruckner as was the Emperor.

What Franz Josef did for music and musicians, and to that belongs the conferring of high orders on Brahms and Bruckner— he did, not out of an active relationship with music but as a correct fulfilment of his regal duty which was regulated by the Spanish Court Ceremonial, his Catholic piety, and by the documents on his writing desk.

The Empress had more feeling for music than the Emperor, for sick souls seek music. The Empress, who was a romantic woman, was a great enthusiast for Wagner's music. She also sent Wagner one thousand gulden when he was weighed down by debts in 1863. The Archdukes of the Austrian court interested themselves primarily in ballet performances, with the exception of Archduke Eugene, who was a good pianist. The relations between the Austrian court and aristocracy, on one hand, and the Viennese corps de ballet on the other, were quite lively for awhile. Folk-singers and art-whistlers catered to the musical needs of Crown Prince Rudolf. His fiacre-driver, Bratfisch, had to whistle Viennese songs to him. With this fiacre-driver, the Crown Prince and Baroness Vecera drove to the hunting castle, Mayerling; and Bratfisch's songs of beautiful Vienna, of St. Stephen's Cathedral, of lovely Viennese women, of the fiacre and of the blue Danube were interrupted by the death-knell of the Austrian monarchy.

Emperor Franz Josef lived music-less and died music-less. The monotonous litanies of the priests at his death-bed in Schönbrunn were the only sounds which recalled music when the Emperor of the greatest musical capital of the world died.

3

Meeting Great Composers

Recollections of Johannes Brahms

I

By the time I first met Brahms on the Ringstrasse he was the greatest musical authority in Vienna. By degrees he had overcome the resistance of the public, with which he met when he had come to Vienna, and was recognized as one of the most serious and solid composers of the time. There he was regarded as a sort of "Burgomaster" of the musical life of the city. He was on the boards of governors of the most distinguished musical societies, and his decisions were final in the choice of professors for the Conservatory and awards of

Brahms Walking on the "Ringstrasse"

state scholarships to musicians. A close friend of Hanslick, Brahms' opinions were certainly duly reflected in the Hanslick criticisms, as well as in many of the other criticisms, since most of the critics were friends of Hanslick and bowed before the verdict of their powerful colleague. In short, Brahms became head of an influential conservative clique and whether he wanted to be thus identified or not, he was the musical pope of the same ultra-conservative society who had hissed even the first performance of his 4th Symphony by the Vienna Philharmonic. This group now gathered around Brahms to wall out modern composers like Wagner, Liszt, Bruckner and Hugo Wolf. Brahms, the Conservative, had come a long way from Brahms the Romantic, the enthusiast who had written passionate music full of love, and heartbreak, who had laid bare his soul, crowded with love for his friend Schumann's wife and the tragic passion of his feeling. Brahms as a composer had learned to quell his vibrant enthusiasm and barricade it behind classical form. He used his craftsmanship to cover his romanticism with a classical facade. He adapted himself to the bourgeois and middle-class Viennese society and in their houses became an honored guest, thought of as an ingenious and conservative composer belonging to the middle class.

* * * * *

My earliest recollection of Brahms is as remarkable as it is surprising. There are few people who have heard Brahms play dance music. I am one. When I was a student at the University of Vienna, I met my friends each night to discuss the happenings of the day. For reasons of strict economy, since we had very little money, our choice of meeting places was narrowed down to a reasonably priced eating place located in one of the oldest streets of Vienna. Here for little or nothing we were able to have a slice of sausage and a glass of beer in one of the two rooms which the establishment boasted for catering to a clientele made up for the most part of hucksters, tradeswomen waiting for the markets to open, and a few others like ourselves. The low-ceilinged rooms were dense with smoke and acrid with the smell of beer. The walls were exceptionally thick and like those of all the other houses in the street, had been standing since the 15th century. In a place like this—and only the Americanism "dive" really describes it—one would never have expected to find a man like Brahms.

One bitter cold night in the middle of winter the door opened and in walked an elegant company of fashionably dressed ladies and gentlemen apparently returning from a late party. One of the group was Brahms and we were all surprised to see the famous composer in our midst. He was also in evening clothes and with his friends sat at a table and ordered beer.

A short time later the door opened again, admitting a rush of snow and three more patrons. In contrast to the other newcomers, these last were eminently more suited to the environment, the feminine member of the trio being a well-known street-walker and inhabitant of this old and dark section of the city. Her escorts were gigolos and all were very drunk. They seated themselves at a table next to Brahms and his friends and ordered drinks—as if they had not already drunk enough—all of them. Suddenly above the talking, the "lady" called over to Brahms: "Professor, play us some dance music. We want to dance." I had the impression that she knew him, which is not unlikely, for Brahms, like Beethoven, was somewhat divided in his patronage of idealistic companionship and the more downright variety found in dark and unfrequented streets. At any rate, he rose from the table and with slow and deliberate steps went toward the old untuned piano which leaned against the dirty wall and began to play—waltzes, quadrilles—tunes which were for the most part *passé* and dated back a good many years. The lady who had succeeded so remarkably in getting Brahms to play, danced with her friends and others joined in. Brahms played uninterruptedly for an hour and then returned to his table, paid his bill and left. I have often thought the proprietor of this establishment should have put up a tablet in memory of this evening: "Brahms played dance music in this pub."

The following day I went to my coffee house and met an elderly gentleman who had been in Brahms' party the night before. This was Mr. Bela Haas, a well-to-do socialite famous for his wit. I said to him: "Please tell me what ever induced Brahms to play dance music for such a gathering," and he answered, "Well, I too was surprised and asked Brahms the same question. He told me: 'When I was a boy in Hamburg I used to play in just such a place the whole night. I played dance music for drunken sailors and their girls. The place reminded me of that time and the pieces I played were those I used to play every night in Hamburg.' "

Shortly after this first acquaintance with Brahms I met him again under no less interesting circumstances.

In the year 1892 a great theatre and music exposition was inaugurated in Vienna. The center of this international exposition was "die Rotunde," a famous building in the Prater, in which rare and valuable treasures of musical and theatrical life gathered from all over the world were on display. Next to the *Rotunde* in the park, a vast theatre was built, and it was here that Smetana's "Bartered Bride" went forth, after a sensational Viennese success, to acclaim throughout the world. However, the main attraction for the general public was "Old Vienna," a skillfully constructed replica of an 18th century Vienna marketplace, with house faithfully reproduced, a stage for comedians who performed old Viennese plays, and a large restaurant where the famous Viennese "Schrammeln" played popular music in the garden. This group of musicians was known for its perfect renditions of Viennese music and was made up of two violins, one guitar and one accordion supplemented by whistlers and yodelers, usually from the audience. Vienna of Franz Josef's time was very enthusiastic about these musicians. They were invited to the palaces of the aristocrats and Crown Prince Rudolf himself liked to frequent the places where the *Schrammeln* played and it was not unusual for him to join in the singing of Viennese tunes.

It was at this restaurant that I encountered Brahms for the second time. He was in the company of Alice Barbi, a marvelous singer who had come to Vienna for the first time in the year 1888, as an unknown artist and rose overnight to fame, acclaimed as the greatest singer of classical songs. I had been present at her first concert, the audience limited to fifty who had been given complimentary tickets to this preview, so to speak, by the concert management. The second concert was sold out as were all which followed. Unfortunately for us she early terminated her career, marrying an Italian aristocrat and going into retirement. She was one of the most striking figures we ever had—a dark Italian beauty with dreamy black eyes, luxurious dark hair which she wore in a low knot on the nape of her neck. The expression in her rich contralto voice filled the soul and she could make an audience joyful or sad with her song. Her program regularly consisted of songs of Schubert, Schumann and Brahms. She never sang music of other composers and I have never heard Brahms' pieces—the simpler composition like *"Vergebliches Staendchen"* nor the more difficult like *"Wie bist du meine Koenigin"*—sung more lovingly than by Barbi. The combination of Italian sense of melody, southern beauty, true musical form and deep expression flowing from the soul was never more perfect than in this singer.

Brahms had come with Alice Barbi to the "Schrammeln" to show her the popular Viennese musicians and typical Viennese popular playing. It was not difficult to see that Brahms was not merely being a polite host to Barbi; he was captivated by her. Usually a somber man, he was in good spirits, his face wreathed in smiles and completely engrossed in this great artist and beautiful woman. He doted upon her and one would have had to be blind not to have seen his devotion and pleasure in her company.

The *Schrammeln* after playing several Viennese selections struck up an American song popular at that time—"TA-RA-RA-BOOM-DE-AY." As the "BOOM" was played, it was customary to strike the table with a walking stick or thump it with a beer glass, and to this day I can see Brahms exuberantly rapping his umbrella on the table—a little boy with a gray beard. There was love, kindled and sparkling, in Brahms that day beneath the old trees of the Prater which overhung dining tables as the musicians played an American song. Perhaps Barbi reminded him of another great singer with whom he had been in love in his youth and who, like Barbi, was also a contralto—Hermine Spiese.

RECOLLECTIONS OF JOHANNES BRAHMS

At the last of the concerts which Barbi gave, an all-Brahms concert was announced. Barbi, wanting to show Brahms her devotion, dedicated a whole evening of songs to him.

We young admirers of Alice Barbi would not have missed the Brahms concert for anything in the world and stood waiting for her appearance. Finally the door to the stage opened and Barbi came out dressed in one of the simply-cut white gowns which she always wore, her black hair knotted softly, and behind her to our surprise, and the surprise of the whole audience, in the place of the usual accompanist, came Brahms. He was somewhat at a loss and came on the stage with the awkwardness of a great Newfoundland dog following its mistress. Later we were told that Brahms appeared unannounced at the singer's dressing room and astounded her by saying that he wished to accompany her at the piano. That night the audience not only heard Brahms' most beautiful songs sung by Barbi but played by the composer himself.

Brahms never accompanied in the manner to which we are accustomed to-day. Accompanists of great singers perform in the same manner as lackeys laying a carpet at the feet of their mistresses. They are in the background, obsequious and bending to the whims of the artist and never step forth to attract attention. But not Brahms. He was still a great musician as an accompanist. At this concert there were two musicians performing with an equally distributed effort and attention. The singer was not the main feature, the song was important, and both singer and pianist worked toward the same goal in the service of the composer.

Brahms' accompaniment had a strong foundation of basses, even in sweet songs like the *Wiegenlied,* the accompaniment of which is usually sublimated and pampering. Brahms himself always used firmness in the basses. His hand was somewhat heavy and his playing was devoid of the complicated shading and nuances of colors which characterizes players of the Liszt school. He was simple and strong. There was spiritual and musical potency in his playing—no nervous over-sensitiveness running amuck in hundreds of little color patches. When Brahms played, the design was important and not the colors themselves.

There was another trait in Brahms' accompaniment which is no longer found. He built up his accompaniment like a symphonic composition. There was unity, gradation and development. The music reached its climax from within by virtue of the musical forces. When he played his songs he was the creator of great symphonic forms, used in the development of a vast musical composite of several ideas, which grew like petals to form a single beautiful flower.

Barbi's concert was the first time I had heard Brahms interpret his own songs, but later I was to have other opportunities of attending concerts at which he played his own compositions. He enjoyed accompanying the Viennese tenor, Gustav Walter. Walter was the first in Vienna to give a concert as a soloist in a concert at which no other artist was programmed. He had a mellifluous tenor voice which he used with fine taste and was accomplished in developing discriminating half-tones and falsettos. He is identified with the history of Brahms' music since it was he who sang the solo at the first performance of Brahms' cantata "Rinaldo." He was especially well known for his charming renditions of Brahms' semi-classical songs like *"Ständchen"* and *"Wiegenlied."*

Brahms, whose hands were heavy, experienced some difficulty in adapting his accompaniment to Walter's hovering pianos.

The last time I saw Brahms on the concert stage was in 1891 when he appeared at the first performance of his Piano trio in B major in the *Kleiner Musikvereinssaal* of Vienna.

It is well known that while in Vienna Brahms revised his first chamber music composition which he had written in 1854. Previously the music was the excited product of a romantic composer—wild, fanciful and copious, but when revised it became a clear logical, classic pattern. Brahms put into the transformation of this music all the many endowments of an experienced and great composer, rounding it out toward greater coherence and unity. When the revised music was first performed, Arnold Rosé played the violin and Brahms himself was at the piano. He played in the powerful and tightly woven classic style which was so characteristic of him and as usual introduced thundering basses. Upon this ponderous structure a magnificent and uniform building was erected. In the great climaxes of the composition ran the undertone of subterranean rumbling like the echo of a remote earthquake which served to remind listeners that beneath the heavy boulders of classic form the romanticism of Brahms' youth was buried.

Brahms attended all the big concerts in Vienna. In the Society of Friends' Concert hall where he had conducted *"Gesellschafts"* concerts for three years, and where Philharmonic and choral concerts were given, Brahms always sat in the Director's box. It was here that he heard his last concert on the occasion of the performance of his 4th symphony, March 7th, 1897. Certainly he must have recalled the first inauspicious playing of his composition——by the same orchestra and conductor (Hans Richter), which was roundly hissed by an earlier Viennese audience. On this night I mention, we were deeply shocked by his appearance. He had the sallow, gray pallor of a dying man, and it was only a month later that he passed away in his Karlsgasse (now Brahmsgasse) apartment where he had lived and worked for a quarter of a century.

II

It was at this apartment that I spoke with Brahms. Then I was a student at the University of Vienna at the time and ambitious to become a musician—or better still, a composer. Without benefit of a great deal of training I had been composing day and night—songs, violin pieces, chamber music— and like many young people I was obsessed with the one thought of giving utterance to my musical feeling. My mother was a friend of Celestine Truxa, the widow of an Austrian naval officer, from whom Brahms rented his apartment and she asked Mrs. Truxa if it would be possible to have Brahms look at some of my work and pass judgment on my talent. Also she wanted his advice as to what she should do with a son so ambitious to become a composer, that he gave himself over to writing musical notes instead of law notes, as a legal career had long been planned for me.

Brahms bade me come and I went to his house carrying under my arm the precious bundle which held my wonderful compositions. I remember the apartment had three rooms furnished in the old Viennese period style. I entered the room that was his "library," with a writing table, and an easy chair with a cushion. The next room was his "workroom" where his new compositions lay on a large old-fashioned table illuminated by the soft glow of the oil lamp. There was also a rocking chair which one found in all modest homes and which seemed to symbolize the quiet-loving German mentality of that time and went with a hearth, slippers, cap and dressing gown. The only adornment the workroom boasted was a picture of Raphael's Sistine Madonna; his piano was placed near the windows and held, besides notes, a large box of cigars. One door of this room opened into the third— Brahms' bedroom, and over the bed hung Bach's picture. White lace curtains hung at all the windows and the apartment was kept meticulously clean by Mrs. Truxa. There was an air of lower middle-class simplicity about these rooms. There was nothing artistic about them and they were certainly a direct contrast to the luxurious suite in which Wagner worked and very different from Richard Strauss' surroundings. Probably Brahms' attachment to his old-fashioned accommodations grew out of their likeness to his father's home in Hamburg.

When I approached Brahms in his workroom, he received me with a few mumbled words which he growled into his beard—as a dozing dog would if disturbed—and took my compositions from my hand. At once he plunged two fingers between the first and third staffs of the score. I was somewhat surprised to see him cover up my middle voices of which I was inordinately proud. At this time the songs of Richard Strauss were new, and songs like "Traum durch die Daemmerung" and "Heimliche Aufforderung" had impressed me deeply, so I had more or less adopted the style, writing the piano part with many voices. But the very nicest of all my notes Brahms hid—the many semiquavers with which I had been so lavish. Seeing my astonishment he growled, "When I look over a new song I always cover the middle voices. I only want to see the melody and the bass. If these two are right, everything is right." Finally he said, "You must learn counterpoint. Go to a good counterpoint teacher for two years and then come back and we shall see what is left of your talent." I asked him if he would recommend someone and with the same gruff tone he said, "In the country there are some old organists who know counterpoint. Perhaps you can find one who will teach you."

With this interview ringing in my ears I left, bent on following his suggestion and I did find an "old organist" and went to him as a pupil. My teacher, however, was not a country organist, or more correctly, was no longer a country organist. He was Anton Bruckner.

Brahms was the Great God of musical life in Vienna, an authority of the first order and a torch-bearer of the classical heritage of a musical city. The whole conservative society paid him homage. But Bruckner lived on the thin edge of Vienna's musical life. He was surrounded and admired by his own circle of enthusiastic friends and students, but the public had no taste for his music. At a concert performance of one of his symphonies the hall emptied after the first movement except, of course, for our own ranks who made up the standees, and we stayed and cheered him until we were hoarse. The critics dubbed his music "drunken Wagnerian." Brahms said of him to a friend of mine, "The whole Bruckner movement is nothing but a swindle. In 30 years no one will know who

Bruckner was," and this was Brahms' opinion of Bruckner, Brahms who was surrounded by mediocre musicians who wrote symphonies, devoid of ideas, according to theory-book prescription and were soon forgotten. We students were anxious to have Bruckner's opinion of Brahms and went to a Philharmonic concert at which one of Brahms' symphonies was performed. Brahms was enthroned as usual in the director's box while Bruckner stood among his students quite far back in the standing-room section. When the concert was over we asked Bruckner how he liked Brahms' music and he answered, "Doff your caps, gentlemen. He is Dr. Brahms—I like my music better."

Fridays Brahms always attended the meetings of the *Tonkuenstlerverein,* an association of Viennese musicians. The new compositions of the members were usually performed at these gatherings, and Brahms' presence was the *bête noir* of every composer, for he was a sharp and scurrilous censurer, sparing not even his best friends. His well-sharpened tongue lashed out with poisonous criticism. Looking back, I think Brahms' sadistic pleasure in giving offense, was a front to cover up vulnerable spots in his own soul—that the poison was the defense mechanism of his softness. A wit of Vienna, who was invited to all parties, invented the story that Brahms leaving a supper said to the hostess, "I apologize if there were any here whom I neglected to offend."

The inventor of this anecdote was Mr. Bela Haas, a wealthy man and friend of Hanslick and Brahms. Many of Brahms' new compositions were rehearsed in his apartment. Brahms liked Haas' witticisms and since they were always barbed and aggressive thrusts, it is understandable that he

appreciated a talent so like his own. Bela Haas did not hesitate to nick even Brahms with his stinging foils. He told me
that he and Brahms were walking in the Stadtpark where the
beautiful memorial statue of Schubert stands. Brahms stood
looking at the statue—an artist with a notebook on his knee
and pen poised as if to write down some heaven-sent melody
which had come winging into his heart. After some moments
of reverent study, Bela Haas said, "Look, Dr. Brahms—in
thirty years there will be another musician's monument erected
here and people will pause to read the name of JOHANNES
BRAHMS in high golden letters." Brahms was quietly bask-
ing in speculated glory when Haas continued, "and reading
the name Johannes Brahms, they will turn to one another and
say, 'Brahms? Brahms? Whoever on earth was he?'"

III

Brahms' character was certainly not simple. Everyone
familiar with his music knew him as a man of delicate, warm
and beautiful sentiment. There are tunes of unusual tenderness
and grace in his works, but his shyness forced him to hide the
free melodious expression behind a barrier of complicated
rhythm and intricate syncopation and it comes to the surface
only as light through chinks in a wall. It is often true that
strong personalities are ashamed of softness and prefer to seem
hard and high handed. One of the most interesting and reveal-
ing stories about Brahms was told me by Bela Haas and
shows clearly how he used rudeness in fear of betraying his
sensitiveness.

When Brahms celebrated his sixtieth birthday, he was

awarded the "Leopoldsorder," the highest order of Austria which Emperor Franz Josef had never bestowed upon a musician, minor orders usually being reserved for them, if given at all. In honor of the occasion a party was given for Brahms and he asked Bela Haas to go with him. Together they walked through the Ringstrasse to the Franz Josef Quai where the festivities were to take place in the home of one of Brahms' friends. It was dark and about midway to the house Brahms suddenly pushed Bela Haas into one of the public lavatories near the pavement, saying, "Come on! Come on!" Bela Haas was dumbfounded, but Brahms finally succeeded in getting him into the washroom and extracted from his pocket a small box saying, "Here, help me put this thing on." The "Thing" was the medal of the *Leopoldsorder* and standing in the men's room, Haas helped him to adjust the ribbon about his neck.

Beyond any question of doubt Brahms was delighted and honored to receive this decoration, but was deeply ashamed of his joy and selected the most ignominious place he could think of to put it on in order to conceal any vanity or pleasure which might escape him.

There were many conflicts in Brahms' soul, many inhibitions. His outer roughness covered inward tenderness and his almost ascetic simplicity in living covered his romanticism. His attacks on his friends were only one of the symptoms which belied the complicated organization of his personality and deep tension in his soul.

Like all great musicians living in Vienna, Brahms loved the landscape around the city. The country to the south of the city was specially dear to him as it was full of memories of Beethoven where on the gates of houses and gardens are marked tablets reminding the passerby that Beethoven had walked there.

One of Brahms' friends, the theorist and musicologist Mandyczewsky, told me a story of Brahms' strolling in the Vienna woods. After many hours of wandering he and his friends had come to an inn and asked for black coffee. The coffee was made with chicory—an economy exercised by many cooks—and Brahms did not like chicory in his coffee. He called the proprietress to his table and said, "My dear old lady, have you some chicory?" When she said she had, he continued in an even more gracious tone, "It's not possible! May I see it?" The old woman retreated to the kitchen and returned with two packages of chicory which she handed to Brahms. He looked them over solemnly and inquired, "Is that all you have?" When she said yes, he pocketed both boxes and said, "Well, now you can go back and make us some black coffee."

IV.

Brahms generally spent his summers at Ischl, the site of Emperor Franz Josef's summer palace. Johann Strauss had his summer house there too, and Brahms used to visit him and play "Tarock," a favorite card game, the Austrian pinochle. It was in Ischl that Brahms composed his last work, the melancholy "Vier Ernste Gesaenge"—an astounding presentiment of death.

As all great composers were—Wagner, Berlioz and Liszt among them—Brahms was fascinated by the melodies of Johann Strauss. The Strauss waltzes were the inspiration for

112

his *"Liebesliederwalzer,"* the most beautiful tribute Brahms could have paid Vienna. Once at a ball in Vienna a lady asked Brahms to write something on her fan. He wrote the opening bars of the Blue Danube and the words "Unfortunately not by Johannes Brahms."

I attended the first performances of the String Quartet in G Major, the revised Piano Trio in B, the Quinetet in B Minor and the two sonatas for clarinet. Along with these the *"Volkslieder"* and several compositions for piano were played for the first time. Brahms was nearly always present at the first performances of his new compositions and would come to the stage to take his bows. His personality and bearing were arresting wherever one saw him; of medium height he gave the impression of being a great boulder of a man and would walk heavily to the stage, his flushed face always belying his sensitiveness and pleasure in being recognized and applauded.

Frequently I saw Brahms in the Vienna Opera House. Of Wagner's work he specially liked *"Die Meistersinger von Nuernberg"* for its festive, brilliant music, and it seemed to arouse his patriotism. For all his many years in Vienna, he was a German patriot—ardently enthusiastic over German victories in France and his political inclinations were those of a middle class man in the Bismarck epoch. When Hanslick was about to publish his vitriolic criticism of *Meistersinger* in a book, Brahms asked him to temper it a little, which he did, but it is still damningly harsh. As composers went, Brahms loved Mozart best, especially for his *Nozze di Figaro*. Professor Mandyczewsky told me that Brahms thought the finale of the second act the finest music ever written for the theatre, and the music the most perfect from a musicodramatic standpoint. It has movement, theatrical action, lifeblood, and is a wonderfully artistic characterization of contrasting personalities. Brahms preferred Mozart to Beethoven. While Beethoven's music had a divine quality, was compelling and often violent, Mozart coped with the reality of human struggling. He often said, "There are spots in Beethoven's music which indicate that under circumstance Beethoven could have become a criminal."

Next to Mozart the greatest musician, in Brahm's opinion, was Bach. He once said to Mandyczewsky, "When the new Handel edition comes out and is sent me, I put it in my library and say, 'As soon as I have time I will look it over.' But when a new Bach edition appears, I let everything else go, for there is nothing more important to me than studying this volume. I know that I shall learn something new."

Brahms had a special predilection for Bizet's *Carmen* and kept the score in his library. He admired this music for its spirited clarity and jewel-like, sparkling orchestration. His own orchestration was compact and heavy and had no brilliancy or color, but he could admire in Bizet the sense of fitness which made him leave a free space between sounds and his aptitude for noting in music true Mediterranean zest and color.

Brahms could well appreciate Bizet, for his music was so different from his own. But he was ever a man of contrasts. Coming from the foggy north, he loved the South. He needed its sunlight and warmth, for there was much that was dark and turbulent in his soul; and he who was so stern and grave took his heart to the gaiety and cheer of Vienna.

The Composer of the "Queen of Sheba"

In the epoch of Emperor Franz Josef, Carl Goldmark was the oldest of the many great musicians who contributed to Vienna's glory as a center of musical life. The lines and wrinkles on Goldmark's face spoke of the many years of hard struggling and working, of despairing and praying he had undergone. He had the face of a kind, good and calm man. He always reminded me of a wise old Rabbi, whose mind was above this life, and who lived in the thought of God. He was eighty-three years old when he died. There were few men in Vienna who grew so old. Franz Josef also lived to the same age as Goldmark, who was a boy when the eighteen-year old Emperor ascended the throne in the midst of the storms of the Revolution of 1848. Goldmark lived through the entire epoch of Franz Josef, experienced all the misfortunes and catastrophes of the crumbling monarchy, and, like the Emperor, finally died during the great war which destroyed it.

It was music which supplied the greatest splendor to the Austrian monarchy during Franz Josef's reign. The waltzes of Johann Strauss, the symphonies of Anton Bruckner, the songs of Hugo Wolf, the brilliant Vienna Opera directed by Gustav Mahler, the famous Vienna Philharmonic Orchestra, the glory of the Vienna Conservatory which supplied the whole world with composers, conductors, singers and instrumentalists—all this comprised the greatest treasure of the Austrian monarchy. During Franz Josef's reign, Austria may have lost wars. It may have lost the Italian provinces and the supremacy over Germany. The everlasting struggles of the nationalities may have destroyed the empire of the Hapsburgs. But the colorful display of music, the wealth of musical life, the sounds which filled the air, and the great composers who were born in Austria, or later came there, gave the time of Franz Josef imperishable fame and glory. To that abundance of sounds, colors and melodies, the music of Goldmark was a very original and peculiar contribution. Little music existed which could compare with his in brightness, exuberance and voluptuousness. An admixture of oriental luxury increases still more the general impression of sensual enjoyment which cannot be separated from Goldmark's music.

Goldmark was born in Hungary, which, of all European countries, is nearest to the Orient. The music of the Hungarian gypsies is oriental music, and the cymbal, which accompanies all gypsy music, an oriental instrument. The primitive colors which the Hungarian peasants use in painting their jugs and plates are oriental colors. These impressions of his youth must have accompanied Goldmark throughout his life. But its oriental color is only one of the elements which join in creating the peculiar value of Goldmark's music. Goldmark is one of the artistic representatives of Franz Josef's era which succeeded for the last time in the history of Austria in gathering the spiritual and artistic forces of German, Slavic and Hungarian peoples in the valley of the Danube, and shaping them into a higher general culture. Goldmark represents the spirit of Austrian culture under Franz Josef, the artistic wealth, the refinement of taste, the predilection for sensual enjoyment, the inclination for decorative luxury which were the gifts of an old European capital. In this sense Goldmark belongs to Austria and Vienna, and the exuberant colors of his music remind us that at the time of sunset, all colors are brighter and more radiant.

Carl Goldmark came to Vienna when he was fourteen years old. He was a poor Jewish boy from Hungary. His father was a cantor and notary of Polish descent. There were twelve children in the family, all of whom grew up with little more than the traditional religious education. In the synagogue, little Goldmark heard the old tunes of the Hebrew service which accompanied the Jewish people from their native oriental country to the distress and persecutions of Europe. Saturdays and feast days he heard the book of the Torah and the prophets sung with the ancient cantillation which adorned the holy words. He did not begin to learn reading and writing until he was twelve years old. He was one of many poor Jewish boys who came to the Austrian capital to study. He lived with his brother Josef, a medical student whose boots and clothes he had to clean. Every day, like other poor Jewish boys, he had his lunch at the home of a well-to-do, charitable family. In Jewish life, it was a tradition that the rich feed the poor. Such meals were called "Taege-essen" ("day's eating").

Goldmark studied violin in the Conservatory with Josef Boehm. Then he was engaged as violinist at the Carltheater where operettas and popular plays used to be performed. Sitting in the orchestra, he listened attentively to the orchestral sounds. He told me often how he acquired experience in how to write for orchestra in the small pit where twenty to thirty musicians sat. He tried studiously to become acquainted with the compass and the technique of producing tones from the various instruments, and questioned his colleagues indefatigably about the peculiarities of their instruments. He studied sounds and the mingling of sounds. While the comedians sang their ditties, he studied orchestration. Goldmark completed these studies of his in a small theatre in Budapest. There were only two first violinists and when the concertmaster fell ill, Goldmark played alone at the first desk of the first violins. He told me how once, as the only violinist, he played a performance of Meyerbeer's "The Huguenots," and remarked in his mild and wise way: "I learned orchestration when I was playing in that orchestra. You cannot learn orchestration in a good orchestra. Music played by a good orchestra always sounds well."

Goldmark was the noblest example of an autodidact I have ever known. He loved to study, even when he was a very old man. When he was more than seventy, I once met him in Gmunden, walking along the beautiful allée which borders the lake. I asked him where he was going and, noticing a small red book in his hand, what he was reading. He replied that every day he made a round-trip on one of the lake steamers, and that, sitting on board, he studied an English dictionary. And he explained further: "Just as one has to exercise in order to keep the body fit, so does one have to exercise one's mind. The best exercise for mental fitness is studying the vocabulary of a foreign language."

In 1848, the storms of revolution were sweeping through the narrow streets of Vienna. Goldmark's brother Josef was one of its leaders, and in the hall of the old university, he shouted for freedom and the brotherhood of man; and finally he had to leave Vienna when the army of Duke Windisch-graetz suppressed the glorious call. He went to the United States, where his daughters still live, wonderful old ladies who preserve the noble features of the Goldmark family. The American composer, Rubin Goldmark, was his nephew, and Justice Brandeis his brother-in-law.

Carl Goldmark, a reserved and shy man, kept away from the bloody struggle and returned to Hungary for three years. When, once more, he went back to Vienna, the new city had been built.

In 1869, the new Opera House was opened in Vienna, and it was for this theatre that Carl Goldmark's greatest work, the opera "The Queen of Sheba" was written. "The Queen of Sheba" was more than a grand opera with a splendid display of voices, many-part choruses, richly colored orchestra, impressive scenery, and imposing processions of masses. Like Verdi's Egyptian opera, "Aida," Goldmark's first great opera which was finished the same year that Verdi's opera was performed in Cairo for the first time (1872), was a masterwork of modern painting of landscape with the lights, sun and the colors of the Orient. Both were romantic operas. A French romantic poet, Gerard de Nerval, who traveled to Cairo, Syria and Constantinople, living outside reality and dreaming fantastic dreams, was the first to use the tale of the Queen of Sheba for an opera book written for Meyerbeer. But the composer of "Faust," Gounod, composed the opera, "The Queen of Sheba," which was performed in Paris ten years before Goldmark's work. Goldmark's "Queen of Sheba" is surely connected with the French romantic tradition. Like "Aida," it is an oriental opera in the style of the French romantic opera school. In both works, the style of the operas of Rossini, Meyerbeer and Halévy, reaches its climax.

But despite all superficial resemblance between Goldmark's "Queen of Sheba" and the great French opera, there is something quite new in the former. The operas of Meyerbeer and other composers of the French romantic opera school were products or fancy, technique and calculation. Goldmark's "Queen of Sheba" is a product of fancy, technique and unconscious remembrances, impressions, feelings and dreams of a Jew who, as a boy, saw the lights in the synagogue and on the festive Sabbath table, heard the recitation of the Torah; and who read the description of the Tabernacle which a Jew in Babylonian exile had imagined as a fairy tale—a wonderful dream of precious material, jewels, gold and silver.

It is strange that Goldmark himself did not want to admit the connection between his work and his Jewish soul. I once asked him if he never had a mind to compose an opera "Esther." I reminded him that Grillparzer, the greatest Austrian poet, had left a wonderful "Esther" fragment and that it certainly would be an artistic deed to unite Grillparzer's verses with his music. He became furious. "It seems that the Jews consider my "Queen of Sheba" a national opera. But in composing this work, I had no other interest than to write music to an interesting and efficient text. I was captivated by the oriental colors. I was interested in this type of subject purely on account of artistic motives. After having composed this oriental opera, I had exhausted this subject. I turned to other subjects."

It was true. After the "Queen of Sheba," Goldmark composed the opera, "Merlin," the text of which the poet and philosopher, Siegfried Lipiner, took from a Celtic legend; another opera, "The Captive" with Greek heroes as characters and the Briseis episode from the "Iliad" as subject; "The Cricket on the Hearth," after Dickens' "Christmas Carol"; and the old German "Goetz von Berlichingen" based on Goethe's play—an opera of mediaeval times in which the composer made his farthest departure from the artistic world and mood of the "Queen of Sheba."

Another time I had an experience which again illustrated how Goldmark misunderstood the very sources of his creative fancy and his unique artistic force. I had been in Prague. I loved this old and somewhat stern city where I had studied at the High School, and where, as a boy, I had often walked to the old houses of the Ghetto, through the dusky streets; and where I had passed the weather-worn tombstones of the old Jewish cemetery, and the Jewish City Hall with the Hebrew ciphers on the clock whose hands moved from right to left, arriving finally at the Gothic "Altneuschule." This synagogue always made a very strong impression on me. The mediaeval room with the pointed arches of its pillars and the traceries of its small windows was always dark, and in the gloom, old Jews prayed ecstatically, their prayer-desks shaking, now murmuring, now singing. When visiting Prague, I never missed going to this synagogue, in which the dark ages seemed still to be alive. After returning, from a trip to Prague, I happened to meet Goldmark, and I told him of this synagogue and how I had been impressed by some phrases of the prayers I heard there, which reminded me of certain passages in his "Queen of Sheba." I asked him whether he had used those Jewish prayer tunes consciously or unconsciously. He was very angry, and absolutely refused to admit that he used synagogal music in his opera. The resemblance of some phrases in the "Queen of Sheba" with the turns and phrases of the Jewish prayers, he insisted, was purely coincidental. Goldmark seemed to have forgotten that he was the son of a cantor, and that the first music he had heard as a child was that of the synagogue. These melodies must have been buried in the deepest layers of his soul, for such recollections of youth are indestructible. Composing his opera, he could not have helped being shaken in the unconscious regions where, as with every great artist, childhood impressions kept living and streaming upward through the roots of his fancy into the images and forms of his works.

When I spoke to the famous chief Rabbi of Vienna, Professor Chajes, about Goldmark, I expressed my bewilderment that this great and wise composer who represented, in his personality, the best Jewish traditions, wanted to escape his Judaism. He did not want to see the fact that his greatest opera was a perfect masterpiece because its biblical subject expressed all the forces of his Jewish soul, his Jewish environment and the beauty of his Jewish religion. As a Jew, he was uneasy and timid, although his greatness was part of the greatness of the people to whom he belonged not only by birth but by the best of his feeling. His wisdom was rabbinical wisdom. His ambition for learning and his impulse to become more and more proficient were an inheritance from the people of the "Book." Excepting Professor Chajes, Professor Freud who honored me by discussing with me some aspects of Jewish

music, and Professor Einstein, he was the most perfect representative of the Jewish personality I ever met. But this he
did not wish to see.

I asked Professor Chajes if he did not think that the
"Queen of Sheba" was a wonderful picture of the Palestinian
landscape in sounds, a colorful image of oriental light; and
how it could happen that Goldmark had accomplished this
without having been in the Orient. The great scholar
answered: "Goldmark did not have to go to the Orient. He
had the Orient in his soul," and he repeated this profound
sentence at the dedication of the honorary tomb of Goldmark.

Even if Goldmark did not want to recognize the Jewish
heritage in his creative faculty, he certainly was intimidated
by the anti-semitic students who stood in the gallery at the
Opera House and hissed at a performance of the "Queen of
Sheba." The music critics of anti-semitic Viennese newspapers
did not fail to depreciate Goldmark's music as that of a Jew.

I always was sorry that so great a composer as Hugo Wolf
howled with the wolves in this respect. When Wolf set
Goethe's poem, "Gutmann und Gutweib" to music, he accompanied the words "Und da kamen Juden" ("and there Jews
were coming") with the contrapuntal combination of two
themes. The first of these is one of the themes of Goldmark's
"Queen of Sheba," the other a theme of Adalbert von Gold-
schmidt, one of the most interesting composers in Vienna,
whose trilogy "Gaea" is a profound and philosophical work.
Hugo Wolf was the last person who should have indulged
in anti-semitic allusions. One of his best friends, at whose
expense his first songs were published and in whose apartment
he lived for a long time, was my friend, Friedrich Eckstein,

to whom I am indebted for having introduced me to Hugo Wolf.

Goldmark could expect no other methods of dealing from his enemies than with abuse and hatred, and the greater and the more successful his work, the greater the abuse and hatred had to be. It was more difficult for him to bear the reluctant praise of friends. He suffered keenly when he heard the criticisms of Eduard Hanslick, who had the greatest esteem for Goldmark's pure and modest personality, but who confessed, in his review of the first performance of the "Queen of Sheba" that he could "put up with this kind of music only for a short time." I quote: "With the obstinacy of a spirited man, Goldmark nestled down into the preference for oriental music with its lamenting, whining tunes, with its augmented fourths and diminished sixths, its disagreeable fluctuating between major and minor, its heavily growling basses above which thousands of dissonant and small tones are crossing. Only a few colleagues of Goldmark have such a lasting pleasure in sharp dissonances as he. I have not always succeeded in becoming friends with Goldmark's music even though my efforts were facilitated by my personal esteem and sympathy for the composer. I never missed spirit and independence in Goldmark's compositions, but I did miss clarity, natural feeling and sense of beauty." In Hanslick's criticisms on the "Queen of Sheba," allusions to the Jewish color of Goldmark's music are not lacking. The song of Astharoth which lures Assad to the Queen is, for instance, a tune "with which one may push pious Jews into a synagogue, but no lover to a rendezvous." The melody of this criticism was the same as that of Goldmark's enemies, only the orchestration was finer and more refined.

The most bitter experience Goldmark had to endure was the harsh, even rude treatment he received from Brahms. Brahms did not like the music of the "Queen of Sheba." He felt about it as did Hugo Wolf, and Goldmark relates in his memoirs[1] some very unpleasant stories which demonstrate how unkindly Brahms acted toward him. One of these stories was told me by Ignatz Bruell, Goldmark's most intimate friend, whose own opera, "The Golden Cross" was one of the most successful and popular works of the time. Bruell told it somewhat differently than did Goldmark himself. The latter tried to extenuate Brahms' very ugly behavior. According to Bruell, he gave a party in honor of Goldmark after the beautiful chorus, "Wer sich der Musik erkieset" ("Who chooses music for himself") was performed for the first time in concert by the Society of Friends of Music. The words of this chorus were by Luther, who loved music. Goldmark's new composition was a great success and the audience took the opportunity of showing him their admiration for his artistic personality, venerable in accomplishment as well as in actual age. All the composer's friends were invited to the party afterwards, and they awaited Brahms' arrival with excitement. Finally Brahms arrived, gloomy, and he did not speak one word. After some taciturn brooding, he finally grumbled: "Wonderful text. Sorry that a Jew composed the music to it!" Perhaps Brahms, when he made this malicious remark, was irritated because he himself had not set this poetical stanza of Luther's

---

[1] Goldmark's Memoirs were translated into English by his niece, Alice Brandeis, and published in New York, 1927. ("Notes of a Viennese Composer.")

to music of his own serious, manly and ingenious composition. Instead of such music, we have inherited the much less agreeable memory of a cruel offense to one of the noblest of his colleagues.

Goldmark's "Queen of Sheba" rises high over the lowland of human weakness, envy and meanness. Since its première, it has been recognized in all the great opera houses of the world as one of the most impressive operas ever written, and as the production of an artist who possessed a fancy of his own and a new kind of imagination nourished upon the images of the Bible, the sublime solemnity of the Psalms, and the intensive and pathetic feeling of the songs of the Synagogue. The "Queen of Sheba" is an opera written for audiences who like beautiful melodies, ingenious climaxes of choruses and ensembles, resounding orchestra, dramatic passions and conflicts. No opinion on Goldmark was more unjust and false than the sentence of Friedrich Nietzsche calling him "the skilful ape of Wagner." There is more in the music of the "Queen of Sheba" than the utilization of Wagner's orchestral devices, which are self-evident in the work of a modern composer. But there is color, the conjuration of a vanished world, glorification of the past, a great epoch of the history of a people illuminated by the lights of legend. The Queen of Sheba's visit with Solomon had often been depicted in painting, frescoes and sculptures by the greatest artists of the dark ages and of the Renaissance. No one of them displayed the imagination, the vividness and the exuberance of Goldmark.

I made the acquaintance of Carl Goldmark in the year 1899, shortly after the première of his opera, "The Captive"

THE COMPOSER OF THE "QUEEN OF SHEBA"

("Die Kriegsgefangene") in the Vienna Opera House.

At this time, I had begun writing music criticism in a small Viennese music paper which had to tolerate my first attempts at reviewing opera and concert. My criticisms on the new tragic and sombre Greek opera was animated by my high personal esteem for Goldmark, and especially by my admiration for his opera "Merlin," a great and fantastic work, which was the most Wagnerian of all his operas, and in which he wished to surpass even the "Queen of Sheba." Only the largest and best staffed and equipped opera houses could perform "Merlin," which requires great voices, a great display of settings, and all the resources that a theatre possesses. Even Goldmark's friends were surprised when, ten years after the first performance of "Merlin" (1896), he wrote an opera in the emotional style of a simple musical comedy. This was his melodious "Cricket on the Hearth," in which, after having been an over-pathetic composer, he transformed himself into a modest, good-natured, typical citizen.

I was sitting at my desk, perpetrating some new critical essay, when my bell rang. I went to answer it, looked through the peep-hole of the door, but I could see nothing but the top of a felt hat. I opened the door and there was Goldmark, a man of such small stature, that he did not reach the level of the peep-hole. I recognized him, of course. He was about sixty-seven at this time, and I had often seen him at concerts, so I showed him, with the natural respect of a young man, to my room. Goldmark told me that he wanted to thank me for my criticism of his new opera, and he made me feel ashamed by his goodness and his tranquillity.

Since that day, I often spoke to Goldmark. I always felt

better after having been in his company. It was a kind of moral efficacy which emanated from him that so impressed me. In my lifetime, I have met many great men, artists as well as scholars. No one else, however, had the superior detachment of mind Goldmark possessed. When I read, later on, the sentence of the philosopher Leibnitz that "justice is the most perfect union of wisdom and kindness," I immediately thought of Goldmark. He was a wise and good man.

Shortly after this first meeting, I was appointed lecturer at the Conservatory of the Friends of Music. My first lecture on the Aesthetics of Music was published in a musical journal. A few days later I received a kind letter from Goldmark, who had chanced to read the article, in which he said friendly words praising the content and ideas as well as the form of my lecture. That was why I went to thank Goldmark. I found him in the coffee-house where he used to drink coffee after his lunch and read the important European newspapers. He was an avid reader, and wanted to know everything that was going on in the world. The coffee-house was on the Ringstrasse, close to the Burgtheater (Café Landmann), and it had a magnificent view of the new City Hall and the park surrounding it. Goldmark was sitting there at a table on the outside terrace with his old friend, Ignatz Bruell. On one side of the table, Goldmark was reading his papers; on the other, Bruell was hidden behind some great daily. Neither one of them spoke a word. In this way, they understood each other perfectly. One was silent, the other listened. I did not want to disturb the thoughtful silence. So I ordered a cup of coffee, took up a newspaper and read, thereby becoming the third silent man.

THE COMPOSER OF THE "QUEEN OF SHEBA"

As in the life of every great artist, there were in Goldmark's, too, happy days and days of sadness and distress. Throughout all those fluctuations of life, Goldmark was always restful, kind and good. Seldom did he complain of the injustices of destiny. And never have I heard him make one of those malicious, ugly and envious remarks which I so frequently encountered among even the greatest artists when they discussed their colleagues or rivals.

All Goldmark's operas had their premières in the Vienna Opera House. The "Queen of Sheba" from here started its triumphal march to Germany, Italy and other European countries, and so did Goldmark's other operas. But when he wrote his "Goetz von Berlichingen," Gustav Mahler was convinced that the opera was a weak work, and refused to perform it. Goldmark was confounded, but did not lose the balance of his spirit. He recalled how, years ago, another Director of the Vienna Opera House had at first refused to perform the "Queen of Sheba," and that, when it had been decided to perform it, the conductor practically cut the work to pieces after the dress rehearsal; and, finally, that notwithstanding all the prophesies of coming failure, the première resulted in a glorious success for composer and artists. So, instead of the Vienna Opera House, the Opera House of Budapest was given the honor of presenting "Goetz von Berlichingen" for the first time. Goldmark asked me to come to Budapest for the occasion. Attending a rehearsal in the beautiful and luxurious Opera House in Budapest, I was astonished at the energy and command the usually reserved and bashful Goldmark displayed. He was not an easy-going artist. His will and intentions were definitely determined. The little man knew exactly how to impose his orders, and the conductor, singers and stage-director had to obey his instructions, even though he expressed them in a soft, polite tone.

The first night of "Goetz von Berlichingen" was a great success. The Hungarians are an enthusiastic people. Since Goldmark had been born in Hungary, the audience loudly cheered the composer; and after the performance, Goldmark's victory was celebrated with inspiring speeches, Hungarian wine and gypsy music at a hotel near the Danube where Hungarian society congregated to celebrate festive events, and where during the reign of Franz Josef, the Hungarian joy of life overflowed every night.

The success of Goldmark's opera in Budapest was so great that the Vienna Opera House had to follow with a perform-ance there. Despite an excellent Vienna presentation, the opera soon disappeared from the repertory. Goldmark's artistic imagination could not easily adapt itself to the musical de-scription of the ancient Germany of rude and simple customs, of knights of the dark ages, of strong castles with thick walls and high watch-towers and of soldiers in armor. His fancy leaned to the burning sun and the brilliant colors of the south. His was (and I quote a word of Nietzsche) a "Mediterranean" fancy. The first composition with which Goldmark had at-tracted the attention of the world had been the overture "Sacuntala" which was played in all the concert halls, and became famous because of its gleaming Oriental colors. All Goldmark's great music had the splendor and magnificence of Oriental carpets. Even in his simple and idyllic musical comedy, "The Cricket on the Hearth," the orchestra is like a trunk full of precious jewels. In his popular orchestral suite, the "Rural Wedding," the orchestra is anything but rural. It is artistically embroidered, heavily loaded with gorgeousness, refined and ingenious. His imagination was related to the one which created the tales of "A Thousand and One Nights." How true were Professor Chaje's words: "He had the Orient in his soul!"

When I spent my summer vacations in Gmunden, one of the most charming resorts in the Austrian Alps, I met Goldmark almost every day. He liked the place, and had bought a low farmhouse on the outskirts of the town. On the wall of that house there is now a commemorative tablet with his portrait.

While we walked together, he would tell me of his youth, the memoirs he intended to write (he began writing them when he was eighty) and especially of his meeting with Richard Wagner. He told me how well he loved the Alps and how he spent every vacation in the mountains. Until his seventieth birthday, he used to climb high mountains and swim in the icy, green waters of the Alpine lakes. Goldmark was very angry at the physicians who, when he was seventy, prohibited him from continuing such youthful activities.

Sometimes I accompanied Goldmark to other sections of the Salzkammergut when he wanted to visit friends who summered in that wonderful country of snowy peaks and green lakes. One might say that the Salzkammergut was divided into several musical districts. In Gmunden Carl Goldmark composed. Not far from there was the charming village of Traunkirchen where Hugo Wolf was busy writing songs. At Ischl, two famous Johanns—Strauss and Brahms—spent their vacations. On the shores of the Attersee, Gustav Mahler had rented a small house which had once been used as a laundry, and there, on a meadow under flowering fruit trees, he composed his Second Symphony. A few miles farther on, Ignatz Bruell and his family owned a wonderful house, and it was here that Goldmark liked best to visit.

Ignatz Bruell was not only a successful composer, but a man of most fascinating personality. Nothing could be more impressive than visiting this fine and cultivated man who lived with his beautiful wife and his two just as beautiful daughters in perfect harmony. Bruell's great blue eyes were like those of a good child. He was a friendly, naive man who did not understand that there could be wickedness and ugliness in human beings. Bruell had the reputation of being one of the most musical pianists in Vienna, and Brahms liked hearing his own new piano compositions played by Bruell. Sometimes I had the honor of being invited by Bruell to play classical symphonies with him. It was a pleasure to play with this friendly and indulgent man. Still greater was the pleasure when Bruell, lured to the piano by his flattering wife, played compositions of Schumann. His whole soul was filled with romanticism, and I have seldom heard Schumann's works played with such poetic feeling. While he played, Goldmark used to sit in a corner, listening attentively.

* * * * *

I spoke to Goldmark for the last time in Vienna, at his apartment in the Neubaugasse. He was sitting at his table writing notes. Curious, I asked the old man who at that time was over eighty, what new composition he was planning. He said: "I am writing exercises for my grandchild to whom I am teaching piano." As a young musician in Vienna, Gold-mark had made his living by teaching piano. He taught for fifteen years. His favorite pupil had been a seven-year-old girl to whom he gave lessons, receiving a free meal at her home as payment. That little girl later became a famous soprano, Caroline Bettelheim, and she sang the role of the Queen of Sheba in the first performance of the opera. So when, in his old age, Goldmark wrote exercises for his grand-child, he remembered Caroline Bettelheim and his days as a poor young musician in Vienna. The circle of his life was reaching completion.

Since during the first World War, I was an officer in the Austrian army and served far from Vienna, I could not be present at the funeral of Goldmark. But when, after the war, a commemorative tablet was affixed to the house in the Schuet-telstrasse, from where, sixty years before, Goldmark had walked with his violin on his way to the Carltheater, and where he had written his first successful compositions, I was asked to make the speech of the day. Representatives of the Ministry of Education were present, with those of Vienna's musical life. I was given the opportunity of recalling the figure of the little man who was a great composer, and whose imagination was one of the most personal and unique in the history of music.

Hours with Hugo Wolf

It was in the standing-room section at the Philharmonic Concerts that I met Hugo Wolf for the first time. He stood there during one of the rare performances of Anton Bruckner's Fourth Symphony, leaning with his back to the great mirror which ornamented the rear wall of the great concert hall. He was a slender man in his thirties, dressed in a brown velvet jacket, a wide black artist's tie around his neck, extremely pale in the face and with eyes which burned like live coals— the eyes of a fanatic.

Around him stood young people, enthusiastic followers of Wagner, Liszt and Berlioz, the stormtroopers of the new musical generation. Many of them had long, streaming hair and wild looks. All excitedly awaited the appearance of Hans Richter, the conductor whose baton was the magic wand that exorcized the ghosts of great music. Everyone discussed music with enthusiasm. Some held scores which they studied like mystical books.

Hugo Wolf was one of the most passionate enthusiasts. Although his wonderful "Moericke Lieder," which now belong to the repertoire of all concert singers, had been published at that time, Wolf still had to live in the outskirts of Vienna as if in exile. A ferocious revolutionary, he was expelled by Vienna's fashionable society which detected in his songs strong traces of the damned Wagnerian poison. In writing the modern chromatic harmonies and expressive declamatory lines of a new musical epoch, he had committed a crime which was punished with the death sentence by the conservative music critics of Vienna and by conservative musical society. Besides writing modern music, he dared, as music critic of a weekly, to attack Eduard Hanslick and Brahms. Wolf was enthusiastic about the music of Wagner and Liszt, and excited about that of Berlioz. Bruckner was his saint, before whom he knelt. He was furious about the superficial taste of high society, and stormed like a crusader against the walls of the old music fortress Vienna, swinging the banner of Wagner. He was fanatical, enthusiastic, moody, like all true artists. He was unjust, of course, subjective, but courageous and brave. The conservative music critics of Vienna who pretended to defend classical music when they were really defending their own narrow-mindedness, never forgave Wolf the enthusiastic fanaticism of his criticisms. The name Hugo Wolf disappeared from the columns of the Viennese daily papers where musical conservatism had entrenched itself. He was shunned like a leper and had to live outside the pale of a musical society which did not even know his name. He had to be satisfied with the love and admiration of a small group of friends who recognized his greatness and his genius, and who could feel the delicacy of his soul behind the pricks of his personality.

We young musicians, devoted to Wagner, fanatical believers in modern music, who hated the sensual conservatism of Vienna's wealthy society, believed in Hugo Wolf. His songs were new music. The words were filled with a new kind of emotion. A modern, nervous tempo swung through his harmonies. There was a new and fascinating lyrical feeling in his melodies, and more air and atmosphere in them than in

other songs. There were new shades and colors which corresponded to those to be found in the impressionistic paintings
of those days. Hugo Wolf belonged to us and we belonged
to him. There is a secret understanding among young men
of the same generation. So we stared at the pale man who
stood in the standing-room section just like ourselves, while
Brahms sat in a box like God sitting on clouds. Hugo Wolf
was as excited about Bruckner's music as we were; and when
he shouted before the beginning of the fourth movement of
the symphony, menacingly and imperiously raising his fist:
"Attention! Now the sublimest part is starting!" it sounded
like a battle cry.

Shortly after seeing Wolf for the first time, I was given
the welcome opportunity of making his acquaintance.

In the "Prater" of Vienna where people, by the hundreds,
sat in the many restaurants, or rode on the merry-go-rounds;
where young couples, in love, walked under old chestnut trees,
and where on lovely summer evenings the air was filled with
music, songs and kisses, in 1902 a new amusement park had
been opened. It was called "Venice in Vienna." A sort of
make-believe city had been built of canvas and wood. On
water-filled canals, gondolas were manned by gondoliers imported from Venice. They shouted their melodious "Sta-li"
and beat the dirty water with their long, black oars, standing
on the high stern of the gondola and rocking to and fro.
Vienna's best society sat in the restaurants and coffee-houses
of the amusement section, or walked among the cheap settings
of Gothic palaces, laughing, flirting and throwing "confetti."
Italian music floated seductively from the great open-air theatre, and in all the coffee-houses and restaurants, small groups

of Italian singers shook their tambourines and entertained with folk-songs of Venice and Naples.

I had been standing in front of one of the stages, listening to Neapolitan songs, canzonettas and barcarolles, which reminded me of moonlit nights in Naples, of the white-sailed fishing boats heading slowly for Capri, of the wide Gulf of Naples and of Vesuvius. I was so absorbed in reminiscing, that I was not aware of two men who stood beside me and listened quite as attentively as myself. One of them was my friend Fritz Eckstein, a manufacturer and world-traveler, a great scholar in philosophy and calculus, a mystic and music-lover, who was serving as a volunteer secretary to Anton Bruckner, and who had the symphonies of Bruckner and the songs of Hugo Wolf printed at his own expense. (This great man died in Vienna, not long ago, after the Nazis had expelled him from his home where, among books on philosophy and mathematics, piled from floor to ceiling, Hugo Wolf had lived as his guest for a long time.) The other listener was Hugo Wolf. He was extremely pale, and in his eyes a disastrous fire was burning. The approaching catastrophe was already painted in the pallor of that suffering face and in the restlessness of the eyes.

Fritz Eckstein introduced me to Wolf, but a conversation did not start for some time. Wolf remained silent, as if submerged in his thoughts. His glance was stinging, and I was careful not to disturb him, for, to all appearances, he wanted to be left alone with the dark powers in his soul.

Like many great artists, Wolf went from deep depression to excitement and fits of elation. He struggled between melancholy and agitation, and like Beethoven, the greatest musician of this kind, he knew hell and heaven, the deepest abysses and the highest peaks. I was greatly moved when, after Wolf's death, the director of the lunatic asylum where he died, showed me the chart where the physicians of that institution had recorded day by day the sufferings and tortures of his sick mind. This diary of a diseased soul, as it were, proved that even in the changing moods of mental illness there was the same regular cycle of depression and excitement, of shining day and black night, restlessly revolving until his death, as there had been in the happier days of the creative artist.

Fritz Eckstein, Hugo Wolf and I, after some fruitless attempts to start a conversation with the silent composer, sat down at a table in one of the coffee-houses and ordered coffee, the smell of which accompanies all phases of life in Vienna. The Italian singers there were singing the world-famous can-zonetta, "Funiculi-Funicula"——the rattling rhythms of which had been sung for the first time when Cook opened the cog-railway carrying tourists to the summit of Vesuvius. It seemed as if this melody awakened Wolf out of a deep dream. He became excited, gave the singers money, and had them repeat the tune, which was new to him, again and again. He shouted enthusiastically, "I shall write a symphony about that melody!" He was not, of course, accorded the time to write any such symphony, since he soon became lost in his sickness as in a dark swamp. But somewhat later, the young Richard Strauss used the merry tune in the last movement of his symphonic poem, "Aus Italien," mingling the vivacious rhythms of the "funiculi" with the noises of the streets of Naples.

Shortly after that meeting, Wolf sent me, at the instiga-tion of Fritz Eckstein who knew of my admiration for the composer's songs, the two volumes of his new "Spanish Song Book" ("Spanisches Liederbuch"). Southern countries had been for Hugo Wolf what they had been for the philosopher Friedrich Nietzsche, who was always longing for the splendor and the sun of the south—a kind of spiritual native home. The "Italian" and "Spanish" songs of Hugo Wolf, his exciting "Spanish Serenade," his operas "Corregidor" and "Manuel Venegas" testify to this longing. In his blood was the ardent desire for the colors of the Mediterranean, for the pines and laurel bushes. He was born in southern Styria whose alpine mountains descend to friendly hills where red-wine grapes grow and fan-blowers merrily tinkle in the vineyards. In that country, where on the summit of every hill a little white church is standing, the sun is already as warm as the southern sun. One feels as if one were in a friendly ante-room to Italy.

The ports of Trieste, Aquileja, Dalmatia and Venice are not far away from that country where Slavic races mingle with races of German or Roman descent. Hugo Wolf's grandmother had a Slavic name, Stanko, and her family originated in Malborgetto, an Italian village. The unrest in Wolf's blood proves the heritage of different races in the Austrian mixture.

When I opened the second volume of the "Spanish Song Book" which contains the secular songs, I felt as if I were wandering on the streets and squares of Spanish towns under green balconies. I heard the tinkling of mandolins and the rattling of castagnettes. I saw dark eyes glancing beneath black mantillas and great combs on the top of the heads of the Spanish girls. I heard the clatter of shoes dancing the same dances which, even in Roman times, had brought a bright flush to the faces of the dancers. In those songs was Spain—

not a masked-ball Spain, but the real soul of the country, the colors of the Spanish day and of the Spanish night, the smell of the dust on the streets, the passions and the loves of that country where the blood of Romans, Berbers of Carthage, Visigoths, Arabs and Moors had mingled, heated by the sun of the south like mulled wine by fire.

But still more of the real Spain I found in the first volume of the "Spanish Song Book," in the sacred songs. The striking Catholic devotion of that music is not the Austrian devotion, and Hugo Wolf's sacred songs do not belong to the specific Austrian piety as do the masses of Haydn, Mozart, Beethoven, Schubert and Bruckner. Wolf's is the music of a visionary who evokes in his soul, like the Spanish Jesuits, the apparition of Jesus and Mary by prayer and penance, crying and beating his breast. Whoever knows anything about the devotional exercises of St. Ignatius will recognize that kind of devotion in the songs of Hugo Wolf. Spanish Catholic devotion had ruled for many years in Vienna under Leopold the First. Friars of Spain had built houses and monasteries in Vienna, and in one of those houses Beethoven had died. It was a strange occurrence that a modern composer like Wolf renewed the Spanish spirit of the 17th century. He had been a student in the convent of St. Paul in Carinthia. The convent had been built, on the summit of a hill, like a fortress with thick walls and mighty vaults where thirteen Hapsburg princes lie buried. It was as if the Spanish devotion of these dead Hapsburgs had transferred itself to the composer. The past is great in Austria. Grillparzer, the most famous Austrian poet, wrote plays in Spanish verses, and a modern poet, Hugo von Hoffmannsthal, was inspired by Calderon. Vienna was a city on whose spiritual life many cultures left their traces.

Hugo Wolf was, in his imagination, living in sunny Spain when his spirit dipped into darkness. While I was studying his new songs, he was walking under the arcades of the Vienna Opera House, shouting: "I am the new Director of the Opera House!" Friends tried to calm him, and told him, at last, that he had to drive to the Imperial Castle in order to present himself, as new Director of the Opera, to the Emperor. He consented, and his friends took him to a lunatic asylum.

I shall never forget the day, February 19, 1903, when we brought the mortal frame of Hugo Wolf to the Votivkirche in Vienna. When the priest walked solemnly, with the crucifix and incense, to the door of the church where the coffin had been deposited, intoning the very old Catholic prayers for the dead, from behind the altar a choir began one of the sacred choruses of Hugo Wolf, "Ergebung" ("Submission"). This chorus of the dead composer sounded mysteriously through the Gothic aisles of the church and proclaimed the greatness of the man who, unruly and unrestrained in life, struggling with passionate dark powers in his soul, prayed: "Be a pitiful judge to us sinners." No other composer found more vibrant melodies and harmonies for all the moods of desperation and struggle, no other was more moving and more human in the confession of sin. He was a suffering mortal who prayed, in his sacred songs, for pardon. Heaven rewarded him with fame and immortality.

Studies with Anton Bruckner

In 1890 I entered the University of Vienna, where Anton Bruckner was teaching harmony and composition. That great composer who, with Brahms, had brought the tradition of the classical symphony to a close, was at that time still unrecognized.

Bruckner at the Organ

The most influential music critic of Vienna, and the great adversary of Wagner, Eduard Hanslick, tenaciously opposed any music in which he scented the Wagneresque. He failed to understand Anton Bruckner's music, which proceeds, essentially, from other sources than the Wagnerian, and is imbued, in a Catholic spirit, with the sacredness of the Mass.

Nor did the musical public of that time care for Bruckner's music. When his symphonies were performed at Philharmonic concerts in Vienna, half of the audience left the hall before his number had begun and the other half followed after the close of the first or second movement. By the fourth movement, there was but a handful of young enthusiasts among the standees, who cheered and bravoed until they were hoarse while Anton Bruckner stepped onto the platform and bowed, humble and childlike, to Hans Richter (the great Wagnerian conductor), and threw kisses to the members of the orchestra. The fashionable audiences of the Philharmonic concerts would decide that their behavior had been quite justified when they read the next day in the newspapers that Bruckner composed "like a drunkard," or that he was a composer who had become "confused by Wagner's music."

This attitude on the part of the Viennese public must be viewed in the atmosphere and in the attitude of that specific era. A city which laughed, sang, loved and drank deeply of all worldly happiness could only with reluctance seek or find access to the music of Anton Bruckner, for his music sprang from deeper sources than the superficial life of such a town and had in it nothing akin to the materialism of modern existence. Bruckner's was a profoundly religious nature.

In Vienna his personality was often a matter of mirth. The elegant society could not understand Bruckner, and he was like a stranger in the sensuous, new city—a man who hailed from another planet. Up to his forty-fifth year, Anton Bruckner had lived in rural districts among people who spoke the peasant dialect of Upper Austria. He had spent many years as a teacher and organist among the priests of the Monastery of St. Florian, whose lives were passed between the cloister cells and the chapel. The Abbot of St. Florian and the Arch-bishop were for Bruckner the representatives of God. He could not understand the great city, with its beautifully-dressed people who chaffed, laughed and flirted so easily, as if there were no Heaven and no God. He dedicated his Ninth

Symphony to "Our beloved Father Almighty." Like the mediaeval musicians, he felt that he was a "Musician of God."
But in a great cosmopolitan capital, proud of its own enlighten-
ment, a Musician of God seemed absurd. This international
city believed in cement and iron, in electricity and machines,
in the Stock Exchange and in business speculations.

Such was Anton Bruckner's status in the life of Vienna
when I entered the University there.

"Do come to Bruckner's lecture to-day—there's always
lots of fun!" said one of my fellow-students, and I promptly
agreed to come. It was the first time I had heard the name
of Anton Bruckner. But the prospect of having "lots of fun"
was irresistible for a freshman aged eighteen. I arrived in
good time at the lecture-room of the Philosophical faculty
where this musician, of whom I knew nothing up to that time,
gave his lectures on counterpoint. My colleague had described
him as a "queer fool" and I expected to be amused.

I knew the room in which the entertainment was supposed
to take place. It was the same room in which Professor
Hanslick gave his lectures on musicology, for which I had
registered. How well I remember the quaint, old-fashioned
piano next to the reading-desk. How well, too, I recall the
expectant tension with which I had been looking forward to
the famous critic's first lecture—and how distinctly I remember
my disappointment! The little old man who had dared fight
Richard Wagner, the mightiest genius of modern music, with
the graceful periods of a drawing-room hero, mounted the
podium without raising his eyes, almost timidly. He drew a
manuscript from his pocket and, in a high-pitched voice,
read us a lecture which dealt with the life of Beethoven in a

most superficial way, bare of scientific foundation. Now and then he interrupted his monotonous report, tripped to the piano, played some passages from one of Beethoven's compositions with a very out-of-date fingering, and thereafter resumed the dull ripple of his lecture.

Previous to this I had attended courses of several important men of the University of Vienna, and I was well aware how much inspiration and stimulation the fascinating courses of brilliant teachers could convey to the students. I had become enthusiastic over the elegantly-phrased and witty lectures of Adolf Exner, who, through the description of a Roman journey, had introduced us to the field of Roman Law; and I had been captivated by the stagy declamation of the idealistic philosopher Brentano. Bernatzik's lectures on anarchism, Reich's lectures on Ibsen and Menger's on questions of social politics had introduced me to the spiritual movements of the time. I was most eager to learn and went about listening to all sorts of courses without, as yet, knowing where I would finally settle down. Eduard Hanslick, however, had neither the slightest gift of speech nor the ability freely to communicate with his students. He therefore did not appeal to me and I never attended another of his lectures.

Anton Bruckner had become a lecturer on theory of music at the University of Vienna contrary to Eduard Hanslick's wishes. "That's what he'll never forgive me!" Bruckner exclaimed again and again. Hanslick, extremely touchy like all vain little men, actually never forgave Bruckner in spite of all the bowing and scraping the latter indulged in whenever he encountered the dreaded critic.

The small lecture-room where I sat with my colleague

awaiting the merry performance soon was crammed, and after the academic quarter had elapsed there entered a crowd of people: first Anton Bruckner, bowing again and again, and behind him, like a rustling train, old and young men, and a very pretty girl, too. All of us greeted the queer musician by solemn trampling which my friend and I prolonged for fun, much to Bruckner's joy. We were highly amused at his bows and appearance. Of course he wore his Upper-Austrian loose jacket, comfortably cut out of home-woven fabric. His trousers were loose and baggy. The big head was close shaven, and innumerable wrinkles furrowed his face. When he began telling us a lengthy story in Upper-Austrian dialect, he reminded me of an old peasant, battered by wind and weather.

This was the year 1891 and Bruckner had just arrived from Berlin where Siegfried Ochs had made his "Te Deum" a triumphal success—the work of a "foolish" composer who had been laughed and sneered at in Vienna. Bruckner could not stop talking about the "marvelous director," or the "highly ingenious" performance, or the "most charming" choir. And he did not omit the fact that he had kissed the girls of the choir, one after the other, amid the applause of the audience. With obvious emotion, he reported that there had not been a single Berlin paper which had disapproved. He glanced about furtively when he told us: "Just imagine, gentlemen, one of the honorable critics wrote that I was a second Beethoven! Good Lord, how can anyone dare say such a thing!" and he quickly made the sign of the cross on his forehead as if to avert the sin.

The "fun" I had expected during that first lecture was only partly realized, for suddenly something happened that I can never forget. From a nearby church the Angelus sounded and when that little bell rang, Anton Bruckner interrupted his lecture, knelt down and began to pray: "Ave Maria . . ."

In the churches of many cities I have watched the devout at their prayers. In Vienna, in the great and glorious old St. Stephen's Cathedral one could daily see people of all sorts and of all conditions in life worship before the statue of the Blessed Virgin. In the Cathedral of St. Anthony of Padua, in St. Peter's in Rome, in churches in Barcelona and Valencia I have seen hundreds in ecstatic prayer, but I have never seen anyone pray as Anton Bruckner did. He seemed to be transfigured, illuminated from within. His old peasant face with the countless wrinkles that covered it like furrows in a field, had become the face of a priest. His expression may best be compared with that of the Apostles in the paintings of Giotto. He looked like an aged saint, his countenance transfigured as one imagines that of St. Francis was when he knelt before the Crib and prayed.

I stopped smiling when I saw his face, humble and blissful, refulgent with celestial light, radiant as a church window through which the sun is shining. I saw this face before me when I listened to his first Symphony, and I have always seen it whenever I have heard his symphonies well-played.

Having finished his prayer, Bruckner stepped up to the music black-board on the wall, and began his lecture.

Bruckner had been a pupil of Simon Sechter, that mighty fortress of counterpoint to whose home he made a pilgrimage every week from Linz, where Bruckner was cathedral organist at the time. Sechter's entire life was dedicated to counterpoint. Every day, after he got up, he sat at his writing desk, working out a new fugue. Not before having finished the last organ-point, over which the four voices streamed to the final chord, did he have his breakfast.

Sechter's doctrine, which was delivered to us by Bruckner like a holy heritage, was built upon two strong pillars. The one which inspired Bruckner with greatest respect was the theory of the "Fundamental Basses," a world of spirits in the bass, which accompanied the harmonies like shadows in the depths; and the theory of "natural harmonies" which form the laws of all beauty of harmonic progression. Everywhere there was law and order, even holiness. The fundamental steps of the bass which Bruckner invariably noted in his scores under the last line of the staff, had cosmic importance. Thus we understood the greatness and sometimes, the rigidity and solemnity of Bruckner's harmonies. Bruckner, the pupil of Sechter who was a kind of architect of harmonies, pondered over chords and chord associations as a mediaeval architect contemplates the original forms of a Gothic cathedral. They were his path to the Kingdom of God.

The conductor Ferdinand Loewe, one of Bruckner's pupils, showed me several folio volumes with exercises written by Bruckner when he studied with Sechter. He must have worked on them day and night. Sometimes when Bruckner came to Vienna he visited the opera house. Here he attended performances of Wagner's operas. He was deeply moved when he heard "Tannhäuser." He stood in the standing-room section when he heard Winkelman sing the story of his pilgrimage to the Pope in Rome. When Tannhäuser related how he was cursed by the Pope, Bruckner began to cry and shouted: "Why did he not pardon him! Why did he not pardon him!"

STUDIES WITH ANTON BRUCKNER

Bruckner explained Sechter's principles to us by using many comparisons, taken from everyday life, in the dialect of Upper Austria. He sounded like a peasant telling humorous stories to the children in a farmhouse. For instance, he compared an unexpected dissonance in music with a "dear auntie" who unexpectedly came on a visit, spreading terror and confusion in the household until she is cajoled out of the place again. "Where is dear auntie, where is dear auntie?" he shouted, bending over the piano-keys. He struck a chord again and again until the necessary missing note was sounded. Then Bruckner would beam and bow and exclaim: "Oh, there she is, our dear auntie . . .!" The interval of a second was a "poor fellow" who had "to wait in a corner till he was called"; and the seventh, a "damned wretch whom you may not trust."

Such metaphors were intermingled with memories from Bruckner's life or complaints about Hanslick. One might find such intermezzi scurrilous or naive, but they were the stammerings of a child-like soul in an artificial and complicated world which this pure and saint-like man could not comprehend. It was difficult not to become aware of the radiance in Bruckner's face. There was something in the mobile features of this old man which was far greater than the erudition, knowledge and profundity which we found in other professors at the University.

One time, with infinite care, Bruckner wrote some chords on the black-board and pointed out a certain dissonant sequence which he said was "quite wrong, perfectly incorrect" and "strictly forbidden." Remarking that this very dissonance which he had just criticized so harshly had been used only twice, once by Beethoven, once by himself, he sat down at the piano and began playing a passage from the Adagio of his Seventh Symphony, where this "perfectly incorrect" and "strictly forbidden" dissonance occurred. It was the first of Bruckner's music I ever heard.

The impression was so glorious that from that day on I had not a moment's respite until I heard the living orchestral interpretation of one of Bruckner's symphonies. I still recall vividly Bruckner's serene expression while playing his magnificent music to the audience. I still see the picture of the old man's pathetic face, radiant with divine genius.

During my four years of university studies I did not miss a single one of Bruckner's lectures. I had been led to him, first, by the prospect of "having fun." I had been disappointed in this expectation. The new "Brother Gaudeamus" (that was Bruckner's name for his students), had forgotten how to laugh in this first lecture, but he had been taught how to admire ingenious creative power.

Sometimes Bruckner honored me by allowing me to accompany him, after his lecture, to a nearby coffee-house. We used to sit at the round table which stood in the middle of the room. Since this particular coffee-house was situated near the Stock Exchange on the Ringstrasse, the guests, for the most part, were stock-jobbers who gazed curiously at the strange composer who ordered coffee and read the newspapers. We young students would sit and wait patiently until Bruckner finished reading. Once he read about the great pogrom in Kishinew where hundreds of Jews had been killed. He looked distressed and timid when he laid the newspaper down. Anxiously he looked at the guests who were sitting in the cafe, discussing rates of exchange and market quotations, and said to us, with a half-shy, half-respectful glance at the Jewish guests: "Jesus and Mary! Now they have killed, in Russia, so many (—with lowered voice) Jewish gentlemen!"

I often heard Bruckner play the organ. In the Court Chapel, in St. Stephen's Cathedral, in the church at Klosterneuberg, I admired his art of improvising. The sound of his organ-playing is still preserved in his symphonies. Their great climaxes are the kind Bruckner built up at the end of his improvisations, pulling all the registers of his instrument, unchaining all the glory of magnificent sounds. Sitting at the organ, treading the pedal and loosing all the power of shining chords, he saw the Heavens open, with God and the saints in the clouds. The concept of God descending from Heaven is the final vision in all Bruckner's symphonies; and that was exactly what he wished to express on the organ when, before the close, his music soared in celestial splendor of sound, soul and song. Often he would end his improvisation with a great fugue, which was crowned by a chorale. The colossal last movement of his Fifth Symphony, when, over the massive orchestral fugue, brass choruses unfold, rising majestically above the climax like the voice of eternity, is essentially the same as one of his organ improvisations. Had Bruckner ever written an opera, it would have had the same character. He often said to us that if he were to write an opera, he would need a libretto whose theme would be the descent of the Holy Spirit.

Anton Bruckner was the last greatest musician of the nineteenth century whose music ascended from Earth into Heaven. His pathos and splendor came in large part from the Catholic Church, which, during the Counter-Reformation, had developed the style which inspired him. Bruckner may be called the last great musician of the Baroque, which was still alive in new Vienna, in his music. He had nothing in common with modern realism and materialism, which reproduced the visage of the world masterfully and vividly. The metropolis in which he dwelt was foreign to him. He was a man who lived in God and whose music is a cathedral with high pillars, bold arches, brilliant windows, divine services and a glowing altar at which a lonely worshipper kneels and prays.

Meeting this humble genius in Vienna was the greatest experience of my life. I let elegant Viennese society laugh about Bruckner. But I quietly sat down at my writing-desk and wrote an essay, which was published in one of the great German magazines, and gave the first thorough account of the greatness of Bruckner's music. Thus I entered the musical life of Vienna as music critic. I pushed open the door, shouting: "Hats off! A genius!"

4

In the Opera House and Concert Halls—1891-1914

The Musical Capital of Nations

The presence of so many great musicians gave meaning to musical life in the period of Emperor Franz Josef. Each year new works by Brahms were performed. Hugo Wolf had his songs published. Bruckner's symphonies were new works. All this music had not, as yet, been catalogued by the music historians. It was the music of the day, and came fresh from the pots of old Vienna's music-kitchen. The music-critics took their testing ladles, dipped them in the steaming pots, tasted, and found the fare good or bad.

Like any educated, cultivated society, Viennese music circles enjoyed well-written, witty or malicious newspaper criticisms. The daily papers which appeared in Vienna were a great power. In 1867, the "New Free Press" was founded which, along with the London Times and the Paris "Figaro," quickly became the most widely-read newspaper in Europe. For it, the best pens wrote on politics and art. The jewel-piece of a feuilleton was zealously cultivated after Parisian models. But here it was a Vienna feuilleton: tasteful, cultured, charming, instructive in a gracious form. The strongest German stylist in the world of journalism, the Suabian Ludwig Speidel, wrote on the theatre, and all Vienna waited for four or five days after a première for his feuilleton; since, after first-nights, for a few days he went walking under the Prater trees to assemble his thoughts and bring them into clear form. When, distinguished by his majestic scholar's head, he appeared in the Burgtheater and lowered himself heavily into his aisle-seat, his hands resting on the silver knob of his cane, everyone would turn respectfully toward this great critic who would let the Viennese public know how the new play had pleased him. After the performance Speidel would go to the "Winter Beer House," where the best Pilsener was served, and sit there until the early morning hours with a few learned friends.

Hugo Wittman, the second great Viennese feuilletonist, was also a Suabian, but he wrote in a light conversational tone, like a Parisian. The third of the "New Free Press" feuilletonists was the music critic, Eduard Hanslick, and what he wrote about music was read by all Europe.

Every evening Hanslick went to the concert hall or to the opera, and when the little old man made his appearance, a

Hanslick and Bruckner
(O. Bohler)

movement would go through the audience. Seldom did a musical society and a critic understand each other as well as the Viennese public and Hanslick. Viennese society loved classical music, Italian opera arias and French music, and so did Hanslick. For a long time Viennese society wanted to hear nothing of Wagner, and Hanslick wanted this still less and still longer. Viennese society was elegant. So was Hanslick. Society loved wit, and Hanslick was witty. Society enjoyed life, and was superficial, and so was Hanslick, even though he possessed a keen mind and great culture. Hanslick said in his criticisms what the most mentally limited member of Viennese society thought, but he wrote it down in most ingenious form.

When I began to write music criticisms, I had to introduce myself to my famous old colleague, and I learned to know him as an amiable man. On this occasion, he removed a silver-snuff-box from the back pocket of his black Biedermeyer coat and offered me some of the black powder. Then he himself took an ample pinch, and, taking out a colored handkerchief, sneezed with quite some thoroughness. Then he began to recount the latest anecdotes. He loved the lively things in life. He liked to go to parties, enjoyed good food, was gallant to the ladies, told jokes, and played Strauss waltzes.

Hanslick came to Vienna from Prague, and his name is undoubtedly Czech. Indeed, most of the critics and writers of Franz Josef's time came from outside Vienna: Hanslick from Bohemia, Speidel and Wittmann from Suabia, the great art-critic, Luwig Hevesi, and the brilliant feuilletonist Theodore Herzl, who was the founder of Zionism, from Hungary. All of them became Viennese, and leaders of Viennese taste. What one calls the Viennese spirit sprang from such mixtures and minglings. The great architects who had built the palaces on the Ringstrasse were a North German, Schmidt, a Dane, Hansen; and only one of them, Ferstel, was a native Viennese. The foremost professors of the University of Vienna came from many different countries. Without this racial combining and fusing, Vienna would not have become a European capital; nor would the city's musical life have preserved its richness; its universality and its color. Music in Vienna was brought to life through the musical talent of many nations.

Of these contributing nations, the Italian was especially important up to the beginning of the nineteenth century. Even in Emperor Franz Josef's time there was a large Italian percentage in Vienna's population. Austria, until 1859, possessed Milan and Lombardy, and only in 1866 did it lose Venice. From this time on there were many families of Italian officials in Vienna. For ages, the trade in Italian fruits and oils had been in the hands of Italian merchants who resided in Vienna. Italians, too, were the peddlers who sold salami and cheese in all the Prater inns and whom the Viennese nicknamed "Salamucci." The Viennese folk-dialect still to-day contains many Italian words.

Even in more modern times Italian music had a second home in Vienna. From 1815 to 1859, the Milan La Scala was, of course, an Austrian theatre and the Austrian officers and soldiers who were garrisoned there went there to hear the operas of Verdi and Donizetti. The greatest Italian singers appeared in Vienna, and Italian composers were quite at home in the Vienna Opera. In 1821 Rossini conducted there. Donizetti, who also was an Austrian court-composer, wrote his operas "Linda di Chamounix" and "Maria Rohan" for the Vienna Opera. In 1871, Verdi conducted his "Requiem" and "Aida" in this theatre.

When Emperor Franz Josef began his reign in the revolutionary year 1848, enthusiastic nationalists ripped the Italian placards from the Vienna Royal Opera. But Vienna musical society refused to be deprived of Italian singers and operas. Each spring, when the Prater chestnut-trees flamed into bloom, an Italian opera season moved into the Vienna Opera House, and the Viennese went wild over the brilliance of the Italian voices.

With each new Italian opera composer, Vienna's enthusiasm for Italian voices and operatic works was renewed. Just such a wave of excitement resulted from Mascagni's "Cavalleria Rusticana" when the naturalistic opera was given in Vienna in 1891. And enthusiasm came to an even higher pitch the following year when Mascagni himself, famous overnight, appeared in Vienna.

When I met Mascagni at that time, he was a slender young man with jet-black hair who looked like a Roman Proconsul. The handsome Italian, who had a modest and charming manner, had completely devastated Viennese women of all circles of society and of all ages. Every morning the postman brought hundreds of love-letters to the Hotel Imperial where the composer was living. Frequently Mascagni conducted his successful opera himself at the Vienna Opera House, and on such occasions was showered with applause. Of his later operas, "L'Amico Fritz" and "Die Rantzau" were performed in Vienna, but despite Mascagni's personal popularity, they met with no great success.

In 1892 Leoncavallo's "Pagliacci" was given for the first time by an Italian opera troupe which presented guest performances frequently at the theatre of the Music Exhibition in Vienna. Leoncavallo himself came to conduct this performance. He was a stocky man with a bushy moustache who looked more like a butcher than a musician. In his conversation, he had difficulty disguising his envy of Mascagni's triumph. Leoncavallo visited the editors of all the Viennese papers and declared himself a Jew, which was quite untrue. When I happened to mention this to Mascagni, he was furious. He said that Leoncavallo was a swindler if he pretended he was Jewish. It seems that Leoncavallo had heard that many managers and owners of Viennese papers were Jewish, and he felt he could obtain their good graces by posing as one of them. He also thought that they would beat their drums louder for a Jewish composer than for a Christian. Nevertheless, Jew or non-Jew, the composer and his "Pagliacci" had a great success. The role of Nedda was sung by a young Italian soprano with burning dark eyes, who completely captivated her audience by the nervous intensity of her expression. She represented a new type of tragic opera singer. She was no pompous woman with a voluptuous bosom, as the case had always been up to that time on Italian opera stages. She was cat-like, slender and haggard. This was Bellincioni. When she appeared on the stage in one of the new naturalistic operas, she was like a woman of the people, an Italian from the south; and in roles of this sort she had no peer. She was to the operatic stage what Duse, with still stronger spiritual force, was to the dramatic—the artist with the soul and temperament of the new era.

In 1892, to her Santuzza and her Nedda, she added a third great role—the main feminine one in the opera "Mala Vita" by Giordano, who with this naturalistic work, introduced himself to the Viennese public. The heroine is a daughter of joy, the hero a consumptive, who makes a vow to marry a fallen woman. The opera closes with the prostitute, after an unhappy marriage, returning to the house of her profession. I can still see Bellincioni before me—pale, pulling a shawl over her dark head, walking back with weary steps to the house of commercial love.

The following year, in the Theater an der Wien, there was another Italian opera season presented. Once more, only Italian realistic operas comprised the repertory. Blood flowed, on the stage, in streams. One had the choice of seeing the leading man stabbed with dagger or knife, throw himself under a moving railroad train, or end his operatic life in a hemmorrhage. The favorite means of death in these Italian operas was, of course, knife-blows, which, in "Cavalleria Rusticana" and "Pagliacci" had world-wide success.

During this season, an opera, "The Willis," by the then unknown composer Puccini, was presented to Viennese audiences for the first time. During the general rehearsal, Puccini, slender and pale, with a well-tended moustache, stood calmly and quietly in the theatre, gazing dreamily at the stage. Quite unlike so many excited composers at dress-rehearsals of their works, he did not say a single word. To my astonishment, I noticed that Mascagni had borrowed from the score of this opera some orchestral effects for his famous "Intermezzo" in "Cavalleria." Even in this opera of his youth, Puccini was already an artist of interesting orchestral sound. His orchestra was far superior to Mascagni's, and much more artistic. He was a more delicate and more subtle artist. Nevertheless, at the time, the performance of his opera did not attract much attention. The great Puccini triumphs only began with "La Bohême" which was not performed at the Court Opera but at the Theater an der Wien, for the first time, because Gustav Mahler, then Director of the Court Opera, considered the "Bohême" by Leoncavallo better than Puccini's.

Puccini regularly came to Vienna for the premières of his works; and the Vienna Opera, where in Jeritza and Lotte Lehmann he found famous interpreters of his feminine roles, was one of his favorite opera houses. His "La Rondine" was composed especially for a Viennese operetta-theater, the Carl-theater. Puccini was the last great Italian opera composer who delighted the Viennese public in the same way as, in earlier centuries, Rossini, Donizetti and Verdi had done. Puccini's was a tender, soft, melancholy love melody which breathed out the perfume of violets when the violins began to sing. I heard this new love melody of Puccini's for the first time at a concert of the marine band in Pola, which played a potpourri of the then new "Bohême." A young conductor stood on the podium, wearing a white linen uniform, and a marine cap on his head. It was Franz Lehar, who, in his own operettas, made the Puccini love melody even more popular.

Through more than three hundred years, Italian music furnished one of the most important and influential components of Viennese music. The feeling for melody and for sound, which distinguished Vienna, was stimulated by Italian music. The most popular Viennese musician, Johann Strauss, was primarily a melody-inventor, like the Italian opera composers. Just how much Italian music flowed in the blood of Viennese composers is demonstrated, in modern times, by Hugo Wolf, in his "Italian Serenade" and in his "Italian Song Book."

* * * * *

The relationship between Vienna and French music was

established through the French education of the nobility and of the upper classes of Vienna. The Viennese aristocrats all spoke French, which was a kind of international language, and the members of high society read the latest French novels. In Vienna, the French mind and the bright and polished elegance of French thought were very much admired. Something of this French clarity was apparent in the French grand operas of Boieldieu and Auber. It appeared, in a new form, in Massenet.

When Massenet's "Manon" was first performed, November 9, 1890, at the Vienna Court Opera, it achieved a sensational success which far surpassed its reception in Paris. At this performance, I was standing in the highest gallery of the opera house, and in the St. Sulpice scene, where Manon persuades her abbé to follow her, I clapped, along with the rest of the audience, until my hands were sore. The leading artists, Renard as Manon, and Van Dyck as Des Grieux, took curtain call after curtain call. This was a genuine, roaring Viennese success.

Everyone looked forward with special excitement to Massenet's new work, "Werther," which was to be produced at the Court Opera the following year. The dress-rehearsal was depressing and it was feared that the new opera would be a fiasco, because the gloomy melancholy of the last act took the listener by surprise. As each act ended, faces became longer. However, to the general amazement, "Werther's" première was a huge success, and Massenet was so delighted that he could not say enough flattering things about Vienna and the Viennese public. Massenet again came to Vienna for the hundredth performance of his "Manon" and personally conducted. The admirable man was no conductor, and he directed the performance with broad, stiff arm-movements. Nevertheless, the jubilation was great.

Of the famous French composers after Massenet, Debussy and Ravel came to Vienna.

Claude Debussy conducted a concert of his own works in Vienna in 1910. I described him at that time as "a broad-shouldered man, with coal-black hair and pointed beard, slightly indolent and ponderous in his movements, with a somewhat sullen and weary glance."

At that time I had already known Debussy personally. Twenty years before, I had spent a year in Paris. That had been a period of artistic movement. There were veritable streams of new ideas in poetry, where the mystic Mallarmé was the last word, and in music, where French musicians were busy attacking Wagner's omnipotence. Up on the hill of the Montmartre, which the young artists had proudly named "The Brains of Paris," the young poets, painters and musicians discussed new formulas of art, and daily made new experiments. In the Latin Quarter I encountered Strindberg, brooding and sunk in mystic thought, sitting outside a café, with an absinthe glass before him. Surrounded by a group of friends was Oscar Wilde, already fat, wearing an unusual green ring on his right hand which held a lighted cigar. At the studio of Léandre, the excellent caricaturist, I met Debussy, shortly after I had seen several songs of his, steeped in a mist of color, published in the progressive "Révue Blanche."

Debussy rarely came out of his shell. He liked to muse and meditate, and only displayed outward enthusiasm when he spoke about the masses of Palestrina, which were sung by the famous choir in the Church of St. Gervais. These he considered the perfect works of religious ecstasy.

When Debussy came to Vienna for the first time, he was forty-eight years old. He had already become famous in Paris through the performance of "Pelléas and Melisande" (1902). Debussy's music was heard in Vienna for the first time at a concert, conducted by the composer. The programme included the "Petite Suite," "L'Apres midi d'un Faun" and "Ibéria." This music, transparent, gleaming, shimmering, was a music of hovering impressions, of melting, indefinite contours; a "music of nerves" belonging to a new age.

Ravel visited Vienna very frequently. The first reception accorded him there was not very friendly. The composer, with the violinist Szigeti, performed his Violin Sonata. Its scherzo, in blues rhythm, seemed, to the conservative Viennese public, to violate classic traditions. While one danced to "Blues" in Vienna as one did to all the members of the Foxtrot family, nevertheless the public did not deem this modern rhythm worthy enough to be employed in chamber-music; although Haydn, Mozart and Beethoven not only had composed dance music, but had incorporated contemporary popular dance music in their symphonies and chamber-music. After the Ravel "Blues" Scherzo, one of those famous Viennese concert riots occurred with which the musical public accompanied the performance of all modern music up to Schoenberg and Stravinsky. But the artistic qualities of Ravel's ingenious and finely polished music quickly conquered opposition, and when, in 1929, he first conducted a concert of his compositions, he was warmly acclaimed. After that, Ravel frequently and gladly returned to Vienna.

After the performance of his beautiful ballet, "L'Enfant et les Sortiléges," at the Vienna Opera, I had the pleasure of meeting Ravel at the home of one of his friends who had planned an evening of Viennese wine and music in his honor. I learned to admire and esteem the intellectual refinement of this musician who looked like a jockey; however, one could easily discern the signs of the malignant disease which eventually destroyed Ravel in the lost gaze in his eyes, and in his absolute immersion in his thoughts.

* * *

Vienna was bound to two great European nations through its enjoyment and appreciation of Italian melody and the French intellect. An especially interesting color was added to Viennese life by the proximity of Hungary.

Since 1867, Austria and Hungary had been bound in a double monarchy, and Emperor Franz Josef had received the crown of St. Stephen in Budapest. Most of the Hungarian aristocrats spent the winter in Vienna, and the two sister cities of the Danube were joined by close social ties. Hungarian music was played in the restaurants of the inner city and in the Prater where in the "Czarda" (so the country inns were called in Hungary), the Hungarian soldiers and the Viennese girls met. The fiery rhythms of Hungarian music were popular throughout all Vienna. The frenzy of a "Czardas" melody was known to old and young; and Hungarian "Goulash" had become a kind of national dish in Vienna.

Hungary, the land of fiery women, fiery horses and fiery wines added still more sensuousness to Viennese life. A Hungarian woman set Vienna's whole life of pleasure in motion: this was Princess Metternich or, as the Viennese intimately called her, "Princess Pauline." The little, ugly woman with the thick, protruding lips, scintillated intellect, and had the temperament of a Hungarian horse of the steppes. Her father, Count Sandor, was a daring horseman. When he rode in the Prater, he jumped his horse over moving carriages. Princess Metternich had inherited her father's temperament, and first demonstrated it in Paris, where, as the wife of the Austrian ambassador, she led the gaiety of the social life at Napoleon III's court, and stormed the gates of the Paris Opera in order to secure the performance of Wagner's "Tannhäuser." She was also popular in Vienna for her brilliant energy. Every year she organized balls and concerts, theatricals and folk-festivals, for charitable purposes, and Viennese society spent money freely on them. No P. T. Barnum knew his business better than she, nor devised cleverer ways of attracting huge audiences.

Johann Strauss, who understood Viennese life and atmosphere better than anyone else, allotted considerable place in his works to music in Hungarian style. One of his most popular operettas, "The Gypsy Baron" owes its success in no little degree to its enchanting Hungarian melodies. The only "grand" opera that the Waltz King composed, "Ritter Pazmann," contains some of the most tempestuous Hungarian ballet music imaginable. While the Emperor ruled over Austria and Hungary, Johann Strauss ruled over Austrian and Hungarian melodies.

From Hungary came the composer Carl Goldmark, the conductors Hans Richter and Arthur Nikisch; Franz Lehar, the most successful operetta composer in the world. From

Hungary, too, came Kalmann, who in his operetta, "The Czardas Princess," had made the passionate Hungarian tone popular. Lehar's and Kalmann's operetta successes went forth from Vienna, which was a sounding-board for music of every description and of every nationality. Hungary was inexhaustible in talent, which sprang to its full bloom in Vienna's air.

If the Hungarians gave additional color to the life and music of Vienna, the Slavs gave it softness. They contributed more than other influences toward banishing the German stiffness and rudeness from Viennese culture. From Vienna, Anton Dvorak's music started its course through the world. It was Brahms who discovered this primitive musician and who procured him a publisher, Simrock, in Leipzig.

Also in Vienna Bedrich Smetana's music was discovered for the world at large. I was present at the performance of "The Bartered Bride" in Vienna, on June 1st, 1892, which secured for Smetana's masterpiece its first real international recognition. For up to that time the opera was known only to the Czech audiences in Prague, where it was very popular.

I first heard the opera in a little Czech village, during my boyhood, when I was spending a vacation there. It was a typical Czech village which lay in a valley surrounded by woods. At the entrance of the village was the castle, where a toll-gate barred the road. Then came a long row of farmhouses with their accompanying stables and barns. In the center of the village, on the promontory, stood the church, and nearby, the inn. On Sundays the peasant boys and girls, who all week had worked in the fields, went to dance at the inn. The girls wore many petticoats, and tied colored kerchiefs around their heads. The young men kept their pipes in their mouths if they wanted to dance; walked up to one of the girls, removed the pipe, and spat the tobacco juice on the wooden floor. This was the invitation to the dance. The musicians sat at a table, their music propped up against beer glasses. Thus they played Smetana's music, while the dancers revolved in the smoky room, and we children stood at the door and listened and watched. And that was how I heard Smetana's music in the landscape from whence it sprang.

In Vienna, it was played again in different surroundings. At the Vienna Theatre and Music Exhibition of 1892 there was a theatre where troupes of different nationalities presented their performances. Here Judic played French comedies. Italian singers sang Italian operas. Reinhardt came from Berlin and gave Shakespeare's "Winter Tale." The Czech National Theatre gave Smetana's "Bartered Bride." Right from the end of the overture the surprised and delighted audience started applauding. The duet, "You know a girl" had to be sung four times, and the beautiful quintet in the last act was also encored. This was the greatest operatic success that Vienna had experienced. Hesch, the bass who sang the role of Kezal, was engaged for the Vienna Opera by Gustav Mahler, and became one of Vienna's most beloved singers.

Vienna again demonstrated its faculty of understanding and evaluating foreign culture when it uncovered Janacek's opera, "Jenufa," to the eyes of the world. Old Janacek came to Vienna for the performance of his work. With his bushy moustache, he looked like a colonel, but his shining blue eyes betrayed the artist. Seldom have I met a more charming old gentleman. He had radical and original views about music.

In fact, his opinions might well have belonged to a very young man. He attended a festival of modern music, one time, at Salzburg. After a concert, where the most modern music had been played, I spent an entire night with him, walking through the ancient streets of the town, discussing the problems of modern music until the sun rose over the mountains. At that time Janacek was seventy years old, but he was younger than the youngest of us all.

Janacek's opera, "Jenufa," kneaded out of the strong Slavic earth, was at first refused by the Czech public and music critics. Its keen realism, related to the realism of Moussorgsky, was not understood, and the great Slavic compassion which, at the end of the opera, transfigures the Czech village tragedy, struck few responsive chords in the hearts of that first audience. Vienna had no prejudices in its regard, and the Viennese success of this genial work opened to it the doors of the opera houses of the world. In Vienna, the title role was sung by Jeritza, who came of Slavic ancestry. Leo Slezak, the tenor, came from Moravia. Both artists still had their Czech accent. Young Jeritza, with her Slavic nose, her blonde hair, her expansive, sensuous smile, always looked like one of the young peasant-girls who worked and laughed in the Moravian fields. In her was the unbroken strength of nature, and in her radiant voice sang the female sex.

In the period of Franz Josef, the Italian, the Hungarian and the Slavic still mingled in Vienna's music. A great river has many tributaries.

In the Opera House

New Vienna's best society congregated every evening in the boxes and parquet of the new Opera House which was opened by Emperor Franz Josef on May 25, 1869.

Up to this time the "Kärntnerthor Theatre," which had stood in the old fortress-city near the southern town portal, had been Vienna's opera theatre. It had been built during Empress Maria Theresia's reign and operas had been performed there since 1810. From 1819 on it had been named the "Royal Court Opera Theatre." An old Viennese music lover told me that in the old theatre the acoustics were so wonderful that one not only heard the tones, but the very breath of air which surrounded them.

For the Viennese this theatre had been the scene of great enthusiasm for sixty-nine years. Here the ovations of the public had roared about Rossini and Donizetti. Here the delight had been great over the great and brilliant operas of Meyerbeer. History was at home in this theatre, as in all Vienna's theatres. Weber had composed his opera "Euryanthe" expressly for the Kärntnerthor Theatre. Here Beethoven's "Fidelio" was produced in 1814 for the first time in the version we know it today. Here in 1824, the deaf Beethoven performed his Ninth Symphony for the first time. The house was filled to capacity. Beethoven, wearing a black frock-coat, with black satin knee-breeches, silk stockings and buckled shoes, stood at the conductor's desk. He no longer could hear anything at all, and when, at the end, the audience shouted and applauded, one of the singers had to turn the deaf master around so that he could see the members of the audience waving their handkerchiefs.

Distinguished history and living present dwelled in this theatre. Nothing could bring more fame to it than the letter which Richard Wagner wrote when, in 1861, he heard his "Lohengrin" here for the first time: "That is a heavenly Opera! A mass of wonderful voices, one more beautiful than the other; chorus, orchestra—enchanting!"

For new Vienna, which had found the old fortress walls too confining, the old opera house was likewise too small. People wanted a new opera house, beautiful and large, like the new city; elegant like the city's society. They wanted a palace, not an old building with dark nooks and corners and low-ceilinged corridors. A prize-competition was instituted for the building of a new opera house, in which Van der Nuell and Siccardsburg were the winners. Both architects were Viennese, and they proudly erected the new theatre on the Ringstrasse, which was the Via Triumphalis of Vienna, at the entrance to the city. Past this new music palace the life of the new city flowed into the old from dawn to dusk. The majestic building faced the Ringstrasse, and its bright loggia was decorated by Schwind, Vienna's greatest painter, with illustrations from legends. This was a festival theatre in early French Renaissance style, with marble entrance-halls and a broad, splendid staircase, which the beautiful women in fur wraps and jewels slowly ascended on the way to their boxes. The great auditorium itself, with its rows of boxes laid out on the Italian model, was lavishly decorated with gold and extravagantly lighted. The ceiling was bordered by an enormous wreath of golden fruit, and in the center of glorious frescoes, hung a brilliant chandelier. The orchestra pit was comfortable and the stage was broad and deep. It was a magnificent theatre, worthy of a rich and magnificent city.

Strangely enough, the Viennese at first were not very well satisfied with their new opera. They were accustomed to the more intimate acoustics of the old opera house and found that they did not hear well in the new one. The comic journals made fun of the bronze winged horses which stood atop the building, saying that they were too thin, and went so far as to hang feed-bags around their necks. Finally, the problematic horses were sold, in 1877, to the city of San Francisco. One of the architects, Siccardsburg, committed suicide by shooting himself because of the continuous attacks and criticisms of the building. Only when the Viennese had gotten used to the house did they recognize its beauty.

Among the important opera houses of Europe, the Vienna Opera had its own special style. The Paris Opera was more elaborate, and, as the theatre of the financial and stock-exchange period, was overloaded with costly porphyry pillars, marble and gold. The Vienna Opera is festive, but middle-class. It is not obtrusively elegant. It is, to be sure, a large theatre, but when one enters the auditorium, one does not have the feeling of being in a large theatre. The society people, who sit in the boxes or in the orchestra on comfortable red plush chairs, form, like the society of a salon, a complete unit.

In this opera house, Vienna's society was like a painting within a golden frame. In the boxes at the right and left of the stage, and in the large festival box, sat the members of the Imperial family. In the orchestra were the officers, decorated with many orders, and the brilliantly dressed men and women of the wealthy official families. Toward the rear stood the young officers, who, as guests of the Emperor, were admitted to the opera for a very small sum, amounting to about ten cents. In the boxes were the families of the old noble houses, and the new plutocrats of Vienna. In the galleries were the young music enthusiasts, many holding piano scores—girls and young men, sometimes in a close embrace for double enjoyment.

In the Vienna Opera, one encountered more color, more vitality and more musical élan than in other German opera houses. It lay on the map between Germany and Italy and bound the operatic art of two great nations.

In the first third of the 19th century, during Rossini's time, the most famous Italian singers sang in the Vienna Opera. Every year one heard Lablache, Rubini, Donzelli, Ambrogi, the mesdames Lalande, Dardanelli and other great international favorites. The uproar over Rossini, which almost made the Viennese forget that Beethoven was living among them, is quite understandable when one considers that such amazing artists performed his works. Even Weber, when he came to Vienna for the performance of his "Euryanthe," was caught up in the general delirium, and wrote: "I have never encountered such artists before" and that they "represent the highest, purest perfection." After the period of the Rossini opera came (after 1830), the Meyerbeer period, with new singers like Adolphe Nourrit who, in Auber's "La Muette de Portici" and in Meyerbeer's operas, from "Robert le Diable" to "Les Huguenots," first sang the leading tenor roles, and brought an elegant, French style of tenor singing to the operatic stage. Another exponent of this energetic, yet charming French style was Roger, who was the first Johann van Leyden in Meyerbeer's "Le Prophète." After Meyerbeer, it was Verdi who, in Italy, evolved a new, vigorous tenor type—the stretta singer with the stormy high "C." The Vienna Opera, during two generations, reveled in such singers and such vocal artistry. This created a tradition which remained on its stage and with its public. For this reason it was that the Viennese derived more joy from beautiful voices than opera audiences in other German cities. In Vienna, the charm of sound held sway as it did in Italian opera houses, and this delight in sheer tonal beauty reigned also in the chorus and orchestra.

When the Vienna Opera was opened, the Wagnerian period had already dawned. The older Viennese wanted nothing to do with Wagner, but the women and the youth displayed a colossal enthusiasm for the composer's colorful romanticism. Since the younger generation belonged to him, the world belonged to Wagner. "Die Meistersinger von Nürnberg," "Der Ring des Nibelungen" and "Tristan und Isolde" were set in the golden frame of the Vienna Opera, and Franz von Jauner, who became Opera Director in 1872, engaged Hans Richter, the famous Wagnerian conductor, to perform them.

Hans Richter's life was closely bound with Wagner's. He had, in Wagner's villa, Triebschen, copied the score of "Meistersinger." He had been present when Wagner laid the cornerstone of his Bayreuth Theatre; and had played the tympani in the performance of Beethoven's Ninth Symphony which consecrated the festival theatre. Again at Triebschen,

Richter had played the trumpet at the performance of the "Siegfried Idyll" with which Wagner greeted his new-born son. Richter prepared the chorus for the first "Meistersinger" performance. At Bayreuth, he conducted the first performance of the "Ring." Finally, he died in Bayreuth, where he had spent the last years of his life, like Kurvenal at the feet of his master. In Hans Richter, the Vienna Opera encountered Wagner's great representative and the most famous general in the Wagnerian wars.

I have often seen Hans Richter conduct at the Vienna Opera, and I dare say that never again, as many great conductors as I have seen standing in his place there and elsewhere, have I seen a conductor so full of naturalness and simple strength. Nikisch, the pale salon gypsy with the romantic curls, was interesting; Gustav Mahler a bundle of nerves with the highest kind of intelligence; Weingartner, elegant and formally impressive; Toscanini, a firebrand and a volcano. None of these was so imposing as Hans Richter, of whom Debussy wrote, after hearing him conduct in London: "He conducts as dear God would conduct if He had learned conducting from Hans Richter." I was deeply moved when I read this sentence of Debussy's, since I had often asked myself whether my great admiration for Hans Richter had not been influenced by the fact that he was the great conductor of my youth, and that I had heard all the masterworks of music first under his powerful baton. But here I saw that Debussy felt exactly the same as I on the subject.

In the Vienna Opera, Hans Richter sat on a comfortable wicker chair in the centre of his musicians. He was a massive man, broad, heavy, and his large blue eyes behind professor-like spectacles looked calmly out as far as the most removed members of his orchestra. His beard flowed down over his breast. Holding his baton powerfully in his hand, his beat was clear and visible from the distance. At the climaxes he swung out with a broad movement. Strength and brilliance emanated from Richter's conducting, and all details merged into a great symphonic line. Every kind of pathos, whether it was the festive pathos of the "Meistersinger," the tragic pathos of Beethoven's Ninth Symphony or the religious pathos of the Bach Mass, Richter achieved without exertion. He did not have to raise himself on his toes or strain his nerves when he wished to draw the fullest degree of sound from his orchestra. As complete master of his craft, he was natural in every moment; he possessed an instinctive feeling for perfect truth which was undimmed by the slightest shadow of a mannerism. I have never heard anything so powerful as Hans Richter's conducting of the third act of "Walkyrie," which was unified and rounded from the Ride of the Walkyries of the beginning—which really sounded like a ride through clouds and tempest—to the great climaxes of the end, where the orchestra roared up from the depths. Nor have I ever heard anything so solemn and awe-inspiring as his prelude to the third act of "Meistersinger," which rose from the depths to the heights, all feeling and thought, solitude and pomp.

Hans Richter conducted everything at the Vienna Opera, not only Wagner, but Mozart, Rossini and Bizet. For Mozart, Richter, whose hand was heavy and mighty, lacked a certain lightness. Even Mozart's "Don Giovanni," conducted by him, took on great symphonic lines, as if Beethoven had composed it. But whenever Mozart's music became really monumental, as in the Overture to the "Magic Flute," Richter was unsurpassable. This music really ascended to the light and had a sunny brilliance. Richter conducted Rossini, Verdi and Bizet with more routine than enthusiasm, and most of the time with his baton in his left hand, which he had schooled to the same extent as his right. But in Wagner's works, he sat commandingly and filled with his mission as Wagner's apostle, in the middle of the orchestra, with all the strings grouped at the left and the winds at the right, like two armies which he led to victory.

For the Wagner performances, the Vienna Opera had at its disposal singers who, like Herman Winkelmann, Amalia Materna and Theodore Reichmann, had been trained by Wagner himself for his new style. Winkelmann sang the role of Parsifal at the first "Parsifal" performance in Bayreuth. Materna had been the first Brünnhilde, and Kundry, Reichmann the first Amfortas. Winkelmann's manly heroic voice, in which there also seemed to flow a tear, his heroic gestures, his straightforward glance, made him the born singer of Tannhäuser and Tristan. He was the bold knight in "Meistersinger" who is a poet and a lover. As Lohengrin, too, he was manly and knightly, when he left his swan-boat and stood there, holding a sword over his breast, his glance directed upward as in prayer. His high "a" sparkled like a golden shield on which the sun is falling. In Materna's voice, there was heroic jubilation; and Reichmann's elegiac baritone was shrouded as if by a veil. All these singers had been favorites of Wagner, especially Materna, whom Wagner, in his letters, addressed with particular tenderness: "My dear, good child— my true, faithful Wagner-daughter." Once he closed a letter to her: "God, when I think of the last Kundry evenings! Adieu, my dearest, good and best one!" Such artists made Wagner's performances into impressive events which had far-reaching influence. In the Vienna performance of "Meister-singer," a young baritone sang the role of the Town Watch-man. Later, this singer, Angelo Neumann, traveled through the world with a Wagnerian touring company. One of the most magnificent conductors of our times, Arthur Nikisch, was a violinist in the Wagnerian orchestra of the Vienna Opera.

But the Vienna Opera was not alone a great Wagner theatre. Since 1891, when Mascagni's "Cavalleria Rusticana" brought filled houses, it was also a Mascagni theatre. After the première of Massenet's "Manon" in 1890, it became a Massenet theatre; and it was a Goldmark and Verdi theatre as well. A French writer on art, Ritter, in one of his books, called the Vienna Opera "the gayest theatre in the world. There they perform earliest what there is of note in Europe; here singers and dancers from the four corners of the globe congregate, and costly productions and ballet performances play an eminent part."

The Vienna Opera would not have been a typical Viennese theatre had not ballet performances played a significant role. Vienna was the city of beautiful women, and, moreover, the city of the dance. Although, according to an unwritten law, the prima ballerina had to be an Italian, the other ballet members came from Vienna homes, had the Viennese laugh and the Viennese love of life. For them, new ballets were written which, like Baier's famous "Puppenfee" ("Doll Fairy"), were graceful, playful and charming. Ballet per-formances attracted all Vienna's best society. Young aristocrats, after the performance, took the pretty ballerinas to supper at the Hotel Sacher nearby. Wealthy old men sat in the first row and gazed through large opera-glasses at the girls on the stage, as if this was their principal occupation in life. The Viennese called these old gentlemen "ballet uncles," and folk-singers delighted in singing mocking songs about them.

The opera was Vienna's focal point. The great musicians who were its artistic leaders came from many foreign countries. This had been the case also at the old opera house, the Kärntnerthor Theatre, where Otto Nicolai (the founder of the Vienna Philharmonic concerts) had come from Königsberg, Heinrich Esser from Mannheim and Otto Dessoff, the greatest conductor of earlier days, from Leipzig. In the new opera house, there were, among the leading musicians, only three native Viennese: Herbeck, Franz Schalk, Clemens Krauss. Hans Richter came from Hungary; Wilhelm Jahn, the excellent Opera Director from 1880-1887, from Moravia; Gustav Mahler also from the Bohemian-Moravian borderland; Felix von Weingartner from Dalmatia; Richard Strauss from Bavaria; Bruno Walter from Berlin. All these men created the tradition which covered the new opera house with its patina. Their achievements there became history, and the ghosts, which cast their spell in the beautiful halls of the Vienna Opera, bound the present with the past and future.

New Concert Halls and Old Traditions

One year after the new Opera House, the new Concert House—the Music Society Building—was dedicated. Here, ever since 1870, the large concerts have been given. This building, too, is near the Ringstrasse. Emperor Franz Josef had donated the ground, and among the sponsors of the new house were the Empress, the Archdukes, Princes, Counts like the Liechtensteins, Schoenborns, Schwarzenbergs, Lobkowitzes —all members of the eighty aristocratic families which, according to the words of Napoleon, ruled Austria. Other sponsors included bankers and industrialists. In compliance with the taste of new Vienna's society, the building was decorated in that pompous style which characterizes all the buildings of the Ringstrasse epoch: paintings of the Nine Muses on the ceiling, golden Caryatides whose hands were clasped beneath their bosoms, framing the boxes, and with gas-lit chandeliers.

Two years later, in the Herrengasse where the Liechtenstein, Gallas and Kinsky palaces stood near the Imperial Palace, the intimate "Konzertsall" (Bösendorfersaal) was opened. Here Rubinstein, von Bülow and Liszt played the piano, the Joachim quartet performed, and Barbi sang. The piano manufacturer, Boesendorfer, built it. On this site had formerly been the riding school of the Duke of Liechtenstein. Because of this fact, the Viennese pianists, when it came time for the building's dedication, refused to play there. Hans von Bülow was courageous enough to perform at its inauguration, on November 19, 1872. Since the lighting had not been completed in time, stable lanterns were brought for illumination. The Emperor's Chief Stable-Master, Count Gruenne, regretfully remarked: "It's a shame such a beautiful riding-school is gone!"

The most important concerts were those of the Vienna Philharmonic. The members of the orchestra of the Opera managed these performances and themselves chose their conductors. This fact explains the enthusiasm which poured forth from the orchestra under great conductors, the freedom of execution and the brightness of its sound. The personnel comprised the best musicians of the city who played in these

Hans Richter leaves the stand after a
Bruckner performance
(O. Böhler)

concerts for their own enjoyment. They would not tolerate much pressure from the side of the conductor, any more than a spirited, thoroughbred horse will stand hard pressure from the spurs. Hans Richter told me: "One must allow this orchestra its free-play and lead it only to the point where it can develop its forces freely." All of the great conductors observed this rule when they directed the Philharmonic, best of all Hans Richter during the sixteen years of his leadership, and

Felix von Weingartner who was at its helm for eighteen years. Two other conductors could boast of having aroused the orchestra's greatest enthusiasm and admiration—Arthur Nikisch and Arturo Toscanini. Men like they, and Muck, Mottl, Furtwaengler, Richard Strauss and Mahler knew how to unleash all its powers of brightness and virtuosity. Mediocre conductors were lost with this orchestra.

The most eminent members of the orchestra were, at the same time, professors at the Conservatory which was housed in the same building. They educated pupils who adopted their way of playing, and who later became teachers themselves of the following generation of musicians. Thus there developed a special style of Viennese orchestral playing which was transmitted from one epoch to another like a precious heirloom. No concert orchestra in Europe had a similar tradition.

The Viennese public was musical, sensitive and capable of enthusiasm, but was, to a high degree, conservative, because it was surrounded by ghosts of old traditions which had become memories and habits. Each new musical movement had to battle these ghosts. Vienna had little interest in the progressive development of music. Every new musician encountered resistance in Vienna, even Robert Schumann. Up to the year 1854, the Society of the Friends of Music had not played a single one of his works. When finally, in this year, his C Major symphony was performed, it was coolly received.

The first orchestral work of Franz Liszt, "Les Preludes," was performed by Hellmesberger. It was hissed by a part of the audience. In 1858, Liszt himself came to Vienna. Twice his "Graner Festival Mass" was performed, both times with dubious success, although Liszt at that time was one of the most famous composers in Europe. In 1861, Carl Taussig gave three orchestral concerts of Liszt's compositions. Attendance was very poor.

Until 1850, nobody in Vienna had even thought of performing an opera by Richard Wagner, although, through the successes of his "Rienzi" and "Tannhäuser," he was Germany's most famous musician and the man of the hour. When finally the Director of the Vienna Opera wanted to perform "Tannhäuser," the censor forbade it because of its "immoral" libretto. At that time, Wagner's music was known in Vienna only through the concerts given by the Waltz King, Johann Strauss. Even the music of "Tristan and Isolde," which had been declared "unplayable," was first played by Johann Strauss at his concerts in the Volksgarten. The first performance of "Tannhäuser" in Austria did not take place in Vienna, but in Graz (where Richard Strauss's "Salome" was also performed before its Vienna presentation). When finally "Tannhäuser" was given in Vienna, it was at the Thalia Theatre in Ottakring—a theatre far out in the suburbs which was nothing more than a wooden barn. The performance, according to all reports, must have been terrible. Tannhäuser was hoarse or voiceless, Wolfram shouted, Venus sang off-pitch. Hanslick called the Singer's Contest "the Battle of the Invalids." Wagner considered the performance only as a means for making money, and wrote to the Theatre Director: "The devil take Vienna if it doesn't bring me in some money. Otherwise the cozy nest means damned little to me."

This suburban performance of "Tannhäuser" at least had the merit of having paved the way toward the Wagnerian performances at the Vienna Court Opera. In 1858, "Lohengrin" was performed for the first time, at the old Kärntner-thor Theatre. "Tannhäuser" followed in 1859. Fourteen years had passed since this opera's Dresden première, and it had been produced on all the German stages, as well as in Brünn, Lemberg and Linz before its performance in Vienna. The criticisms in the Vienna newspapers were so malicious that the Leipzig "New Magazine for Music" reproached the authors for their narrow-mindedness and lack of restraint.

In 1861, Richard Wagner came to Vienna from exile. Here he heard his "Lohengrin" for the first time; and the audience gave an ovation to the pale, small man who sat in a second-tier box. Wagner was so enthusiastic about the performance and the public that he immediately wanted to bring "Tristan and Isolde" to Vienna for its première, and wished to compose "Meistersinger" expressly for Vienna. At this point, Vienna had the wonderful opportunity of becoming Wagner's music city—perhaps his Bayreuth. The spiteful attacks on the composer in the newspapers destroyed this plan. I have read a letter of Wagner's which is still unpublished, where he exclaims, up in arms, that he will never return to a city where he could not even go to the men's-room without being scolded. His "Tristan and Isolde" was removed from the repertoire after seventy-seven rehearsals as "voice-murdering." And when, in 1879, in the new Vienna Opera, the "Meistersinger" was given for the first time, the "Prügel" ("Thrashing") Scene at the end of Act II was continued in the orchestra. One section of the audience hissed, and the other half attacked the hissers.

In 1872, the Vienna Philharmonic rejected the second symphony of Anton Bruckner as "unplayable." When Bruckner's symphonies were finally performed, the public was so antagonistic and the criticisms so spiteful that Bruckner writes in a letter: "They scared me to death in Vienna." In a letter of 1875, he complains desperately that he had to go begging in Vienna. In 1875, he asked the Philharmonic not to perform his Seventh Symphony because of the opposition of Brahms and Hanslick. When Bruckner was seventy years old and, in 1892, his Eighth Symphony, dedicated to Emperor Franz Josef, was performed, the Viennese hailed the shy old man, who stood helplessly on the concert platform, with great enthusiasm. The Viennese public made life hard for composers, but if a musician were great enough to outlast a period of being misunderstood, or if by any chance he had meanwhile become famous somewhere else, nowhere could more enthusiasm be demonstrated than by this same public.

For all great composers of modern times, this period finally arrived. When "Thus Spake Zarathustra" was performed under Hans Richter, the audience laughed at the cock's-crow of the trumpet and hissed at the end. The same thing occurred with "Ein Heldenleben" ("A Hero's Life"). A few years later, no more violent applause could be heard in Vienna than after Strauss performances. First performances of works by Bartok, Ravel and Hindemith were duly hissed. At the first performance of Stravinsky's "Sacre du Printemps," the whole hall changed into a real inferno. People laughed, jeered, mocked, hissed and it looked as if this genial work could not be heard to the end. A man shouted from the gallery into the tumult to the conductor (it was Franz Schalk): "Play Bruckner!" Thirty years before, the same man would probably have shouted: "Play Mozart!" In Vienna, the town of the musical classics, it was a favorite sport, if a problematic work had been played and a classical one followed, to greet the latter with demonstrative applause. When Liszt's "Prometheus" was played for the first time, the G Minor Symphony of Mozart was given a riotous ovation, although Mozart certainly needed the applause far less than Liszt.

The biggest concert scandals in Vienna occurred at the Schönberg concerts. Even as a very young musician, Schönberg had a talent for infuriating the public. When, in 1900, two songs of his were sung in a concert hall, the public laughed as if it had just heard the most enormous joke. At the end came violent hissing. Somebody kept whistling on his housekey (another favorite Viennese concert-sport) and Gustav Mahler turned upon the indefatigable whistler and shouted: "Sir, won't you stop?" Whereupon the whistler calmly retorted: "Why? I hiss your symphonies, too."

Even in 1912, when Schönberg arranged a performance of a song by his later famous pupil, Alban Berg, the public had just as good a time as if it had been composed by Schönberg himself. A Schönberg adherent slapped a Schönberg adversary in the face, and the concert had to be stopped. When, twenty years later, Berg's "Wozzeck" was performed at the Vienna Opera, it had a spectacular success. Berg was, by that time, already a famous composer abroad, and there is nothing which so enthuses the Viennese public as great fame to which it has contributed nothing.

The fame of most of the great Viennese musicians originated abroad. The successes of Bruckner began with the performance of his Seventh Symphony, under Nikisch, in Leipzig in 1884, and the performance of the "Romantic"

Symphony in Munich the same year under Hermann Levi. The acknowledgment of Hugo Wolf as song composer originated in Mannheim where Wolf had made a large circle of friends. The success of "Wozzeck" by Alban Berg started with the performances in Berlin under Kleiber, and in Philadelphia under Stokowski. All the Viennese musicians who, in official musical circles, established themselves slowly, had a group of friends who supported and extolled them. The unconditional admiration of these friends provided these musicians with what the general public lacked in warmth and interest.

The fault for the public's lack of understanding was certainly, to a degree, on the side of the Viennese music critics, but not entirely. After all, those critics who are most read by the public stand dependent, to a certain degree, upon the taste of that public. "Que voulez-vous, je suis leur chef. Il faut que je les suivre,"[1] said a witty French party-leader. The power that the influential and widely-read critics wielded over the public consisted to a degree in the fact that they wrote what their public enjoyed reading. More important than the critics, however, was the spirit of the town, which was unfavorable to new and great art in other fields as well as in music. The city of Vienna was, at the time when the new industrial age roared through its streets, full of the enjoyment of life. From the arts, too, it demanded entertainment, not mental exertion. Music should be melodious, lively, clever. For such Viennese music, Brahms was too serious, Bruckner too full of Catholic piety and Mass solemnity, Mahler too cabalistic and too mystic, Schönberg too intensely occupied

[1] "What would you, I am their leader. I have to follow them."

with problems. Vienna, so long accustomed to sensuous enjoyment of its music, was weak in that intellectual power which was more prevalent in northern Germany. Intellectual problems in music, which the works of every great new composer presented, were uncomfortable in Vienna.

Another important instance which demonstrated that while Vienna was a musical city, it was not one which showed understanding for new musicians, was the conservative mind of the monarchy whose capital was Vienna. The Austrian empire was an old monarchy, and the old order penetrated new forms of life. In new Vienna, a time of technical wonders had arrived, but the spirit of the city was old. The construction of society was the same as that of the old feudal court-society of the seventeenth century. And the modern political innovations, like the parliament, and political movements such as those of the workers, changed nothing of this. Despite its Ringstrasse and new palaces, Vienna was a baroque city, just as Rome will always be.

The Spanish Ceremonial, which had ruled the life at the Court of Charles V still ruled at Emperor Franz Josef's. As in the Madrid of the seventeenth century, the Emperor's guards passed with slow steps through the streets where now modern traffic hurried. The horses of the imperial riding school lifted their feet to the beat of a bygone age. On Good Friday, all Vienna was changed into old Spain. On the road from St. Stephen's Cathedral to the Imperial Palace, four altars, decorated with fresh green, were erected where the four evangels were read. From the giant portal of St. Stephen's came a great procession. After the cross came armies of priests and monks, and under a baldachin walked the

Cardinal Archbishop of Vienna, carrying a chalice which blazed with gold and precious stones. Behind the baldachin walked the old Emperor, bareheaded, holding a lighted candle and the Archdukes, the ministers and generals, the high officials and courtiers. All the spectators fell to their knees, and the bells rang. One felt himself back in seventeenth century Madrid, where an ancient Hapsburg, in the Escorial monastery, had himself laid, alive, in his coffin, and prayed the litany of the dead which the monks were chanting in the church. An hour later, automobiles passed through the same streets.

The Viennese lived in modern houses, but the German they spoke was full of old forms dating from the middle-ages. In no other dialect of the German language can one find so many expressions extant which dated back to the time that the Song of the Nibelungs was composed. Besides, the whole history of Vienna is preserved in the folk speech: French words from the time when Napoleon lived in the Castle of Schoenbrunn, Spanish expressions from the time of Leopold I, who had married a Spanish woman, and Italian words. The customs, too, are filled with the past. Viennese men kissed the hands of the ladies whom they met the way the Spaniards had done in the 17th century. From the same period dated the practice of addressing people of higher social standing by the noble title "Herr von"—a custom specially beloved by waiters, who flattered every well-dressed guest by thus addressing him. If the waiter expected an especially good tip, he called the customer "Baron." If he did not get it, the guest had to be satisfied with the more simple "Herr von." One lived in an ancient noble city where the world began with a baron.

Every second Viennese had a long-winded title of some

sort. The longest and most pompous, of course, belonged to the Emperor. Upon them lay the dust of ancient history. So even the title "Emperor of Jerusalem" was not missing, as if Vienna still dwelled in the time of the Crusades. The Court was old, the Church of Austria was old, and the Emperor himself was old. An empire of this sort is not easy to set in motion, even though it is through modern, technical, political and social movements. For a long time during Emperor Franz Josef's reign, the militia was called out at every worker's strike, and fired upon the strikers. The demands of the nationalities and social classes were only slowly satisfied. This conservative spirit naturally worked upon the mentality of the Viennese. In an empire where all was regulated, music could not progress rapidly. In an old police state where every free word was considered dangerous and where the police watched any casual movement with suspicion, strong personalities were apt to be thought dangerous. The appreciation of strong artistic personalities who had destroyed a bit of the old spirit, could not readily occur. So it was with musical life. Every new artist was a threat and a danger.

Classical music was, in such a state and in a city so bound by the old order, of especial importance. It was itself an old order which had been given over in flesh and blood. Even Beethoven's greatest and most daring innovations were not taken into the old order without opposition. It surely took time until the works of Beethoven's last period, even the Ninth Symphony, were given recognition and appreciation. The greatest Austrian poet, Grillparzer, heard in this music only revolution and chaos, and Hanslick only recognized this music against his will. But finally these works, too, became old music, and, as such, in Vienna, classical music. Classical music was the same for the Viennese public as the Constitution was for political life. It was the cornerstone of Viennese musical art and the temple to which one fled in times of need.

Not even in the time of the classicists was the great musical city great because it had understood new music better or more rapidly than other European cities. As early as 1738, Reichardt, the Prussian Court Conductor, complained: "The works of foreign masters have a hard time succeeding here." In music, Vienna was an aristocratic city, proud of its past, rich in tradition. It was the great musical city because here, more than anywhere else, music was a part of its life and the lives of its inhabitants. The city had a musical soul. There were other cities in Europe which thought more intellectually or conversed more brilliantly, as Paris, for instance. Others had stronger political power, like London. Vienna was the musician.

Franz Schalk at the desk.

Modern Music in Vienna

Richard Strauss, Gustav Mahler, Arnold Schönberg

Around the year 1900, the old conservative music city was set into motion. Along with the national and social movements came a general unrest upon artistic fronts. A new epoch was announcing itself. Old orders were shaken. Revolution was in the air, and the life-enjoying, amusement-seeking public of Vienna was frightened.

In literature, painting, theatre and music, the naturalistic tendency had the upper hand. Every year there would be a new social drama by Henrik Ibsen who had turned away from the romantic, and now analyzed the morals of bourgeois society, the modern marriage and the stricken conscience. Strindberg's plays portrayed the battle of the sexes. Zola, Maupassant and Flaubert delighted in depicting everyday life. Tolstoi and Dostoievsky, in powerful novels, described people who lived in hate and love, passion and crime. From France came new impressionistic pictures which released the landscape in a play of colored spots and disintegrated the sunlight. Claude Monet, Sisley and Pissaro painted momentary shadings and color vibrations. Liebermann painted factories. In Germany, a new poet, Gerhardt Hauptmann, appeared on the scene, and with his "Die Weber" ("The Weavers") and "Hannele's Himmelfahrt" (Hannele's Ascension to Heaven") awoke the social conscience of the time.

In the colored, make-believe world of the theatre, too,

changed perception and feeling of a new time were reflected in a new and naturalistic style of dramatic portrayal. Each year Duse came and transformed the stage into reality with her pale, Mater Dolorosa face, her sad eyes, her tired hands, and the voice which was pure soul. In Vienna's Burgtheater, a fortress of the classic dramatic style which Goethe had founded in Weimar, modern actors like Mitterwurzer became established, and when this genial and unpredictable actor died in 1897, Joseph Kainz, the greatest of the new "nerve" actors was a famous and worthy successor. In Berlin, Brahm assembled actors for a naturalistic Ibsen ensemble. He was followed by Max Reinhardt, who in "A Mid-Summer Night's Dream" had the woods fantastically staged with shimmering birch boughs, and the gloomy Cyclops wall in "Elektra" built up high. In Paris, Antoine played, in his "L'Oeuvre" Theatre, the dramas of Ibsen, Strindberg, Hauptmann and Bjoernson.

All at once in Vienna, there was a new literature which bound modern naturalism with Viennese dramatic art and Viennese tenderness. Arthur Schnitzler brought the ladies of Vienna society and the girls of the suburbs to a stage become realistic. Hugo von Hofmannsthal, even when he was still a boy, wrote marble-smooth verse, in which the Viennese baroque lived once more. A great modern critic, Hermann Bahr, traveled throughout Europe and visited all the battle-fields of modern art between Paris and St. Petersburg. All at once, Vienna, too, had a famous modern architect, Otto Wagner, who no longer, like the designers of the Ringstrasse buildings, thought in terms of Greek pillars or Renaissance arches, but in those of cement and iron. In 1903, he erected a new Postal Savings Bank Building in the most modern style on the Ringstrasse, and Vienna conservatism cried and screamed. The same thing had happened in 1900, when the painter Klimt exhibited his ceiling paintings which he had done for the university.

The Viennese public was terrified by so much new art, and saw the end of the world coming when Ibsen and Gerhardt Hauptmann, even, managed to penetrate the classic portals of the Burgtheater. I was present when in the "German Folk Theatre," Ibsen's "The Wild Duck" was presented for the first time. Ibsen himself had come for this performance. He sat in the box nearest the stage, with his ruffled white hair and white beard. He watched, without changing his expression, while the audience laughed at every phrase in the last act; while it applauded everything which was meant ironically, and ridiculed everything which was meant seriously, with jeers and cat-calls. When the curtain fell amid the monstrous clamor of aroused theatre-patrons, Ibsen rose in his box and laughing heartily,tossed his high top-hat to the parquet below. Similar uproars followed every performance of a modern play. When Maeterlinck's "L'Intruse" was given at the Josef-stadt Theatre, every breathing pause called forth laughter. No comedy could have made the audience more hilarious.

Music was carried along with the intellectual movement of the era, and it became naturalistic and impressionistic. The classic harmony began to dissolve. Classic forms, like all the constructions of the period, began to shake and tremble. In France, Claude Debussy, influenced by the impressionistic painters, and by the poetry of Mallarmé and Verlaine, began to compose oscillating tone colors. His faun began to play the flute in the sunlight of an antique landscape. His Spain was a canvas full of color daubs and dust. In Germany, Richard Strauss became the leader of the modern music movement, after he had turned away from the Parsifal-like solemnity of "Guntram," the opera of his youth. He boldly applied himself to every-day life, became the greatest naturalistic champion of the orchestra, and painted the noise of Naples' streets. When his Neapolitan descriptions were hissed in Munich, he wrote von Bülow: "I had a wonderful time. The first step toward independence!" Daring, ironic, full of zest for life, for pranks and jokes, rich in voluptuous melody, young Richard Strauss appeared in a musical world which was tired of Wagner's pompous romanticism. Once I had dinner with Strauss (who was a young man at the time) and Zemlinsky in Vienna. Strauss scratched his fork on his plate and it gave out a squeaking noise. "Could you reproduce that in the orchestra?" he asked Zemlinsky. And as Zemlinsky was shaking his head, Strauss said confidently: "I can do it!" What sound in the world was Strauss unable to copy with his orchestra?

I became acquainted with Strauss in Munich when he was a young court-conductor. The "beer-friendly" city on the Isar had its epoch of genius, and about 1900 Strauss introduced Frank Wedekind to me. Wedekind had already written his bold drama of adolescence, "The Awakening of Spring," which had completely horrified the whole city. Also through Strauss, in Munich, I met the artist Thoma, whose sharp, stinging drawings appeared every week in "Simplicissimus." This paper was the most courageous opposition paper that appeared in Germany. On every street corner one saw its placard—a red pug-dog, showing his teeth. For this paper, Thoma drew his cartoons of Prussian Junkers, German university students, fat industrialists on whose laps young girls were sitting, and conceited officers. It was fresh opposition air in Munich. Berlin, the German Kaiser Wilhelm, the Junkers were the enemy. Richard Strauss lived in this air. He composed with preference to revolutionary modern poets, Dehmel, Liliencron, Bierbaum, Falke, Christian Morgenstern, Hart; and his song, "Der Arbeitsmann" ("The Workman"), on a text by Dehmel, which waves the red flag, will outlive many other songs he has written. At that time, I already knew the songs of Richard Strauss, the naturalistic declamation of which, combined with their lyric tenderness, was something new. Especially the "Traum durch die Dämmerung ("Dream through the Twilight") had made an impression upon me with its fragrance and atmosphere. A girl of my acquaintance sang the beautiful melody, I accompanied at the piano, and at the end, we kissed each other. This was certainly not the worst way of hearing modern music.

Oscar Fried, who later made himself a name as conductor and composer, spoke to me in Munich about Strauss, saying that he was a genius, and I was anxious to meet him. With great interest, I had heard him conduct a performance of "Tannhäuser" at the Munich Court Opera. At that time, he still had his bush of red hair, and his slender hands, of which he was a trifle vain, and which also, later on, he kept carefully manicured. He held the baton gracefully, almost floating in his hand, as opposed to the conductors of the old school who used to grasp their batons firmly, like a commander's staff. Most striking was the supple, delicate sense of sound, the nervous shading, and above all, the many accelerations and retardings of tempi, the modern accentuation. These shiftings of tempi were still more obvious to me when Strauss conducted Mozart's "Don Giovanni" in the small Residence Theatre. His was a non-academic Mozart which stressed the orchestra and the drama on the stage—Mozart, 1900.

When Oscar Fried introduced me to Strauss, who was his teacher, I saw a tall, slender man with fine blue eyes, who was simple and natural. His nature was sharply critical. One had the impression that he knew exactly what he wanted and clearly spoke his thoughts. I well remember our conversation that day. We spoke of Mozart, and Strauss was very polemical against the conception that Mozart was a naive musician. He insisted that Mozart had always chosen sensational subjects for his operas. "The Marriage of Figaro" was the revolutionary play of Mozart's day, and it had been banned in Paris. "Don Giovanni" had an erotic subject, and Mozart was accused of immorality when he composed it. "The Magic Flute," too, with its employment of Masonic rituals, had a sensational subject for its day and age. His love for Mozart, Strauss had inherited from his father. Later on, when I visited Strauss at his country house in Garmisch, I would often see him, after he returned from an automobile excursion, lie down on a sofa and study the score of a Mozart string quartet which, for that purpose, always lay ready on a music stand nearby. This was his refreshment and inspiration too. Afterwards when Strauss had become Director of the Vienna Opera and gave parties at his home there, he always had a Mozart string quartet played at the beginning of the festivities. On one such occasion, I observed that Strauss, who was sitting in a corner, was hardly able to restrain his tears. I asked him later what had moved him so much in this quartet (it was the

C Major). He answered that his father, in his will, had ordered the quartet played in church at his funeral. This had been done, and Strauss recalled it. With a young modern musician like Strauss, this admiration for Mozart was striking. We young musicians were first Wagnerians, then Mozartians. Strauss was first a Mozartian.

Otherwise, Strauss was respectless, not at all pathetic, and Munich was shocked when he wrote his opera "Feuersnot" ("Fire Famine"), on a text by Wolzogen, a cabaret director. In this opera, Strauss ridiculed the people of Munich and glorified the first love-night of a young girl in a naturalistic symphony. The bold opera failed in Munich and Strauss went to Berlin. Here he was in a modern atmosphere. He always needed spiritual inspiration. He found it, mainly, in the new theatre of Max Reinhardt where, for the first time, he saw Oscar Wilde's "Salome" and Hugo von Hofmann-stahl's "Elektra." He found it, also, in "The Weavers" of Gerhardt Hauptmann, and wanted to compose an opera based on the drama. Berlin, during this period, was rich in intellectual forces of all kinds. There were excellent modern magazines, brilliant journalists and critics (like Maximilian Harden, who wrote articles against the Emperor, and on the theatre in a lush, colored style), the best German actors of the younger generation like Bassermann, Sorma and Lehmann. Nikisch conducted the Philharmonic, Weingartner at the Royal Opera. For Richard Strauss, a musician with modern temperament and élan, this Berlin was the right place. Here he became the musician who collected all modern intellectual and artistic movements in his compositions as in a burning-lens.

Richard Strauss first appeared personally in Vienna as a

composer of songs in 1902. He gave a "Liederabend" (Song Recital) at the Boesendorfer Hall, and his wife, Pauline de Ahna, sang his songs. Strauss sat modestly at the piano, like someone who did not wish to draw attention to himself. He was a fine, delicate pianist who shaded the tones with good taste. The Vienna public, who so often had gathered in the same hall to hear the first performance of songs by Brahms and Hugo Wolf, found the Strauss songs beautiful and full of warmth of feeling, but not exactly original. Songs like "Wiegenlied" ("Cradle Song"), with its easily grasped melody and the bells in the accompaniment appeared quite banal and based on a cheap effect. Also, the impressive melody of the "Heimliche Aufforderung" did not impress the audience as being something novel. People had been expecting, in Richard Strauss, a wild innovator, and found, instead, a tasteful lyricist. Hanslick, Vienna's chief critic, called Pauline, the singer of the evening, "the better half of the composer."

Strauss's music had already been heard at the Philharmonic concerts. Hans Richter had conducted "Don Juan" in 1892, and "Tod und Verklärung" ("Death and Transfiguration") in 1893. But even in these performances, no one felt that he had heard the works of a new musical genius. It all sounded too beautiful and too virtuoso. Only with the performance of "Also Sprach Zarathustra" ("Thus Spake Zarathustra") did the uproar and tumult begin like the ones reserved for a genius.

Strauss first became known as a conductor in Vienna the year he came there as guest, directing the Munich Chamber Orchestra. With the long steps of a stork he stormed on to the podium, and began to conduct Wagner's Prelude to "Meistersinger" with the stabbing arm movements which resembled the sallies of a fencer, and the jerking knee-bends which, not much later, made him a notable conductor in the concerts he directed. Vienna was accustomed to the all-powerful, prevailing calm of Hans Richter, and to the Richter breadth of baton technique. Now there stood a young musician of a new generation who was not mighty and broad, but slender and nervous on the podium. His red hair gleamed like a torch borne at the head of a revolutionary mob. In the course of years, Strauss became more concise and more calm as a conductor, and later conducted almost entirely from the wrist with quite brief, short motions.

Once I went to congratulate Strauss, after he had conducted the first act of "Tristan and Isolde" in a most thrilling way, using only short, precise movements. "Feel me here!" Strauss said to me, and placed my hand on his armpit. "Absolutely dry! I can't stand conductors who perspire!" But at that time, in concert, he must have perspired since he often, in conducting the "Meistersinger" prelude, gave the impression of being ecstatic.

In his conducting of this Prelude, also, Strauss showed every inclination to special accent and to the dramatic quickening and retarding of tempi which had already impressed me in Munich as the nervous characteristics of a new time. Even as an old man, conducting this prelude, he still used many of the self-willed tempo variations. He loved to conduct it with the Vienna Philharmonic, to improvise with all the accents, and enjoyed it immensely when the orchestra followed him perfectly through the sudden changes of tempi. Once, after conducting the Prelude of the "Meistersinger," he rushed up to me, red and excited, and cried out, radiant with joy: "Everything improvised! All without rehearsal!"

Later on, Strauss disliked anything unusual in conducting. He used to like to tell me how his father, who had played horn in the Munich Orchestra, had come home after Strauss conducted his first opera performance, and said: "You young conductors imagine God-knows-what when you sit at the conductor's desk. We old musicians already know when you walk to the podium what you are. You don't even have to hold your baton in your hand before we know all." And another time, he remarked: "How many good conductors did I have to see—Bülow, Hermann Levi, Hans Richter, Fischer, Muck, Mottl, Schuch—and how much did I have to conduct myself, until I could do what I now can do."

But this was the wisdom of old age. As a young musician, Strauss conducted as young musicians have always done, and will always do—with enthusiasm, with tense nerves, with new nuances which correspond to the transformed mode of feeling of a new epoch; and never in a calm and clarified way, for these are the qualities either of the highest maturity or of stagnant routine.

As opera composer, Strauss first appeared in Vienna with his exuberant work of youth, "Die Feuersnot." At the dress rehearsal, Strauss, interrupting the conductor, Gustav Mahler, suddenly rushed forward and shouted: "Please, dear Mahler, start again at the 'Nachtlager in Granada' ('A Night's Camp in Granada') spot." Actually, in "Feuersnot," there is a quotation from the Biedermeyer opera "Das Nachtlager von Granada," by Kreutzer, just as in "Salome" there is a quotation from "The Barber of Seville," concerning the use of which in the over-ripe beauty of the "Salome" music, Strauss himself has made the best of jokes. In the "Feuersnot" music, again Strauss did not impress the public as revolutionary. Some people found the libretto frivolous in many respects, and others were shocked about the way Strauss glorified himself in it, but the music, with its folk-like choruses and its zestful lyrics, appeared neither offensive nor particularly bold, though it was harmonious and brisk. Public opinion changed when the horrifying "Salome" was performed for the first time at a private theatre, the "Deutsches Volkstheater." At that performance there was already an actively hissing opposition.

Thus Richard Strauss entered Viennese music life when the great Brahms and Bruckner epoch had come to an end Bruckner had died 1896, Brahms had died in 1897, and with these two symphonists, classical music itself terminated. One was now in a new world of orchestral sound, of virtuoso description, and of crass realism, and Richard Strauss appeared more and more as the eminent master of the period.

For Vienna's musical life, it was of greatest importance that, at that time, Gustav Mahler took over the direction of the Vienna Royal Opera. Mahler conducted a performance of "Lohengrin" on May 11, 1897, and was appointed director on October 8th. Emperor Franz Josef had, in Mahler, appointed a man who, next to Richard Strauss, was the strongest musical personality of the time. Franz Josef was sixty-seven years old, Mahler thirty-seven. Old and new eras stood opposite each other in those two men, the aged monarch and the fanatical musician. With Gustav Mahler at its helm, the Vienna Royal Opera of Franz Josef moved itself right into the center of the European intellectual world, and became, like the theatre of Max Reinhardt in Berlin, and L'Oeuvre Theatre of Antoine in Paris, one of the leading theatres of the intellectual movements of the time.

From the personality of Gustav Mahler, who was a demonic man, streams of nervous energy emanated, and pervaded stage, orchestra and audience at the Vienna Opera. Long before Mahler appeared in the orchestra pit, the audience became excited. When the house grew dark, the small man with sharply-chiseled features, pale and ascetic-looking, literally rushed to the conductor's desk. His conducting was striking enough in his first years of activity in Vienna. He would let his baton shoot forward suddenly, like the tongue of a poisonous serpent. With his right hand, he seemed to pull the music out of the orchestra as out of the bottom of a chest of drawers. He would let his stinging glance loose upon a musician who was seated far away from him, and the man would quail. Giving a cue, he would look in one direction, at the same time pointing his baton in another. He would stare at the stage and make imploring gestures at the singers. He would leap from his conductor's chair as if he had been stung. Mahler was always in full movement like a blazing flame. Later he became calmer. Evidently he controlled himself which only augmented his inner tension.

Mahler was conscious of the extreme tension which emanated from him into the theatre. He once told me, during one of our first talks, "Believe me, people only realize what I am when I am gone. Then it is as if a storm had broken over the theatre." The Viennese public, directly after Mahler's arrival, realized the additional artistic energy which had been bestowed on it in such a personality. In the first year of his direction, the operas of Mozart were performed ten times more often than in other seasons. Wagner had twenty evenings more than in the previous year. Even smaller-scale, lighter operas like Lortzing's "Czar und Zimmermann" played to sold-out houses. Mahler worked according to a broad programme, on the renovation of the ensemble and the repertory. He told me shortly after his arrival that within the next ten years he wanted to revive and re-stage "Fidelio" and the works of Wagner, Mozart, Weber, Lortzing, Gluck; and to put these works together in the form of a great cycle. Then, this accomplished, he wanted to leave the opera.

Rarely has any theatre operated according to a larger-scale plan, and in the first half of Mahler's directorship, what was accomplished corresponded exactly with the ideal picture set forth at the beginning. The intensity with which Mahler attacked the re-studying of a classic work was unusual. Of every work which he prepared and performed, Mahler said: "This is the greatest opera which has ever been written!" He was filled with solemn enthusiasm after he had brought out a new work. Stage and orchestra, décor and singing had to form a complete artistic unity according to his ideas. Each opera was a dramatic work of art. The Wagnerian conception of a comprehensive art work was applied by Mahler to every opera.

For this purpose, Mahler developed a new ensemble. The great Viennese heroic singers of the Wagner epoch had grown old. Winkelmann, Reichmann and Materna had to be replaced by younger forces, and Mahler found the noble tenor Schmedes and young Slezak. In Mildenburg, he had a modern Wagner tragedienne, in Weidemann and Deumuth great baritones. He had Gutheil-Schoder as an interesting singer for lighter roles. Hers was a realistic talent of the first rank for tragic as well as comic parts. In Kurz he had found a new coloratura. All these singers blindly followed the dictates of the genial musician who had formed and trained them. Mahler clung to this ensemble with great love. I can remember how disturbed he was, when he had Gutheil-Schoder sing the Eva in "Meistersinger," and read the unfavorable criticisms about her. He sat sunken down behind the mountain of newspapers, like a wicked dwarf, and nervously chewed his finger-nails—something which he was accustomed to do in moments of stress.

One time, to Mahler's horror, his tenor Schmedes walked into a smoke-filled coffee-house where Mahler was sitting, holding a fat cigar which emitted powerful blasts of smoke. Mahler used all his wiles to get his Siegfried out of the place. He asked him to go, he begged him, and when nothing helped, he flattered him and told Schmedes how the audience only wanted to hear him, and described how horribly disappointed people would be if he had to cancel and someone else replaced him. Schmedes hung on Mahler's every word while so much flattery was being poured over him, and finally left the smoky place, swollen with pride like a freshly inflated balloon. Surely he must have sung especially well that night. However, Mahler could also be very hard and unjust toward singers when he felt any opposition from them.

Mahler was a modern musician with the temperament of his period. As such, he introduced a new Mozart style to the Vienna Opera which was taken up by young musicians and carried to all the German opera houses. Mahler's Mozart performances had spirit and dramatic liveliness, grace and wit. The orchestra had rich nuances, polished like Venetian glass, and worked out in detail like fine lace. Thus, through the artistic mind of an artist of the Ibsen period, Mozart's music achieved a new popularity. "The Marriage of Figaro" and "Cosi fan Tutte" shone like jewels. "The Magic Flute," which became a great box-office attraction, gleamed with intellectual sparkle. As in all people of high intelligence, there was in Mahler a kind of child-like merryness which came as a release after work. When in "The Magic Flute," the animals appeared—lion, hippopotamus, rabbit and monkeys—attracted by Tamino's flute-playing, none of the opera audience laughed more than Mahler at his conductor's desk. He fairly shook with laughter. All comic opera music, whether it was Lortzing, or French music like Boieldieu's "La Dame Blanche," found in Mahler a magnificent interpreter, for no one understood liveliness better than this man who also knew demons in his breast.

With Mahler, the tragic reigned in his interpretation of "Tristan." There are several possible interpretations of this Wagnerian work. Hans Richter conducted it as a symphony with tremendous climaxes and a unified line. Felix Mottl, whom Toscanini specially praised to me, produced the most nature-like sound when working toward his climaxes, and the richest fulness in the music. Strauss conducted the music of the second act—Strauss-like—as an ecstatic hymn, as he did the love music of "Heros Life." Mahler conducted the same music with modern temperament, making vibrant, intense, hysterical climaxes of the period of Charcot and Freud.

At the performance of "Tristan" in 1903, which Mahler

arranged on the anniversary of Wagner's death, for the first time stage décor designed by Professor Roller was used. Roller, that artist who translated Mahler's visions into painting, was one of the principal leaders of the group of modern Viennese painters who, in 1897, banded together in the so-called "Secession." According to the pattern of Claude Monet,

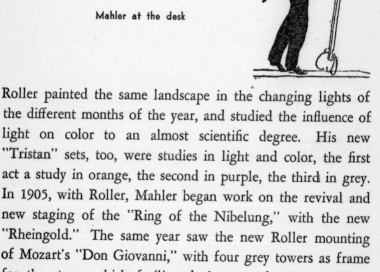

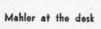

Mahler at the desk

Roller painted the same landscape in the changing lights of the different months of the year, and studied the influence of light on color to an almost scientific degree. His new "Tristan" sets, too, were studies in light and color, the first act a study in orange, the second in purple, the third in grey. In 1905, with Roller, Mahler began work on the revival and new staging of the "Ring of the Nibelung," with the new "Rheingold." The same year saw the new Roller mounting of Mozart's "Don Giovanni," with four grey towers as frame for the stage, which facilitated changes of scenery. When Roller designed the new "Don Giovanni" sets, he was strongly influenced by the ideas of Gordon Craig. Modern ideas of staging and painting found a most forceful expression in Roller's stage.

Through the combined efforts of Mahler and Roller, the

Vienna Opera had suddenly become the leading opera house of Europe. One may safely say that during the first years of Mahler's direction, the highest level was achieved which can be attained in an opera house where performances are given daily, in the perfection of these performances, in artistic spirit, and in the unity of musical and scenic faculties.

The great successes of Mahler led to Hans Richter's departure from the theatre. Mahler and Richter were direct opposites. Physically, Richter was tall and broad-shouldered, Mahler small and slender. They belonged to different generations, Richter the pathetic and powerful, Mahler the intellectual and nervous. Richter had a great nature, Mahler a great intelligence. Richter was a blond German with Wotan's eye, Mahler a dark Jewish type. Mahler did everything in his power not to hurt Richter, but he could not do away with their differences. The enthusiasm which swept about Mahler after each new revival gave Richter the feeling that his work in Vienna was at an end. He had brought Wagner's works of art to a whole generation of Viennese opera-goers. For this he had fought, for a large part of the public had wanted nothing to do with Wagner's music dramas. When I started to go to the Vienna opera, the house was half empty for "Tristan und Isolde," in spite of Winkelmann and Materna. "Siegfried," too, at that time had not as yet any public, and "Goetterdaemmerung" could only be given with cuts. At performances of "Meistersinger," half of the audience in the orchestra rushed away after the third act quintet. Richter had been Wagner's apostle. That fact gave his conducting of Wagner the inner greatness, the élan and morality it possessed. To Richter, measured by his own achievement, Mahler's

Wagner must have seemed less great than it was, for Mahler no longer had to fight; while Richter and the other enthusiasts who had surrounded Wagner, had.

I observed the difference between the two conductors when Mahler conducted "Walkyrie." After the performance, Mahler rushed to me and asked: "Well, how was it?" I answered: "A marvelous performance, but the tempi at the end seemed too fast to me." Mahler frowned, and I quickly noted that I had committed a faux-pas. Artists, like cooks, when they come from the kitchen, want to hear praise and not criticism. Therefore I added, in order to put him in better humor, that probably I was used to the broad tempi of Hans Richter. Mahler became furious and said: "Stop that! Richter has no idea about tempi!" Now it was my turn to be angry, and I reported that Richter had conducted the first "Walkyrie" in Bayreuth under Wagner, and therefore must know the Wagnerian tempi. But Mahler replied curtly: "Maybe he knew the right tempi then. Since then he has forgotten them." I realized it was no use talking to Mahler at this moment, and went on my way. Walking home, I saw Hans Richter ahead of me. Joining him, I asked him whether he had heard the "Walkyrie" performance, and when he replied that he had, I asked him whether he had not thought the tempi at the end had been too fast. He answered: "What of the music, at the end, is "Fire Spell"—that was brought out very well by Mahler. But that this end is a transfiguration (and he put his hand on his heart) and a painful resignation—of that Mahler has no idea!"

When the news of Hans Richter's resignation from the Vienna Opera became known, there were demonstrations by the Wagnerian party at the opera whose sound took on an anti-Semitic character. Just during those years when Mahler was opera director, the anti-Semitic party which Dr. Karl Lueger had founded became successful in the elections of the Municipal Council. Dr. Lueger, a Viennese with the wit of a folk-singer, became mayor of Vienna in 1897 after Emperor Franz Josef had twice rejected him because he hated demagogues. Gustav Mahler, as a Jew—even though he had been baptized, as required by the Spanish Court Ceremonial of all holders of court positions—had been the object of anti-Semitic attacks. At such moments, Mahler felt as a Jew. Once he told me that an artist who is a Jew had to achieve twice as much as another who is not, just as a swimmer who has shorter arms has to make double efforts in order to gain his goal.

A large part of the opera orchestra was connected with the anti-Semitic party, so that Mahler, after a short time gave up the direction of the Philharmonic concerts. In the newspapers, too, hostilities began. Disgruntled opera singers sought and found newspaper connections. Incidents which easily occur in any theatrical organization were published and widely spread abroad, by reporters. Mahler once said to me: "I am not afraid of the opera critics. I'm only afraid of opera reporters." However all this unpleasantness for a long time had no influence on Mahler's position. The high court officials who were his superiors lent their support and confidence to the successful and interesting Opera Director. The opera critics of the important newspapers with whom Mahler had social relations and with whom, at tea, he developed and

211

elaborated his plans, also stood by him. The opera public celebrated him.

Not Gustav Mahler, the Opera Director, but Gustav Mahler, the composer, was the one who, in a fit of anger, gave up his Vienna position. The great symphonies which Mahler composed during his Vienna period, the fifth to the seventh, show that the inner excitement in his soul had increased during this time, and that he sensed as tragic the collision of the ego with the world. External events could increase this excitement, but it lay in the blood of this artist who, like Strindberg, belonged to the tragic modern type. A brother of Mahler's, who also was a musician, died a suicide. Mahler freed himself from his inner tensions, from time to time, through his creative work. Then material for conflict again piled up in his soul. Occasionally there were explosions. Such an explosion was his offering his resignation in 1907.

Gustav Mahler was conscious of his importance as a composer. "In forty or fifty years, they will play my symphonies at orchestral concerts as they now play Beethoven's," Mahler once told me. These symphonies he composed in the summer, during opera vacations, mostly at the Woerthersee. There near his summer house, he had a hut in the forest for composing, where he could be alone and undisturbed. Once I asked him why, apart from songs which are pre-studies to his symphonies, he wrote only symphonies and not, like many other composers, chamber-music and independent choral music as well. Mahler answered: "I have time to compose only in summer. During this short holiday, I have to write large works if I want to go down into posterity." But that is not the only explanation for Mahler's urge to symphony, and to colossal creations at that. There is no doubt that through his philosophic inclinations, Mahler was driven to symphony. In his music, he wanted to solve the riddles of life and death, of nature and humanity, of destiny and the individual. He had the nature of a Faust who wanted to encompass the world's spirit. From that came the great conception of his symphonies, from that the unredeemed, Ahasueristic, deep excitement of his personality.

With the second symphony, which philosophized about death and resurrection, Mahler in 1899 gave proof to the Viennese public for the first time that he was endeavoring to solve the riddle of the cosmos. In 1901 he performed his "Klagende Lied" ("Plaintive Song"), a work of his youth; in 1902, the Fourth Symphony with the heavenly music of the angels, in 1904 the Third Symphony, in 1905 the Fifth. The success of the Second Symphony was unquestionable. Later on, an opposition appeared, as it usually did with new works in Vienna. The holy saints of the classic arts were invoked to aid against the modern devils. The Viennese humorists made their jokes about the modern musicians as well as about the painters and architects. And a composer of bad operettas wrote daily in a widely read Vienna newspaper that Gustav Mahler had no talent and no musical invention.

Nevertheless Mahler continued his magnificent work during the uproar of the attacks. Each revival was still a festival, as was the last, "Iphigenia in Aulis" with its sublime Greek style. But in his heart, Mahler, who fought for his symphonic work, was stirred up, and in his excitement, he handed in his resignation. It was certainly a sudden, impulsive action which Mahler soon regretted and would have liked to take back. But

Mahler's superiors, who for some time had tried to change his mind, had become embittered, by this time, and there was no longer any turning back.

What Mahler left behind him in the Vienna Opera was a repertory, prepared in the style of the new era, a new ensemble, Roller as principal scenic designer, and two conductors whom he had engaged and trained as his helpers—Franz Schalk and Bruno Walter. Moreover, he left the memory of the Vienna Opera's most splendid artistic period which became the yardstick against which everything which was achieved later was measured.

Mahler's successor was Felix von Weingartner, who as an elegant, amiable, smiling, worldly musician was a kind of antithesis of the demonic Mahler. When after three years Weingartner resigned, the operatic businessman, Hans Gregor, succeeded him. Weingartner left no lasting traces behind him upon the opera, and Gregor was merely a businessman. This time was far removed from that when Mahler elevated the opera to a masterpiece of his high, striving spirit. The greatest artist during this period who came to the Vienna Opera was Richard Strauss, who always came back as guest when one of his new works was performed. Strauss conducted "Elektra" especially often, and with great pleasure. One time, years later, after he had conducted "Elektra" with particular élan, he came home and called to me: "I am still the only one who can conduct Eyektra." He conducted this work with very brief movements, and appeared, in the first scene, unintentionally to collect the brooks of music until they flowed together into a river. Everything melodious in the following scenes was broadened out in a noble manner. The breaking-out of the sound in the Elektra-Orestes scene, when after the recognition, the keys rush together, was held and welded by a strong hand, and at the end, the dance rhythms were mightily formed into one bow. At the climaxes, the usually self-controlled conductor sprang excitedly from his chair. The orchestra was always kept subordinate to the stage and the singing, no matter how strongly its naturalistic painting and vivid coloring flared up. One time when I visited Strauss in Garmisch, he was telling about the Italian performance of his opera which he recently had seen in Milan, and went on: "In Milan, I realized for the first time that my 'Elektra' is an Italian opera. The singers can stand on the ramp quite calmly and all they have to do is sing—then there is everything there that the work requires." I heard "Elektra" at least twenty times under Strauss's direction. There was always the most perfect equality between the singing and the orchestra.

At this time, Strauss had advanced to the point where he was the recognized leader and greatest exponent of modern music. Despite this fact, his most Viennese work, which brings to the stage the old Vienna of the period of Empress Maria Theresia, "Der Rosenkavalier," had only a very moderate success at its Vienna première. After the second act, there was scarcely any applause. Strauss had not expected that. At the dress-rehearsal he sat in the first row and enjoyed the antics of the excellent Ochs von Lerchenau, to whom he often called "bravo"; and he beamed when the horns rang out their waltz coloraturas in a brilliant virtuoso manner. And now the work was presented before a cold audience who considered the many waltzes in this score unworthy of being called opera music. Strauss was greatly distressed, and finally said to me, sadly: "If only the people knew how hard it is to compose such waltzes!"

In "Rosenkavalier," to my astonishment, I discovered a place which recalled to my mind a little experience I had had with Strauss in Vienna. During the time when he was working on "Rosenkavalier," I went walking with him in the vicinity of Hietzing. From an inn came the sound of dance music, and Strauss stood there for a long time, listening with interest. Finally he said, laughing: "Do you hear the false basses?" I said yes, since the false basses, some of which were being drawn from their instruments by the contrabass players, were obvious enough. Imagine my surprise when in the inn-music of "Rosenkavalier's" third act, I heard the jolly false bass notes! They are a small, characteristic trait in the Strauss picture of Vienna, and they intensify my delight at every performance of the work as reminiscences of my walk with Strauss.

The modern music of the Richard Strauss period was not rejected by the Vienna Opera, no matter what difficulties the Viennese public made every time a new work was performed. Still under Mahler's direction, Hans Pfitzner's "Rose vom Liebesgarten," an opera with pure, romantic fairy-tale atmosphere, mystic solemnity with gloriously-colored nature pictures, was given for the first time. Under Gregor's direction, Debussy's "Pelleas and Melisande" was performed, with its dreamy scenes—a modern, sad ballad in fragrant, floating, vibrating tones. Under the same director, Schreker's "Das Spielwerk und die Prinzessin" ("The Toy and the Princess"). a symbolic opera and a glowing color fantasy, had its première.

The music of the new era had gotten a foot-hold at the Vienna Opera.

During the time when Gustav Mahler was Opera Director, Richard Strauss was writing his finest operatic and symphonic works. Debussy set people's nerves tingling with his impressionistic tone poems which had the artistic delicacy, the tenderness and refinement of Japanese wood-cuts; Hans Pfitzner bound the atmosphere of "Tristan" and "Parsifal" with that of the German fairy-tale and saga; a new generation of musicians was growing up in Vienna.

The most mature of the Viennese musicians was Alexander von Zemlinsky who, while still a pupil at the Vienna Conservatory, had attracted Brahms' attention by composing a colorful symphony, and whose opera, "Once Upon a Time"— a tender, spiritual work—had been performed by Mahler at the Vienna Opera. Zemlinsky belonged to my circle of friends who, of evenings, used to meet over black coffee at a coffeehouse near the old Burgtheater. This coffee-house—the Café Griensteidel—was the headquarters of literature in Vienna. In its three low rooms could be seen all the men who, as poets or as critics, played their part in the city's intellectual life. The coffee-houses of Vienna still had their special types of patron, like their special kind of coffee. At the Café Fenstergucker, for instance, one found the fashionable Viennese society. At Café Imperial, the owners of stables and race-horses held forth; at Café Pucher, the ministers and high state officials from the ministries situated nearby; at Café Central, the journalists, the chess-players and the intellectuals, among them for a few years a fugitive from Russia, a Dr. Bornstein, who later, as Trotsky, made world history.

At the Café Griensteidel, Hermann Bahr, the leader of modern criticism, gave his fiery talks every evening, with a Virginia cigar in his hand and a brown lock on his forehead. Arthur Schnitzler came there, elegant and melancholy. Hugo von Hofmannsthal was there, too—still almost a boy and already famous, drawling in the tired aristocratic Viennese dialect. A strange man who wore large horn-rimmed glasses and had the drooping mustaches of a walrus—Peter Altenberg—had just published his first sketches which glorified women's soft, tender legs and innocent children's eyes. A

Schoenberg

small hunchback, Karl Kraus, was the greatest satirist of the time.

We young musicians sat in a corner. Alexander von Zemlinsky, although he was only twenty-eight at the time, in the maturity of his judgment, had a visible superiority over the rest of the musicians. Another young musician of our circle was Arthur Bodansky, who was then a violinist in the opera orchestra, and shortly after, became a conductor at an operetta theatre. Zemlinsky brought with him a young man who was a pupil of his. He had the face of a Pierrot, and tossed pointed and stinging paradoxes about. One of them was the assertion that a C Major triad is an effect which can only be applied rarely, and then after most careful preparation. In this sentence, all classic harmony was turned upside down. The young man was Arnold Schönberg. A short time later, one of his first works was performed at a concert—a string quartet in D Minor in classic style influenced by Brahms and Schumann, with moonlight sounds in the slow movement which were quite novel. I had, meanwhile, been promoted to the post of music critic of a weekly newspaper, and wrote an article praising that quartet; and I closed with the prophetic words: "One should remember his name. It is Arnold Schönberg." Of course, Schönberg himself took good care that his name should be remembered. Soon after the performance of the quartet, he brought me a sextet, "Verklaerte Nacht" ("Transfigured Night"). The music sounded new, the harmonies were unusual. Since I did not trust my judgment I gave the score to Gustav Mahler, at that time Opera Director. Mahler wavered in his opinion, as I had done, and asked Arnold Rosé to play the sextet with his musicians, in Mahler's office. He invited me to come to this private performance, and we both were enthusiastic. Mahler said to Rosé: "You must play that!" and Rosé played it at the next of his chamber-music evenings, to the great displeasure of the Viennese public who hissed loudly. This hissing increased in volume in proportion to Schönberg's boldness, in Vienna and in other cities.

The age of classic harmony which had been founded in Vienna came to an end there. The world had changed. Political, economic and social problems rose, like dark storm-clouds, on the sky. Vienna, the gay, elegant town, saw shadows falling over the Ringstrasse which seemed to belong exclusively to the rich, when in 1905, thousands of workers paraded over it and demanded equal voting rights. The people of Vienna—the "common men"—were not satisfied any longer to stop at the curb of the street and cry "Heil" when a court carriage passed. They demanded their social and political rights. The Viennese small citizenry united in a big party, with anti-Semitic slogans, which took possession of the Town Hall in 1895. Dr. Lueger, its leader, raged against capitalists, Jews and the Stock Exchange. He succeeded in frightening the court, the high clergy and wealthy society. The Social Democratic workers strengthened their organizations, too. They had a great leader in Dr. Victor Adler who, since he stuttered, gained power by purely intellectual means. Reason, idealism, calm superiority were his weapons, and even the Emperor esteemed his wisdom which was created by passion. Thus in Vienna, the old town of the court and the aristocracy, the masses pressed restlessly upwards.

Popular Music—Johann Strauss

The political, social and intellectual changes which became apparent in Vienna around 1900 were also of the greatest importance to musical life.

Up to that time, the small Viennese citizen contented himself with simple folk-like music. He stood, so to speak, on the outside of the festive music life of the great city. His life took place in the low houses of the suburbs where the women washed their laundry in the small courtyards and the children played in the streets. In the suburban inns, popular musicians played, mainly harpists and violinists. Such folk-musicians had played back in mediaeval Vienna, and only in 1889, the last of the harpists, Magdalena Hagenauer, died.

What these folk-musicians played was music of the Austrian Alps. The Austrian mountain dances were called "Laendler" (country-music), and turned slowly in three-quarter time. Lanner, the waltz-composer, still wrote "Laendlers." Johann Strauss, the son, still wrote waltzes in "Laendler style"—his opus 247. His waltz "Grillenfänger" (Whim Catcher) bears the sub-title "In the style of Laendler." Suburban inn music was accompanied by whistling and hand-clapping. There were yodelers, too. Old Vienna knew famous lady-yodelers, such as "Tanzerl Leni" (Little dancing Leni) who died in 1870, or "Juden Lisl" (Jewish Lisa) who sang at the inn "Zum Mondschein" in Matzleinsdorf, one of the southern suburbs of Vienna. In gay Vienna of the '70's, the aristocrats amused themselves with that kind of suburban folk-music. They had their favorite yodelers and whistlers. One of these latter, whose nickname was "Baron Jean," whistled at all the fashionable parties of Vienna around 1880. I knew him myself.

Most of this folk-music came on the ships which traveled from Linz to Vienna. There would be Linz musicians aboard, either two fiddlers, a guitarist and a double-bass player, or one fiddler, one clarinettist and a double-bass. During the trip, they played their country dance music, and its sound hovered over the Danube and the landscape. Arriving in Vienna, they played in the inns along the Danube's banks— "The White Lamb," "The White Cock," "The Golden Bear" or "The Blue Star." In one of these Danube inns, Johann Strauss's father was born. There he heard the Laendler of Upper Austria, as a boy, and later on he ennobled it to the rank of waltz.

Some of these Linz musicians would wander to the Spittel-berg, where the inns and taverns of Vienna's high life were situated, and where there was music day and night. Not far from these inns is the house where Lanner, Vienna's first waltz composer, was born.

Music and song were not absent, either, from the small wine gardens of the Vienna environs. In the beginning of the nineteenth century, quartets were the principal performers here. The most famous of these Viennese "wine-quartets" of Emperor Franz Josef's time were the "Schrammeln." Viennese painters often used such quartets as subjects for their paintings. The motion pictures, too, introduced them for local color in their sentimental Viennese films. Members of the quartet used to sit on a small platform in the winegarden. On the table stood wine glasses on which they propped their music. Their Viennese faces would become redder and redder in the course of the evening and their music warmer. The violins would sound sweet and soft. A grateful Vienna has not forgotten these musicians. In Ottakring, one of the suburbs, stands a fountain. At each of its four corners is the figure of a musician, round bowler hat with a flat brim on his head, with violins, harmonica and guitar in hand. When older Viennese pass this fountain, they smile appreciatively and understandingly.

Numerous popular songs were written and composed for the so-called "folk-singers." When the oldest of these, Johann Baptist Moser, sang in 1828, the fiacres of the Viennese aristocrats drew up in long lines in front of the inn where he was performing. The same thing happened with Johann Fürst, whom Princess Metternich introduced into the palaces of the nobility. There were also famous women folk-singers like Antonia Mansfeld, who was tall, slender, and piquant when she sang her songs. She was revered by society as well as by the people, and when the Emperor Napoleon III came to Vienna in 1873, she was called to sing for him. Another songstress, "Fiacre Milly" (the name of this 100 per cent Viennese woman was Czech—Turrecek), was embodied in an opera of Richard Strauss's—"Arabella"—and in the second act she sings her yodel song.

Many of the songs which were composed for the folk-singers became, in turn, folk-music. Vienna had no "Tin Pan Alley." Simple musicians wrote these songs for the folk-singers, who paid them a few gulden as recompense. The most popular of them were written by Karl Lorens ("Ja, da fahr'n wir halt nach Nussdorf 'raus"[1]; "So lang der alte Steffel"[2]; "Menschen, Menschen san mir Alle"[3]; "Die Linzer Buben"[4]); by Alexander Krakauer, "Du guter Himmels-vater"[5]; by Johann Sioli, "Der alte Draher"[6]; by Siczinsky, "Wien, Wien nur du allein"[7]; and Ludwig Gruber ("Es wird ein Wein sein"[8]; "Mei Mutter ist a Wienerin"[9]). Old and young, noble and commoner sang these songs. The Viennese was touched when he sang the praises of his town, the tower of St. Stephen's, Viennese women and wine. As long as there is a Vienna, those songs will be sung.

Of all the songs of Emperor Franz Josef's time, none became so popular as the Fiacre Song. This song is as characteristic of the period as the fiacre itself. On every corner of the city stood the fiacres—distinguished carriages with two horses whose owner was a great, great man, proud of his art of holding the reins and whip lightly in his hand. On his head, he wore the bowler hat of the aristocrat when he sat on the coachbox. Black jacket and striped trousers completed his costume. He kept a meerschaum pipe in his mouth. When a stroller passed, he would tip his hat gently and ask casually: "Shall we go, your Worship?" If one said yes, then the "waterer" who had watered the horses, and the "coach-door opener," both of whom belonged to the entourage, would appear and receive their respective tips. These preliminaries completed, the driver would click his tongue and the horses began trotting. As a man of high standing, the fiacre-driver was discreet. If one drove out to the surrounding districts of

---

[1] "Then we will drive to Nussdorf." [2] "As long as the old Stephen." [3] "Human, human are we all." [4] "The boys from Linz." [5] "Good Father in Heaven." [6] "The old stroller." [7] "Vienna, Vienna, you alone." [8] "There will be a wine." [9] "My mother is a Viennese."

Vienna with a lady, one only had to say the word "Porzellan" ("China ware"), and the driver knew that he must drive carefully in order not to hurt the fragile cart-load which was resting happily in the arms of his passenger.

This was the fiacre driver which a genuine Viennese, Gustav Pick, glorified in a song which became a kind of Viennese folk-hymn. Pick, who like the old-fashioned poets, composed both text and music of his song, like so many other "genuine" Viennese came to Vienna from Hungary. He enjoyed the gay life in Vienna, and loved to go driving in a fiacre. Where he was to find the money for such excursions did not worry him very much, so long as he had friends. From the rhythm of trotting fiacre-horses he evolved the song in which a fiacre-driver describes his art; and the trotting rhythm changes into a waltz when the fiacre-driver sings: "Anyone can become a coachman, but only a Viennese knows how to drive a fiacre." The Tirtaeus of the Viennese fiacre-drivers whistled the melody to a musician, since he himself knew nothing about notes; and the musician wrote down the easy song, which became immortal.

In 1885, the new song was sung in Vienna for the first time. This was at a charity festival in the great Rotunda of the Prater. Girardi, the most popular actor in all Vienna, appeared, seated on the coach-box of a fiacre, and drove right into the Rotunda. When he reached the center of the gigantic enclosure, he brought his horses to a halt with a jerk of the bridle, stood up on the seat, flourished his hat in greeting and sang the new song which swept through the city like wildfire and is popular even to-day. Not once, even when the fiacre-driver was replaced by the automobile chauffeur, did

the song become old. After the war, it took on a new meaning. It became the ballad of happy Old Vienna, where life
was as easy and carefree as in a fairy-tale; and the fiacre-
driver, not the old Emperor, became the symbolic figure of
this golden age.

Only two other songs achieved a popularity similar to
that of the Fiacre Song. One was the "Deutschmeister Lied"
("Teutonic Order Song"). The "Deutschmeister Regiment"
(Regiment of the Teutonic Order) was the real Vienna regiment in which all native Viennese served, and whose blue
lapels belonged to the color-picture of Vienna. This regiment
was considered especially plucky and dashing. Viennese wit
and frivolity were at home in its barracks. A Viennese by the
name of Tureck who was an official of the state printing-works,
belonged to this regiment. He was an under-officer and sat
in his office very bored. His duty was to stamp the passes
which permitted the soldiers to enter the barracks after the
retreat. This was not a very entertaining business, and to
distract himself, Tureck began to hum as he stamped the
seal of the regiment again and again on the pass where one
could read the regiment's full title: "K. und K. Infanterie-
regiment Hoch und Deutschmeister Numero 4" ("Imperial
and Royal Infantry Regiment of the Teutonic Order Number
4"). From the rhythm of these words and the methodical
stamping a melody began to form itself—the melody of a
march song which Tureck sang to his comrades when he
marched with the other soldiers to the drill grounds. Soon
the whole town was singing it, because wherever the soldiers
went, they sang it.

During the 17th century, when Austrian soldiers marched

to Serbia under Prince Eugene, the famous "Prince Eugene Song" developed in similar fashion: one of the soldiers sang it, and the others joined in the dashing melody. In the same manner, all true folk-songs came into being. Verses flew from somewhere into the mind of a man of the people. These verses began to sound. A poem, a melody arose and took wings.

The last Viennese folk-song dates from the year 1918—the "Grinzing Song" of Ralph Benatzky. An excursion to the wine gardens in Grinzing was responsible for the song, and there it was sung first. ("Ich moecht' wieder einmal in Grinzing sein, beim Wein"—"I would love to be in Grinzing again, at wine). From here it traveled all through the city, for the desire to be in Grinzing drinking wine was a lively one in the soul of every Viennese. In gratitude for the song, a memorial plaque, with Benatzky's portrait, was put up near the Grinzing wine garden which the song glorified.

All this music belonged to the people of Vienna. "Art" music for the common man was available only in restaurant gardens where military bands or civilian orchestras gave concerts. These circumstances began to change about 1900. Vienna had grown enormously. In 1892 the suburbs were incorporated into the city, and the small townspeople of the suburbs became "big-city" Viennese. They also developed into a political power and wanted their say in Vienna's musical life. They demanded more and more good music for low prices. The fruitful work of the "Volksbildungverein" ("Society for the Education of the People") and the cultural organizations of the workers contributed to the fostering of musical activity. Musical Vienna, like the town itself, was growing.

In 1898, the inhabitants of the Vienna suburbs decided to build a second national opera house in the outskirts of the city, which should make the masterworks of the opera accessible to people of modest means at modest prices. Rainer Simons, the Director of this theatre who named it the "Volksoper" (the People's Opera), was a very clever theatre expert. From small beginnings, he brought the theatre to great heights. Simons had a special feeling for young talent which gave promise of a great future. A long line of singers became famous in this theatre, while being badly-paid but well-directed artistically. None of these singers attained such fame as Jeritza, whom Simons discovered in a small operetta theatre at Ischl. I remember her first performances. She was a glowing, laughing blonde with a Czech snub-nose, long hands and legs which gave her quite some difficulty on the stage. But her voice was sensuous and brilliant, and Simons knew exactly how to make talent of this sort free and uninhibited.

When I asked Simons what he had done to make Jeritza lose her clumsiness on the stage, he told me that he had had the impression that the young singer was being dominated entirely by her husband. Her inhibitions were apparent when he gave Jeritza her first great role—the feminine lead in Giordano's "Siberia." During rehearsals, in the beginning, she had no idea of what to do during the main scene, in which a girl who has been deserted by her lover, a Russian officer, meets him again by chance, and whips him. Director Simons during this scene stood in the wings, and when Jeritza raised her whip, called to her: "Imagine that it's your husband!" Jeritza flew into a fury and beat the unfortunate tenor so passionately that the scene became one of her first great realistic interpretations. It was a tremendous success for Jeritza. Soon after, she was engaged at the Court Opera where she became a sensational singer of naturalistic roles, and from where she journeyed through the world with her wonderful "Tosca."

When, in 1913, Wagner's works became public domain, the Volksoper made them available to the public in good performances. Richard Strauss conducted "Feuersnot" and "Salome" in this theatre; Battistini sang there as a guest. Zemlinsky was the first conductor. Later Felix von Weingartner became Director. Even beside the Opera of Gustav Mahler, the Volksoper could be esteemed and considered a very serious opera theatre.

In 1900, two new symphony orchestras were founded— the "Konzertvereinsorchester" (Concert Society Orchestra) and the "Tonkünstler Orchester," both of which attracted a people's public, by virtue of their low admission prices. At these concerts, also, famous conductors of the present day conducted—Weingartner, Strauss, Bruno Walter, Furtwängler and others. Bruckner's Ninth Symphony, Richard Strauss's "Sinfonia Domestica," and Mahler's "Das Lied von der Erde" (Song of the Earth) were given their first performances in Vienna by these orchestras. The Vienna Social Democratic workers also had their own symphony concerts—"the Workers' Symphony Concerts."

Thus the tree of musical Vienna put forth new shoots. Enjoyment and understanding of serious music did not remain confined to the wealthy and the aristocratic. Great new layers of the population had entered the cultural circle of music. When Emperor Franz Josef began his reign, there was no such thing as a large public concert in Vienna. There were neither regular orchestral concerts nor choral concerts, and just a very few virtuoso recitals to be heard in Vienna. But after the Emperor died there were in Vienna, in addition to two opera houses, three large orchestras, two large choral societies, two large concert houses with five halls where concerts took place every day. The old musical city had broadened out, and the radio, which conveyed serious and popular music to the smallest house in Vienna, increased the democratizing of musical enjoyment to an extent which previously had been unimaginable. Music came into the houses like water and electric light. Opera performances, symphony concerts and chamber-music were accessible to the poorest people, like the public parks in Vienna which belonged to everyone, and whose lilacs and roses had an equal fragrance for all.

Thus around 1900, in Vienna, there arose a broad popular society around the ancient courtly and feudal musical society. They were separate groups. With the courtly-feudal society, which was destroyed in the war years 1914-1918, ended the three-hundred year development period of Vienna's past. With popular society, a new development began. Their paths ran parallel for a time, then crossed and were borne on by the political movements of the present. And there was a man in Vienna who united both societies. What the old Emperor had not been successful in accomplishing—the harmonization of the social antithesis—a musician who was a genius succeeded in doing. This musician was Johann Strauss.

His music was just as much music for the high-born as for the man in the street. It was perfect art-music, and at the same time, perfect folk-music. His waltzes were highly esteemed by Richard Wagner, Hector Berlioz, Franz Liszt and Johannes Brahms, and loved by all the people.

The two great forerunners of Strauss, the son: Lanner and Father Strauss, also grew with Vienna. Then it was small, with many dreamy, quiet corners, with ladies in crinolines, and clean-shaven men in buttoned black coats and high hats. This little Vienna, under the reign of a silly emperor, led a comfortable existence. A pound of beef cost only twelve kreuzer and a bottle of wine just as little. People called this period of Vienna's history the "Backhendlzeitalter" ("The Age of the Breaded Chicken"), because even the poorest could eat the cheap chickens in his small restaurant. Dance halls were in every nook and corner. Dangerous modern intellectual ideas were not allowed to penetrate the city. The police and censor saw to that. Pleasure and sensuality seemed less dangerous than thinking, and the new Viennese waltz developed from sensuality. When Lanner began to play his romantic waltzes, he played with two violins and a guitar. Later his orchestra grew to five musicians, and afterwards it become larger. Strauss, the father, played at "Sperl's" with a small orchestra. All that changed when Johann Strauss, the son, wrote his waltzes. Hanslick was still complaining about the Wagnerian noise and the Wagnerian dissonances of the Strauss waltzes, and the old Viennese sentimentally cherished the quiet, feeling old waltz music of the Lanner period. Johann Strauss, though, wrote waltzes for a new epoch in which Vienna was a metropolis. He was fiery and brilliant, powerful and elaborate. He raised his violin and played like a teller of fairy tales—stories of new Vienna, the Vienna woods and the Blue Danube. He grew up with Vienna, but his Vienna belonged to the whole world. His waltzes were no longer like those of Lanner and of his father still, romantic dreams—but a hymn to Vienna which sounded throughout the world.

When I first met Strauss, he was leading the life of a well-to-do Viennese aristocrat in his small palace on the "Wieden." He was fashionably dressed in old Viennese style, in dark coat and striped trousers. Strauss was not a musician who gave much reflection to his art. I can quote no sentence of his which would cast a new light on music, any more than I can quote any wise speeches of Schubert on the subject, because he was full of music which streamed forth from his inner soul without constraint, and without reflection. Strauss was the same sort of musician as Schubert. His music sang out when, at night, he sat at his desk, knowing that the woman he loved lay sleeping in the next room, and an erotic atmosphere hovered about him. This erotic atmosphere he needed, for he wrote music for dancing couples who held each other embraced. That these melodies were secretly bound to the city of Vienna and its landscape, no one was less aware than Strauss. By day he was like the other Viennese, speaking the dialect the way they did, and playing cards like them. In the night, all the voices of Vienna became loud in him, and he wrote down what he heard without thinking much about it.

In no work does the voice of Vienna sound more enchanting than in the famous "Blue Danube Waltz," which still to-day symbolizes Vienna for the world. This waltz of waltzes was first sung in 1867, at a concert of the Vienna Men's Choral Society, since it was originally a waltz for male voices with orchestra. Strauss meant it to console the Viennese over the defeat in the War of 1866, and the chorus begins: "Viennese, be glad!" Not only the Viennese, but the whole world was glad that Strauss composed this waltz. The horn call at the beginning sounds like Oberon's, calling the fairies, elves and pixies together. The atmosphere of Shakespeare's "Mid-Summer Night's Dream" is there—moonlight, woodland charm, dances and games of the fairies. It is a far cry from the customary introductions to waltzes. An enchanted light is cast even over the old Danube when Strauss makes music. The Danube looked nothing but a dirty grey to a Viennese. But with Johann Strauss it became blue, and since that time, the whole world believes it is blue.

In his other great waltzes, like "Tales from the Vienna Woods," "Wine, Women and Song" and "Vienna Blood," Strauss also told such fairy tales. He is the greatest poet of Vienna, and gave it the colors of a beautiful dream, like a city in Paradise. Every Viennese saw his city in this Strauss light.

Strauss waltzes were the last fairy-tales told in Vienna. Reality was earnest, care-worn and gloomy. Social tensions kept becoming greater, the labor pains of a new period more severe. A crisis arose, from which feudal society could find no exit except the outbreak of the first World War. To the sound of merry march-music, the Viennese regiments of 1914 passed through the city and on to the battle-fields of Russia and Italy. In this war, the old feudal order, which, in many guises, had reigned in Vienna from the end of the sixteenth century on, finally perished. The social foundations upon which Vienna's musical life had been erected, were drowned in blood and destroyed.

5

The Last Hours

1918-1938

Richard Strauss in Vienna—
The Festivals in Salzburg—
Toscanini in Salzburg

On a dull November day in 1916, in the midst of the first World War, Emperor Franz Josef died. During the last two years of his lifetime, the frail old man arose daily from his army cot, put on his old military coat, sat at his desk and received his generals who reported on the battles in Russia, France and Italy. Then he went into the chapel to pray.

I, an Austrian officer, stood with my fellow-officers on the Ringstrasse when the enormous hearse passed, drawn by six heavy horses. On the same street, I had often seen the Emperor ride. Now it was a sad procession which passed the Court Opera and progressed to the old Capuchin monastery where, in a dark cellar room, the coffins of the Hapsburgs rested, guarded by the brown-garbed monks. When the procession arrived, the monastery gate was closed. A dignitary of the court, according to the prescription of the Spanish Court Ceremonial, knocked at the door. A Capuchin monk opened, and asked "Who is there?" The dignitary answered, "Franz Josef." Then the Emperor's coffin was carried through the low passages and down the staircase to the crypt.

Two years later the Austrian monarchy fell apart. What was left of old Austria was a small, mountainous country of six million inhabitants, a third of whom lived in the capital,

Vienna. Most of the great industries of Austria belonged to the new state of Czechoslovakia, the oil wells to the new Poland, the harbors of the Adriatic Sea to Italy. Austria was small and poor, cut off from world-traffic, and Vienna seemed too large for such a small state. Could Vienna preserve itself as a music city? That was the question which all of us who had contributed to its musical life asked ourselves. Vienna's position as capital of the Austro-Hungarian double-monarchy had been destroyed. The political affairs of half Europe no longer were concentrated there. The various national states had become independent, and took, in part, a hostile or distrustful attitude toward Vienna. What could Vienna mean as capital of a small alpine country, from which the neighboring states closed themselves off? Nothing proves more positively the vital powers which existed in Vienna even after the world-shattering chaos of the first World War than the general conviction that Vienna had to be preserved as the center of European music.

Each of the ruling political parties was convinced of the greatness of Vienna as a musical city and of the importance of the Vienna Opera. Every opportunity to set forth the weight of small Austria as a music center was utilized. The Social Democratic Party, which governed Vienna, immediately after the end of the war, arranged a great music festival in Vienna which described the whole heritage of Austrian music from Haydn and Schubert up to Schönberg. The Beethoven Centenary in 1927 was festively dedicated as a celebration for the world, and from all parts of Europe representatives came from the great nations as they did to the League of Nations. From Paris came Herriot, Minister of Education.

He compared Vienna, as the music city of the world, to the Acropolis as a symbol of the cultural consciousness of humanity. One year later, according to plans laid out by me, Vienna had a large Schubert Festival. The modern Viennese composers, right after the war, invited the musicians of the world to a music festival at Salzburg. Composers came, bringing the scores which they had written during the war. They all understood each other, and in music spoke a common language of the new era which turned away from romanticism and no longer wanted to dream, but wished to be matter-of-fact. The "International Society for Modern Music" was founded on this occasion, at the suggestion of the young Austrian musicians.

Above all, the Vienna Opera had to be preserved in a grand style. After the break-down of the monarchy, it was no longer a court theatre, but a state theatre. As such, it was to proclaim the cultural will of Austria to the world. Two new directors were appointed. One was the oldest conductor of the Vienna Opera, Franz Schalk, a man of great musical culture and sharp intellect. The other was the most famous musician of the present, Richard Strauss. "The goal will be set high and great, pure throughout and without concessions," Franz Schalk wrote me after taking office on November 26, 1918. "Once more we want to try whether it is possible to direct a theatre without a glance forward or backward, up or down, but with a higher artistic intention alone." Richard Strauss came to Vienna in 1919. In a rather long conversation which I had with him, he assured me he wanted to devote himself especially to the direction of the classical operatic works. As if to underscore these words, he began his Viennese activities by conducting Beethoven's "Fidelio" and Mozart's "Magic Flute."

In the past years, Richard Strauss had become more closely bound to Vienna. Every year he appeared there, conducting his own works. In Rodaun, near Vienna, lived the poet and librettist of Strauss's operas, Hugo von Hofmannsthal, who drew him deeper and deeper into the magic circle of the Viennese baroque. The collaboration of Strauss and Hofmannsthal was a perfect one. Hofmannsthal had an inspiring mind, and Strauss needed such inspiration. In his letters and in his conversation, Hofmannsthal met the need of the musician whose bright spirit liked to enflame itself with the modern spirit of artists. Hofmannsthal, who was at home in the baroque theatre of Goldoni, in the Venetian comedy and opera, in the Viennese miracle plays, led Strauss in this field. With

Richard Strauss
(portrait of Mopp)

a fine mind, he guided Strauss away from Wagner to a lighter, more gracious style of musical creation. For Strauss, he created a whole series of female characters, from the Marschallin in "Rosenkavalier" to the Viennese "Arabella." He led Strauss from comic plays to meaningful fairy-plays. When Hofmannsthan sent the text of "Rosenkavalier" to the composer, Strauss was so filled with music that he could not get the continuation of the libretto quickly enough. This Viennese comedy of Hofmannsthal's, with its tender renunciation and the elegy of age, brought all Strauss's most inner music to light, and "Rosenkavalier" became his most successful opera. When, in 1924, I went to Garmisch, Strauss showed me Hofmannsthal's libretto for "Egyptian Helen," and I saw on the margins of the manuscript, already pencilled in, the most important motifs which had resounded in Strauss's mind immediately upon his first reading of the text. Hofmannsthal possessed the gift of awakening music in Strauss. Sometimes, however, things came to a standstill. Such an occasion occurred when Strauss was supposed to compose the second act of "Egyptian Helen." For a long time he had no inspiration. To overcome this hindrance, he made a trip to Spain and Greece. On February 15, 1925, Strauss wrote me from Paris that he hoped that at the walls of Granada, something nice for the Desert King, Altair (one of the characters in the second act of the opera), would occur to him. This hope was fulfilled. On May 20, 1926, he sent me "best regards from the native country of Helen and Elektra," from Athens.

Strauss was not an uncritical musician who accepted the opera texts of Hofmannsthal without having looked at them. The second act of "Rosenkavalier" was exactly indicated by him, since the original sketch of the poet was not to his liking. The beautiful "Elektra" aria, also, after the recognition of Elektra and Orestes ("Orest, Orest"), was written by Hofmannsthal according to the wishes of the composer. To me, the most perfect understanding between Strauss and

Hofmannsthal seems to be in "Ariadne on Naxos," in the beautiful prelude to this opera which Strauss composed for the Vienna Opera. This prelude is an example of a winged and soulful modern comic opera style, in its spirit of tenderness and in its vivacity.

Vienna attracted Strauss more and more and finally captured him completely. He felt at home there. At first he lived in one of the Mozart neighborhoods, not far from the square where the "Magic Flute" theatre had been. From the balcony of his apartment, one could see the fountain erected in honor of the "Magic Flute" where Tamino, playing the flute, walked with Pamina. At that time Strauss loved to compare himself with Mozart. When I once told him that "Rosenkavalier" was his "Marriage of Figaro" and the "Frau ohne Schatten" his "Magic Flute," he said jokingly: "Then there is nothing left for me to compose but my Requiem." In 1926 Strauss moved to the beautiful new house near the Belvedere Park, which he had had built on grounds which the Austrian state had given him as fee for his conducting at the Vienna State Opera. This house, too, stood on Mozart ground, and Strauss enjoyed my telling him this repeatedly. The street where it stood was named the Jaquingasse, so called after Mozart's friend, Gottfried von Jaquin. Young Mozart had composed his opera, "Bastien and Bastienne" for the well-known hypnotist, Dr. Mesmer, who also possessed a house with a theatre not far from there.

Since "Rosenkavalier," Strauss felt more and more like the Mozart of his time. One day he surprised me with the information that he had composed a symphony in four movements in classic style which was not programme music—a symphony like the F Minor symphony of his youth. I had my doubts that this conservatism of the mature Strauss could be productive. His real field was virtuoso tone-painting which depicted modern realism in glowing colors. Here was his greatness and his progress. Strauss himself must have had similar doubts, for he locked the manuscript in his desk and did not even show it to his friends. Apparently it was easier to be a Mozart in the eighteenth century than in the twentieth.

Strauss's Vienna house was built by the Munich architect, Seidel, who had also built his home in Garmisch. It was a beautiful house. Strauss was especially proud of some of his art treasures, and of a beautiful Greco which hung in his studio. He loved to rummage in antique shops for old pictures and other objects of art. In Partenkirchen, on his walks, I often accompanied him into such shops. He had no piano in his studio because he did not use one when composing. In the foyer of the studio, however, stood an upright, above which hung a portrait of Alexander Ritter, the Munich composer who had guided him to the symphonic poems of Liszt and thus had had a decisive influence on young Strauss.

Strauss's practical wife had seen to the arrangement of the house. Strauss loved his original and energetic Pauline whose acquaintance he had made when she was a young singer in Weimar. Strauss told me how he became engaged. Pauline de Ahna was standing on the stage with the other singers at a rehearsal of Strauss's early opera, "Guntram." At the conductor's desk was Strauss, who, as is usual at such rehearsals, had stopped some of the singers and made various corrections. Suddenly Pauline began to cry, threw the vocal score at the conductor's desk and sobbed: "You criticize everybody except me." The consequences of this scene were that Strauss and Pauline became engaged. The art of making scenes, Pauline also exercised as wife of the master. Once I arrived at Strauss's home in Vienna at an inopportune moment when Frau Pauline was just making a very lively scene with her husband. She was excited, screamed, cried, and finally rushed out of the door which she slammed loudly behind her. Strauss looked after her, smiling and said to me: "You see, such a wife I needed!"

There is no doubt that Strauss loved his wife's originality and temperament. Repeatedly he told me that as a young man, he had had a strong inclination to dissipate and make nothing of himself. Then his wife, through her resolute nature, really cured him. Strauss would never tolerate anyone hurting her through a joke or otherwise. When I once permitted myself a little jest about Frau Pauline's love of neatness, Strauss looked at me seriously and immediately said: "Don't make fun of my wife's love of cleanliness!" The regulating of his life was determined by his wife. She was the earthy element in which he found the complement to his genial nervous nature. He laughed when she declared to him that when she had married him—a mere musician—she had made a mésalliance. After all, she was the daughter of a Bavarian general, and according to Munich's standards, a general had a higher rank than a musician. Strauss also laughed when she insisted that he must have Jewish blood in his veins. When he wrote the poem for his opera "Intermezzo," in which he portrayed his marriage and his home-life on the stage, Strauss worked some of these expressions of his wife's into his text with a great deal of love and humor. When Strauss was in New

York for the first time, he conducted a performance of Beethoven's Ninth Symphony at Wanamaker's. At that time, I attacked him sharply since performing one of the greatest and most solemn of all musical works in a department store seemed to me a profanation of art. Strauss replied to me: "It is no shame to earn money for wife and child!"

In Strauss, in addition to his genius, there was also a bourgeois streak. It probably was inherited from his father. Strauss felt comfortable in his family circle, with his wife and child, and led a family life without complication. He subordinated himself to his wife. Once I asked him why he never conducted "Meistersinger" in Vienna. I had heard him conduct it in Berlin, and his had been a beautiful animated and festive interpretation. He answered: "There you'll have to talk to my wife. She doesn't let me conduct long operas." Frau Pauline was tenderly solicitous of his health. She saw that his meals were light, as the doctors recommended, worried about his digestion, and had but one concern—maintaining her husband's good health. And she spread her wings protectively over her son like a hen over a chick.

The bourgeois element was a necessary part of the Strauss family life. As high as the flight of the composer's fantasy was, as bold as he was an artist, just so firmly did this genial man keep his feet on the ground in life. When he returned from his world of imagination into everyday life, his existence exactly resembled that of a middle class citizen who was a good husband and father, happy at his family table. Once I made an automobile trip with Strauss from Garmisch to a place in the Bavarian highlands where some relatives of his lived. He invited these simple, modest ladies into the village inn, and ordered Bavarian white sausages, which are a national dish of the Bavarians. He ate the sausages with great gusto, and as a connoisseur, and talked with his relatives in great detail about the composition, flavor and seasoning as if he had no other interests except Bavarian white sausages.

To his bourgeois side, too, belonged the pleasure which Strauss took in card games. He played Skat, the favorite game of the German middle class. He was very proud of his prowess. When I once asked why he enjoyed cards so much, he answered: "There, at least, one doesn't think of silly music." In Garmisch, Strauss had his regular card "party," which consisted of the head forester, a retired officer and similar citizens. But Strauss also liked to play regularly in Vienna. At the bankers' houses where he was an honored guest, a card table was set up after dinner, and Strauss would play for several hours. The slip on which he noted his gains and losses in his fine script, he would leave to his host as an autograph, after meticulously writing the date over his signature. Generally he won at these games. The circles in which Strauss moved in Vienna were mainly the financial ones of the wealthy bourgeoisie who had acquired tremendous fortunes during the years of the inflation. When I once asked Strauss if he enjoyed moving in such circles, he said: "There, at least, I see that something has become of me. In all those houses, people are anxious to fulfil my every wish." The new barons of finance were, of course, very much flattered to have Strauss in their homes. However, his relationship with the bankers of the inflation had its disadvantages for Strauss. When, in 1929, the house of Morgan led its campaign against speculation in francs, Strauss lost his fortune which had been invested with these bankers.

Pauline Strauss laid special store upon their relations with aristocrats, and she herself came of a noble family. At the large parties which Strauss gave in Vienna, the leaders of the political world, ministers, high officials, the Mayor of Vienna and the most important Social Democrats were invited. I had the impression that Strauss sympathized politically with the Social Democrats. By no means did he love the clerical party. He was a free thinker in religious questions and therefore did not let his son Franz have any religious instruction. That created difficulties when Franz Strauss was to take his entrance exam for the university, since he was also required to pass an examination in religion. Strauss sent his son to a priest to whom it was no secret that he was a freethinker. At the examination, as Strauss related gaily, the priest asked his son: "Do you think your father is convinced in what he believes?" When Franz naturally said "yes," the clever priest replied, "You see, then he too, is a true Catholic," and dismissed the son of this somewhat skeptical believer who thus passed his examination.

Like all Bavarians, Strauss disliked Prussians, even more after the war than before. I remember that after the war, Strauss made a long political discourse to me during a walk at Garmisch. He declared that the best political solution of the problem would be the uniting of Bavaria, Austria and Hungary in a league from which Prussia would be excluded. After the recent upheaval in Germany, as one knows, Strauss put himself, for a period of time, at the disposition of National Socialism. He wanted thus to gain influence on musical development in Germany; and he told me when we met in Salzburg that he had sent three memorandums to the government asking that its attitude on the race question be made more mild in the music field. Doubtless, Richard Strauss made a false step when he allied himself with National Socialism. He placed himself in a difficult position; because not only were his best friends Jews and his librettist, Hugo von Hofmannsthal, a half-Jew, but his daughter-in-law was Jewish and his grandchild, therefore, a half-Jew. A free, European mind, like Strauss, who was bound to all the intellectual movements of Europe and who thought so much in European terms that he had his ballet, "Joseph's Legend" performed first in the Paris Opera by the Russian ballet, is greater than the culture-inimical National Socialism.

I never knew Strauss as anything but amiable, fine, cultivated and thoroughly good-hearted. He could be stubborn, however, and when his face reddened in anger, it was better not to argue with him. But in general, in his great superiority over the circumstances of life, Strauss made an impressive appearance, and lost nothing of his greatness in simpler and more natural forms. I have seen Strauss in the most various situations, and he was always self-controlled and superior. He was a man who always had himself securely in hand and always remained true to character. Of all the genial men I have known in my life, Strauss was the most natural, the most clever and the best behaved. In his eminent self-control, Goethe was his model.

I often visited Strauss in Garmisch where his house overlooked the Krammer. The house, whose windows gave on the powerful mass of the Zugspitze, was protected from the noise and turmoil of the street by a great park whose trees hid it from the eyes of the passersby. Strauss spent his summers there, composing. "In winter I need light occupation," said Strauss to me, "therefore I conduct. You cannot imagine what it means for me when I conduct "Tristan" once in winter, and how it stimulates me in my work." At Garmisch, his mornings were dedicated mainly to composing. Strauss wrote his works either in the beautiful studio, or in the garden where a work table stood under an awning. The afternoons belonged to automobile excursions, to his beloved card games, and to letter-writing which took up a great part of his time, since Strauss was a great correspondent. The number of letters which Strauss wrote in his lifetime must run up to the thousands. They are all in his pointed, nervous yet nonetheless definite and stubborn handwriting which is just as personal as his musical manuscripts.

The first sketches of Strauss's compositions were made in regular notebooks with pencil. These sketch books he could carry comfortably in his pocket. The care with which he wrote, even in these sketch books, is great. There is nothing confused by excitement, as it so often was in the case of Beethoven. Strauss's writing is always clear, as if engraved. Neatness and clarity were essential to Strauss in his work, also. There was none of the disorder which usually surrounds genius in his studio. After he had finished his work for the day, he would collect his sketches and notes from his desk and put them away.

Strauss thought very keenly about the theoretical problems of his art. This was especially the case at the time when the atonal composers appeared upon the musical scene. Though

Strauss had stretched classic and romantic harmony to their utmost boundaries in his "Elektra," nevertheless he had built upon a firm foundation of classic harmony. With pleasure he told me, after returning from the modern music festival at Donaueschingen, that he himself had asked Hindemith after the performance of the latter's string quartet: "Why do you write atonally? After all, you have talent!" In spite of this, he showed me, with definite satisfaction, a spot in the score of his "Alpine Symphony" where he had written several atonal bars. It is the rising progress of the contrabasses at the beginning of the storm, which, as an atonal spot of color, is quite impressionistically inserted in the picture of the storm. In "Elektra," too, there are similar harmonically free coloristic passages. In general, Strauss thought that modern composers knew how to do too little. "They can't do it! They can't do it!" he exclaimed again and again. He meant that modern musicians bring up new problems, but that they are incapable of solving them. How well and how sharply Strauss theorized one sees best from the preface to his opera "Intermezzo" where he analyzes his comic opera style. When he wrote this preface, he had me lecture to him in detail on the history of the opera recitative, and he used the musico-historic information which I could give him in its preface.

The Vienna Opera, the direction of which Strauss had taken over in difficult times, together with Franz Schalk, he loved particularly. He admired the orchestra especially. When, in 1923, he made a concert tour of South America with the opera orchestra, he wrote me on August 7th, from La Plata: "Up to now I have given twenty-one concerts with the marvelous Philharmonic in Rio de Janeiro, San Paolo and Montevideo with greatest success. The first concerts were partly splendidly improvised, the later ones, after polishing rehearsals, a fantastic rhythmic precision in wonderful delivery and paradisiac sound. The orchestra, too, apparently takes great pleasure in playing with me." On August 11th, he followed with a postal card from Buenos Aires in which he said: "The Philharmonic yesterday played Schubert's C Major and the 'Domestica' as if in a fairy-tale."

Repeatedly, in my hearing, Strauss called the Vienna Opera his "Bayreuth." He had already left the Vienna Opera when on June 6, 1931, he wrote from Garmisch: "The precious possession of the Vienna Opera must be preserved at any price. It cannot be that the whole German culture will go to pieces with these damned swine-politics."

In those years when the soil of Austria was shaken, it is immeasurable what Strauss meant for the Vienna Opera and Austrian musical life. Not only had he been the artistic authority which protected the opera against the dilettante meddling of officials and politicians, but he also filled the beautiful house with enthusiasm. He was at the peak of his successes as composer and his work had become established.

Strauss liked especially well to conduct "Tristan and Isolde," to which he gave passionate expression, as if it were a relative of "Elektra," and "Lohengrin," with wonderful solemnity in the Prelude. Strauss's Wagner style was the Wagner style of a new era. He preferred faster tempi, great climaxes, and sometimes—as at the end of "Walkyrie"—real Strauss strettas. Strauss also conducted Mozart's works often, and paid no heed when the Viennese music critics said his tempi were too fast. "I understand that better," he said curtly, and asserted his right as greatest living musician to understand Mozart best. Despite his justified self-reliance, Strauss also knew how to evaluate and honor the opinions of others. He wrote me on May 26, 1922, from Karlsbad, where he was taking the cure: "Your criticism of 'Meistersinger' was a masterpiece of productive criticism—matter-of-fact, instructive in the best sense. It gave me such enjoyment that I especially want to thank you for it."

Under the direction of Strauss and Schalk, a second intimate theatre opened in the Redoutensäle (Masquerade Halls) of the Imperial Palace. It was a true jewel-box—a small, aristocratic splendid hall with large chandeliers of Venetian glass and Gobelins of the Netherland school on the walls. The stage was a mere platform, and from its rear, a double staircase led to a side hall in which the court society had drunk tea in the eighteenth century. The time of Emperor Josef I was still alive in this delightful hall. It was built during his reign, in 1706. One of the halls was dedicated to Italian opera which was presented each year on the empress's birthday. The other was destined for court festivals. In 1744, the last opera was performed, "Hypermnestra" by Hasse. After this, these Halls were used for grand balls. Haydn and Mozart composed dance music for them, and Beethoven conducted there. Now, the greatest composer of modern times sat at the conductor's desk while on the stage there was song and dance amid stylized decorations. There was modern rococo atmosphere in the lovely theatre. Strauss conducted "Cosi fan Tutte" there, and surprised us once with a revival of the old French opera, "Jean de Paris," which had been dear to his heart ever since his youth. For this theatre, where the opera ballet had danced ballets by Ravel and Stravinsky, Strauss composed his "Couperin Ballet." His "Le Bourgeois Gentilhomme," with its clever music, was also presented there.

In the great Opera on the Ringstrasse, Strauss regularly conducted his own operas. The Vienna State Opera, with its exemplary performance of his works, for several years was really his "Bayreuth." Here his great "Elektra" was enthusiastically celebrated by the youth; his "Salome" again and again presented. The warm fairy-tale of the "Frau ohne Schatten" gripped the listener, the Marschallin said good-bye to her youth, and the "Rosenkavalier" waltzes played and joked. "Ariadne auf Naxos" delighted audiences with its intellect and its melody. "Egyptian Helen" presented a modern comedy in Greek frame and a modern problem of marriage in legendary form. "Joseph's Legend" unfolded, in a modern ballet, the beauty of a baroque festival. With "Intermezzo" the present day and Strauss' family life came to the stage. Color, brilliance, modern thought were spread out in the Vienna Opera, and the great composer who had created these works sat there, impressive and powerful, ruling stage and orchestra, surrounded by the reflected light of the orchestra lamps.

With Richard Strauss as leading musician, the Vienna State Opera once again stood in the center of universal worth and meaning.

The opera and the music of Vienna had been saved by the collapse of the Austrian nation. It was more than chance that Hugo von Hofmannsthal, when he wrote opera poems for Strauss, had bound himself to Viennese baroque traditions. For Hofmannsthal, the Austria and the Vienna of the eighteenth century, the Vienna of Charles VI and Empress Maria Theresia, of Prince Eugene and Metastasio, the Vienna of battling Catholicism and of the Roman Empire, was the true one and the one which outlasted all changes of time. This Vienna he revived in his poems for "Rosenkavalier" and "Arabella." The poems of the "Frau ohne Schatten" and "Ariadne auf Naxos," too, were related to the theatre of this Vienna. For the baroque fantasy of Richard Strauss which bathed in splendor and brightness of sound, this world was the right opera world. Strauss loved Vienna and Austria, and one of the most beautiful compositions of his Vienna period was his setting of the "Austrian Song" by Anton Wildgans, a Viennese poet whose ideas were similar to those of Hofmannsthal. In one of the most difficult hours of Vienna's history, Richard Strauss came there as the last of the great musicians who was at home within its confines.

In 1924, differences between Strauss and his co-director, Franz Schalk, arose, in which the wives of the two artists were not without a part. At this time, I received a letter from the Austrian Minister of Education, Dr. Schneider, who invited me to have a talk with him. He told me that one day Richard Strauss came to him and handed in his resignation, and the next day Franz Schalk came and did likewise. I immediately took the standpoint that the departure of the greatest musician of the present would be an unbearable loss for the musical life of Vienna. The Minister seemed to agree with me, but failed to do anything when Strauss handed in his resignation on November 1, 1924. In a letter of April 13, 1925, Strauss wrote me from Garmisch that to that day he had received no official confirmation from the Minister: "Nothing, absolutely nothing! Not even my theatre dress coat did they send me."

The thought that Richard Strauss would be allowed to leave Vienna without anyone's having made an attempt to hold him seemed to me, at that time where every effort had to be made to maintain the Vienna Opera at its high level, so senseless that I went to the Austrian Chancellor, Dr. Ramek, to present the facts to him. The Chancellor listened to me calmly, and promised me that an attempt would be made to change Strauss's mind. A representative of the Ministry of Education was sent to Garmisch to see Strauss, but the gentleman was neither very apt nor did he endeavor very earnestly to mend the torn threads of the situation. In a letter which Strauss wrote me after this visit, dated January 17, 1925, he talked of a "polite beating-around-the-bush about something which one wants to glue together only superficially," and he adds: "If Vienna wants something from me, it should put its cards upon the table, and not only ask what my wishes are, but fulfil them, too. They are completely un-egotistical and refer only to the well-being of the State Opera, about which I still know more than most other people."

Strauss took an active part in the development of the Vienna State Opera's affairs, even from the distance. He saw it, since his departure, in "uncheckable decay" (letter of March 30, 1926) and stormed about the "whole nest of lies and impotence" which had formed there, "from the administrative to the artistic direction" (letter of July 4, 1926). Again and again he made suggestions as to who should be put in the place of Director Schalk, and he collaborated in the nomination of Schneiderhahn as Intendent and Clemens Krauss as Director in 1926. After the appointment of the new Director, he returned for a time as conductor, again, but he would no longer have any part in the management. He had crossed the border of the sixties and looked at life from a higher level. In a letter, he writes: "Complete indifference is already a very strong expression for that which still moves me." (Strauss meant, in regard to the Vienna Opera). He knew that the opera was in good hands with Clemens Krauss. That sufficed him. The Strauss chapter of the Vienna State Opera— a great light in a dark time—was closed for good.

In 1933, commissioned with the direction of a music festival for the city of Vienna, I invited Richard Strauss to conduct "Tristan and Isolde" on the anniversary of the fiftieth death-day of Wagner. Strauss declined and wrote me: "The day before yesterday I conducted, in Dresden, for the last time in this life, "Tristan," in honor of the death of the great master, and with it I definitely finished my activity as conductor of the Wagnerian wonder works. I shall be sixty-nine in June, and I have to husband my strength if I want to complete the compository tasks which still lie ahead of me, with passable freshness. Wagner's dramas are strenuous enough for younger men . . . so it really is not possible, even with the best of will. Such a renunciation is painful, but sometime one has to say good-bye."

One year later I met Strauss, in the company of Opera Director Clemens Krauss, in Salzburg, for the last time. Shortly before, Strauss had celebrated his seventieth birthday, and he looked in the bloom of health. The conversation did not touch upon the Vienna Opera, but on the best methods of catching trout. Strauss held forth in an expert discourse on the subject. One could see he was far distant from the Vienna Opera and its worries.

The fame of the Vienna Opera had become greater and greater. Guest appearances abroad were furthered by the Austrian government. In 1923, the Vienna Opera was sent to Geneva, where it solicited the interest of the League of Nations with its Mozart performances. In 1934, the Vienna Opera presented Strauss's "Frau ohne Schatten" and Mozart's "Cosi fan Tutte" in Venice. Nine years later it traveled to Rome with "Ariadne auf Naxos," which Mussolini wanted to hear. The Opera Orchestra, the Vienna Philharmonic, toured half of Europe and gave its concerts, enthusiastically acclaimed. In 1935, the Philharmonic and the Opera Chorus went to Florence to perform the Beethoven Ninth Symphony under Felix von Weingartner's direction. The music city Vienna seemed to send out rays of its old glory into a new world. Austria had become small but was still large on the map of music. It no longer had any political might, but its musical power seemed unshaken.

New musical fame came to Austria through the festivals which were held every summer in Salzburg, and which, since 1927, became more and more the music festivals of the whole world. In the old Bishop's town on the Salzach, the last great chapter of Vienna's musical history took place.

It can be regarded as symbolic that during the first World War, at a time when the unhappy ending could already be foreseen, in 1917, the "Salzburg Festival Committee" was founded in Vienna. It issued a proclamation for the holding of festivals in the Mozart town. From the very beginning, the programme for the planned festivals was conceived on a grand scale. It was mapped out by Hugo von Hofmannsthal, and approved by the Art Council of the Festivals, which consisted of Franz Schalk, Max Reinhardt, Richard Strauss, Professor Roller and Hofmannsthal. Mozart, of course, was meant to be the center of the festivals, but from this center, one proceeded in the most various directions. The "Idomeneo" of Mozart seemed to lead to the Greek operas of Gluck and to the antique drama. From Mozart's "Don Giovanni," one arrived, according to the ideas of Hofmannsthal, at Molière, Calderon, and at the spiritual dramas of the middle ages. From the "Magic Flute," a double path opened, one branch leading to Goethe's "Faust," the other to Weber, Raimund, the Vienna Folk Theatre, to Gozzi and Goldoni and to Johann Strauss's "Fledermaus." Thus from the outset, the frame of the festivals was widely spanned.

This festival programme was fitted to the spirit of the town of Salzburg, or better, conceived from its spirit by Hofmannsthal. For in Salzburg, the baroque time was not a thing of the past, but something which was still alive in the panorama of the town, in the churches, palaces, yes, even in the simple houses of the people. Lying on the banks of a green alpine stream, and encircled by high mountains, Salzburg is still dominated by its baroque buildings. With the Archbishop Wolf Dietrich (1587-1612) who, as a relative of Pope Pius IV and of Cardinal Borromeo, had Italian blood in his veins, the great Italian epoch of Salzburg began. Under this prince of the church, the cornerstone of the new cathedral was laid, the first plan of which was drawn up by Vincenzo Scamozzi.

Italian art and Italian artists began to overflow Salzburg

under this bishop. Tiburtius Massainus of Verona became the first conductor, and Italian falsetto singers were heard in the cathedral. Dozens of bourgeois houses were torn down by Wolf Dietrich to make room for the new bishop's residence, which was to look like a Roman palazzo with a large court where later the Triton fountain of Antonio Darios let fall its splashing cascades.

The Castle of Mirabell was begun under Wolf Dietrich. Under the melancholy Marcus Sitticus (1612-1619), who, like his predecessor, had been educated in Rome, the new cathedral by Santino Solari rose high in marble splendor akin to St. Peter's in Rome. In the middle of a woodland park, the Castle of Hellbrunn rose up, with water art and grottos, with fish ponds and a stone theatre, with game parks and statues. Under Marcus Sitticus, who sought distraction in festivals and music, Salzburg was filled with theatrical performances of all kinds. In the Hellbrunn stone theatre, worldly as well as religious operas were performed, and Emperor Ferdinand was greeted with the performance of an opera, "Orfeo" on the occasion of his visit in 1618. A Venetian masque-procession was held in the town that same year—the Town Councillors of Salzburg in Venetian costume sat on a galley, pulled by four white horses and driven by Neptune with his three-pronged fork.

The "Gymnasium" (high school) founded by Bishop Marcus Sitticus in 1617, became the fostering-place of theatre-art in Salzburg. In the school plays which were performed there, all the gods of Greek legend appeared normally, or by means of "flying" machines. Choirs sang, rockets flared. The Bishop's praises were sung in choruses and arias. "Labor" entered on a triumphal cart amid the blare of trumpets and Mercury distributed prizes to the best pupils while a large chorus sang hymns. The Court Chapel was completely Italianized under Marcus Sitticus. The court conductor, Peter Gutfreund, had to change his name to "Pietro Bonamico," and his successor was Francesco Turco. In 1628, under Archbishop Paris Lodron, the new marble cathedral was dedicated. Stefano Bernardi, who had become Cathedral Conductor in 1627, had composed a twelve voiced Te Deum for the occasion. From the four pillars of the cupola, the fifty-three part festival mass, which the young Roman, Oratio Benevoli, had composed, resounded solemnly. With its sixteen vocal parts, thirty-four instrumental parts, two organ parts and basso continuo, this music filled the cathedral's huge interior. Before Mass, the relics of the cathedral had been ordered to their new resting place, in a festival procession on triumphal floats where Heaven, the Blessed Virgin, the Saints and Christ on the Cross were depicted. In the afternoon, there was a festival play in the Gymnasium, in which Neptune, Diana and mermaids greeted the festival guests. The finale showed the new cathedral on the stage, above which were angels on a rainbow. The chorus sang and there were comic interludes. At Hellbrunn, in the stone theatre, an ecclesiastical opera, dealing with the conversion of Mary Magdalen, was performed in Italian.

The alpine landscape which surrounds Salzburg and the buildings in Roman style grew together in a unique way. In the seventeenth century, Salzburg was a town of eight thousand inhabitants at the most. Nevertheless, it could boast of churches and palaces which even in Rome, were considered out of the ordinary. The wealth of the old monasteries, of which the Benedictine Order's St. Peter's is the oldest on German soil, was surpassed by only very few places in Europe. All these buildings stand thronged together in the small space between the Capuchin and the Monk's Mountains, between burghers' houses with narrow stairs and flat roofs. German middle-ages as well as Roman baroque splendor meet in Salzburg. Here is alpine country as well as Italy.

This is the town which became the town of Mozart, in whose music German and Italian elements, alpine landscape and the Mediterranean are united. Mozart was born in one of the old merchant-houses in the narrow, crooked Getreide-gasse (Grain Street). His first masses were played in the cathedral and in St. Peter's Church. He was engaged at the court of the Archbishop, whose musicians were still, for the most part, Italians. In the theatre of the University he saw his first theatrical performances. All the characteristics and atmosphere of his beautiful native town made their impressions upon the sensitive, receptive soul of the boy Mozart. And it was this native town of Mozart's which laid the germ of the phenomenal development of his music which became the most perfect synthesis of all European spiritual movements. For Salzburg was a world by itself, and although at that time, it was situated in Germany, it was more closely connected with Rome and Italy.

In Salzburg, just as in Vienna, the earth was drenched with music. From Salzburg the song went forth which became the Christmas song of the whole world, "Silent Night, Holy Night." A school teacher had written the music, a priest the poem. Both lived in a small village near Salzburg, both spoke the Salzburg dialect, both were men of the people.

It was Christmas Eve—December 24th, 1818. In the old church of the small village, Oberndorf, near Salzburg, the priest was celebrating Midnight Mass. Candles burned on the altar, and rosy-cheeked peasant boys, in white surplices, were kneeling behind the priest, swinging the censer. On the side of the altar, as every year, the crib, with freshly painted wooden figures, had been erected. Peasants, in thick winter cloaks, sat praying on the church benches.

The priest had just sung the "Benedicamus Domino" in his shaking, aged voice, when from the choir, two male voices, accompanied by a guitar, began the song. The tenor part was sung by Joseph Mohr, the priest who had written the text, the bass by Franz Gruber, the school-master who composed the melody. At the end of every stanza of "Silent Night, Holy Night," the choir of blond schoolboys, who till this moment had been looking down on the altar, the crib and their parents, joined in with their clear voices.

None of those present, least of all the poet and the composer, had the slightest idea that the song would spread over the whole world. The authors never once thought of having it published. It had been written for Christmas, 1818, and belonged to the divine service, just as the candles flickering on the altar, the crib with the ox and the ass, and the silver censer from which great clouds of incense floated up to the roof of the church.

The melody of this song composed by a peasant's son had a folk-like character. The school-teacher began his "Silent Night, Holy Night" as one sings to a child who is to be sung to sleep. It sounds like a lullaby in which there is something shy and withheld, as it must have been in the looks of the shepherds when they were led by the angels to the Christ Child, and stood there, awed and pious, their caps in their rough hands. Unwittingly the composer gave the melody the rhythm of the songs which are sung in Italy by the Venetian gondoliers and by the fishermen in the boats on the Gulf of Naples. The tune's Italian character is derived from the Salzburg landscape, through which the road leads from Italy to Germany. The houses in Salzburg have the flat roofs of Italian houses, and the sun of the south falls on the Salzburg countryside. Thus the Italian color of the melody belongs to the landscape to which Schoolmaster Gruber was bound. The song is a piece of nature.

Nowhere in the world, during the nineteenth century, was a similar song composed which traveled the whole world. It belonged to the Christmas celebration and brought a powerful message to all humanity.

With such a past, Salzburg was the ideal place for the world's festivals. In 1920, on August 22nd, Max Reinhardt produced the religious play, "Jedermann" ("Everyman"), adapted by Hugo von Hofmannsthal from the English mystery, on the square in front of the Salzburg Cathedral. A simple wooden stage had been erected. From the portal of the church organ music sounded, and at the end of the drama, the bells tolled while the sun set behind the mountains and dyed the marble of the cathedral red. The spectators sat on rude benches and watched the play of the life and death of the wealthy Everyman. At the end, the shroud was placed upon him, and Faith and Good Works led him into his grave.

The theatre had returned to its mediaeval form and had

become once more a primitive mystery play which was equally understandable, plastic and touching for the educated as well as for the folk. Since that day, "Jedermann" was presented every Sunday and holiday during the festival, there, in front of the Cathedral, and peasants came from even the most distant mountain villages to see it.

In 1922, Max Reinhardt produced the "Salzburg Great World Theatre," from Hofmannsthal's adaptation of a play by Calderon, in the Kollegien Church. This time Reinhardt had erected his stage in mediaeval form on the high altar, and

Bruno Walter
(Sketched by Dolbin)

the baroque church of Fischer von Erlach took part in the drama.

The new "Festspielhaus" which Clemens Holzmeister had designed as a simple building which stood between the summer and winter riding schools of the old Bishops, was opened in 1925. A Salzburg painter, Faistauer, decorated its foyer with frescoes. Originally, only plays were given in this theatre, while the performances of the Vienna Opera were held in the small Stadtheater. But in 1927, the Beethoven Centennial year, Franz Schalk had performed "Fidelio" in the Festspielhaus, and from that time on it became the opera theatre of the Salzburg festivals. There, operas were performed, mounted by the great scenic-designers and stage-directors of the present day. Schalk performed "Fidelio" with Roller and the "Magic Flute" with Strnad. For Gluck's "Iphigenia in Tauris," again Professor Roller was engaged. New ideas and inspiration were brought to Salzburg by Bruno Walter. He conducted the much admired "Orfeo." Weber's "Oberon" displayed its oriental magic in the scenic designs by Strnad. Then came the "Abduction from the Seraglio." Later followed the "Marriage of the Figaro" done again with Italian singers. Weber's "Euryanthe" and Hugo Wolf's "Corregidor" were among the revivals conducted by Bruno Walter. Walter commissioned the leading stage-directors for his performances —Karl Heinz Martin, Ludwig Hoert, Herbert Graf and Lothar Wallerstein. Walter's performances, completely thought out, with brilliant intellect, and the greatest intensity within complete unity of style, belong to the art of Salzburg, and were artistic events for the whole world. Clemens Krauss conducted "Cosi fan Tutte," with the charming stage décors by Siebert. The great operatic works of Richard Strauss were introduced, one by one, by the composer, supported in the same spirit by Lothar Wallerstein as stage-director. Thus, the Salzburg opera repertory spread in various directions with Mozart as the central point, in performances which might be considered the most perfect in modern stage technique.

Around the opera performances, concerts by the Vienna Philharmonic were grouped, under the most important conductors; concerts in the Salzburg Cathedral, Mozart Serenades in the courtyards of the Bishops' Residence. In 1934, Max Reinhardt realized his old plan of performing Goethe's

"Faust" in Salzburg. He had a theatre built in the courtyard of the Bishops' summer riding school, and Clemens Holzmeister erected a whole town for the drama. Goethe's "Faust" became a Salzburg "Faust." It was not an educational play—nothing literary—but all theatre, all spectacle and "show." It was as if Goethe's "Faust" had returned to the popular play from which it had emerged. The angels stood high upon the mountain. God's voice thundered from the heights at Mephistopheles below. In one of the openings in the mountain wall, Dr. Faust sat at his work table illuminated by the nocturnal lamp, Mephistopheles behind him. In front of Marguerite's house, a real garden, with green grass and daisies, had been planted. With their girls, the men danced around a real linden tree, and from the church, behind which one saw Salzburg's house-tops, came the sound of choir and organ. Theatre and reality were bound together.

The highest point in the development of the Salzburg Festivals was reached in 1935, when Arturo Toscanini stepped into the circle of great artists who contributed to Salzburg's fame. With this most famous conductor of the time, a man of moral independence and most noble artistic conscience had been won. He was not only a representative of music, but of those ideas of all humanity which had made eighteenth century Vienna the capital of classical music. When in Haydn's "Creation," the creation of man is heralded in the sublime aria, "With dignity and highness arrayed," when in Mozart's "Magic Flute" the godliness of man is glorified in solemn choruses, when in Beethoven's Ninth Symphony men are hailed as brothers—all that was for Toscanini not only music, but faith. No one should approach classical music who is not imbued with the humanistic conception of great music and great artists. Toscanini rejected any compromise such as could be found even in musicians like Furtwaengler and Strauss after the victory of the Hitler movement in Germany, in 1933. One cannot perform great music and at the same time accept the enslaving and brutalizing of humanity. Classical music means music of the noblest humanity. Whoever did not serve this ideal or wished to make compromises had no business in the temple of music.

The three years in which Toscanini was active in Salzburg

Toscanini

were three years of perfect artistic achievement. Music lovers from all parts of the world came to Salzburg to enjoy music which belonged to everybody. For Europe, which was full of nationalistic slogans, of hatred and fear, of force and turmoil, the Salzburg Festival with Toscanini was the last spot left on earth where music was not only beauty, but also faith.

Toscanini began with Beethoven's "Fidelio." Then followed the Italian performance of Verdi's "Falstaff," the wonder-work of the eighty-year old composer. In 1936, the "Meistersinger von Nürnberg" was performed. In the intimate hall of the Festspielhaus, it had the effect of a true comedy, every word understandable, so that every jest, and the art speeches in the shoemaker's room, had wonderful vitality. It was a festival play with joyousness and folklike qualities, with tenderness and resignation. It had a second act, built up high by the stage-director (Dr. Herbert Graf), with many convenient nooks for conversation, for jolly pranks, for confessions, for beatings and for silver moonlight. In 1937, Toscanini conducted the "Magic Flute." Once again one heard a work of humanity with symbolic solemnity, with folk-wit, mystic ceremonies and lively jokes. Toscanini, who was nearly seventy, applied a burning energy to the work. Here was a master-conductor who was only satisfied with the nearest possible approach to perfection, who demanded the finest efforts from artists and colleagues in the production, and who himself undertook the highest and most grandiose.

In addition to his opera performances, Toscanini conducted orchestral concerts and large choral works with classical programmes; and from far away, the whole world came to hear his interpretations. Salzburg could scarcely accommodate the guests who flooded the city on the Salzach on performance days.

Viennese music and Austrian music, during these years, experienced their highest level. For the last time they demonstrated their power of holding the world in their grip. For the last time, also, they confirmed that great way of thinking through which they had become great. It is said that those who are dying often find their moments of greatest well-being right before their passing. All which is life force in dying assembles in a last mounting of strength. From every part, the forces stream together, and a feeling of happiness, health and of a new birth of life takes possession of the dying man, who is deluded into feeling strong and happy. Such a moment in the musical life of Vienna was provided by the Salzburg Festivals. It seemed as if all the powerful forces of Viennese and of Austrian music assembled themselves again at this time; and as if Vienna and Austria were again capable of sending forth the ideas which had made Vienna the music city of the world—a city of mingling and uniting. There is great meaning in the fact that Vienna (for Vienna's musical spirit reigned in Salzburg) returned, in the Salzburg Festivals, to the foundations of that time in which it became great. The rise of Vienna to the status of a European music capital began with the Italian composers and conductors of the Viennese court—with Cesti, Draghi and Caldara—and its glory ends with an Italian conductor—Toscanini. The circle, the first lines of which were drawn in sixteenth century Vienna, was closed in 1937, in Salzburg.

6

Past and Future

An Outlook on History and New Life

It was the end of a development such as had never taken place in a more unified and complete way in the history of music. The city which, through so many centuries, had made music for the world, was destroyed. The war of 1914 ruined the old Austria, the invasion of the year 1938, the European music city, Vienna. Between the spirit which had created Vienna and nationalism, there could be no relationship. They belong to entirely different worlds.

Shortly before the destruction of Vienna as a musical city, the devastation of Europe began. The two events were connected. All over Europe, an old epoch went up in flames, to the accompaniment of murder and hideous cruelty. Both great wars, that of 1914 and of 1938, represent, perhaps, only horrible episodes of a great revolution which destroyed an old order, and which will lead, through streams of blood, to a new one. The social and national tensions in Europe were already great around 1900, society shaken, and its balance destroyed. All these tensions exploded, like a great tempest, in the two wars. As it has been in any historical crisis, this too, is not only the bloody disruption of an old epoch which is no longer capable of controlling its intellectual, social and political problems, and which resorted to force to prevent the forward surge of a new power. It is, at the same time, the painful birth of a new era. From the

273

crisis a new Europe will arise. The way may be long, and lead through want, devastation and misery; new crises may mount up before the ground is prepared for new harvests in a peaceful world, and a new Europe of work, community of nations and harmony of all forces be created. Only the past will be dead, and a fresh chapter of world history will begin. To-day, too, one can say what Goethe said, in the midst of the storms of the French Revolution, when the cannons of the Battle of Valmy were thundering: "From now and from here on begins a new chapter of world history, and you can say that you have been there!"

A new era and a new society, new intellectual values and new forms of life also mean new art and a new relationship of life and society to art. In this connection, the question of Vienna's future as a music city becomes important. Vienna can never rise again in its old form. Here, too, a new development begins, and I should not like to close this book without having answered the question as to under what circumstances and conditions Vienna could become a great musical city once more.

When I conducted the reader on a trip through new Vienna, along the Ringstrasse, the past kept peeping through into the present. The new city of trolleys and busses again and again changed itself back to the old fortress city of the seventeenth and eighteenth centuries. The society which reigned in Vienna until 1918 was only the old feudal society of the baroque period in modern dress. Vienna was old and new at the same time. The past, in this vivid and beautiful city, was everywhere alive, and belonged to its life and existence.

Vienna had scarcely changed since the seventeenth century. Imperial Palace, nobles' palaces, churches and town houses are almost as they were. To be sure, modern banks and a few modern apartment houses have been built, but they did not change the essential picture of the city. Should Mozart return there to-day, he would find the neighborhood where he wrote his "Marriage of Figaro" quite unchanged. Schubert would find his old inns in quiet streets, Beethoven his stately Pasqualatti House. In modern Vienna there are still many narrow, winding streets through which vehicles have difficulty passing.

In a city of this type, the past is a strong power. It was so in the political, social and musical life. Old musical periods did not die when those musicians who lived and worked in them passed away. In the sound of instruments and voices, there were ghostly voices from bygone days. Thus past and present were united. Tradition bound to-day to yesterday. One cannot speak of Vienna's future as a music city without understanding its past. One and the same law ruled in the whole development from the seventeenth to the twentieth century.

It is this law of life of Vienna that we wish to understand that, unchanged, set in motion all the changing characteristics of Viennese music and which will continue to work into the future. This law, as long as Vienna was a great musical city, possessed living strength. Costumes had changed. External forms of life had changed. Generation followed generation, new buildings were erected. Only the personality of the music city remained unchanged during the change of times and customs. Should Vienna begin a new development as a musical city in a new epoch of world history, it would only be possible if it continues to observe this law of its existence. That does not mean that it should copy its past. Nothing is further from my mind than to attempt to preach a dusty conservatism. A great, modern city is no museum. A new time is here with its demands, with new people, new aims and new work. The past is thoroughly dead—a cemetery and a pile of debris. A return to the old forms of life is impossible, for from dead life only a dead art could emerge. Music can only be vital as the expression of a new time, and only from living forces can new music grow. The only thing which remains unchanged is the law which formed Vienna into a great musical city.

The question which is to be answered is what, exactly, made Vienna into a world music city? When and how did Vienna become this music city? What spiritual forces were active which produced in Vienna music which had meaning for the whole world? What is the law which ruled these spiritual forces?

Only history can answer these questions; and we must ask it, if we wish to receive a reply about the future which would be more than mere idle thought. Therefore, after I have sketched the last chapter of the music city, Vienna, from my own point of view and from my personal experience, we must call up the vision of the time when Vienna raised itself to the position of first musical city of the world.

* * *

I

There had always been music in Vienna ever since the Roman soldiers built the fortress on the Danube. We know

276

of the music and of the musical instruments of this period. But Vienna, in those days, was nothing but a fortress with a market-place, and not a music city. In the following eras, twice in the city's history, the musical life became richer and music began to sound more loudly through the Danube lands. One of these times fell in the days when the Babenberger dukes built their castle on the Danube and the Minnesingers, in the thirteenth century, sang their songs of spring, of women, and of love. The greatest of all German poets before Goethe, Walter von der Vogelweide, composed and sang, accompanying himself on the viola. But Minnesingers also sang in other castles, and in the chateaux of southern France there was considerably more music than in thirteenth century Vienna. In the fifteenth century, under Maximilian I, there was again a great deal of music in Vienna. The court chapel was founded where boys from the Netherlands sang the Masses. Great musicians of that period, like Paul Hoffheimer, Ludwig Senfl and Heinrich Isaak were in the service of music-loving rulers. This fact demonstrated, however, more the love for music of the princes than of Vienna's love of music. There were, at that time, many devotees of music among the aristocrats—the Estes in Ferrara, the Gonzagas in Mantua, the Sforzas in Milan, the Kings of France and England, the Dukes of Burgundy. The fifteenth century was a great musical era. The cities of Holland and Paris, not Vienna, were the great music centers of Europe.

It was otherwise in the sixteenth century. At this time, the Austrian landscape—Graz, Innsbruck, Vienna—began to sound. From 1567 on, there were Italian musicians at the court of Graz. At Innsbruck, half of the court chapel orchestra were Italians, directed by a musician from Milan. In Vienna, in 1619, Archduke Ferdinand of Steiermark (Styria), mounted the throne as Emperor Ferdinand II, and brought his orchestra from Graz. He had sixty musicians, mainly Italians, who were then joined to the Vienna Court Orchestra under its conductor, Priuli. Vienna, which even under Rudolf II had had an Italian Court Conductor (Camillo Zanotti, 1586, Orologioo, 1603) now became an Italian music city and grew more so when Ferdinand II married a princess from Mantua. With the new empress came a whole suite of Italians—secretaries, poets, musicians. It was the same under Ferdinand III whose wife, likewise, was an Italian.

During the same time, Vienna developed into a capital where the destiny of European politics was decided. As early as 1438, Vienna had been the capital of the German Empire, and its rulers, who resided in the Imperial Palace of Vienna, were crowned with the crown of the German Emperors. In 1526, the Austrian Empire was formed, in which Bohemia and Hungary were joined to Austria. Ferdinand of Austria was also crowned King of Bohemia and Hungary, and the Slavic, Hungarian and German peoples were united. The great historical hour of Vienna had struck. The Emperors, who lived in Vienna, could consider themselves the center of the world. They were the German kings, the rulers of the Danube territories. They were the champions of the Catholic religion which, in Rome, assembled all its forces to fight against Protestantism. They felt themselves more than Austrian and German rulers. They had become monarchs of the European world. In the sixteenth century, Vienna became a supernational city which remained so until 1918.

For all Europe, these faithful rulers of the new monarchy waged the wars against the Turks who first besieged Vienna in 1527. All Europe waited for the news from Vienna when, in 1683, the Turks pitched their tents on the slopes of the Kahlenberg. The bells were rung throughout Germany and the Te Deum Laudamus was sung when the citizens of Vienna defeated the Turks and the great bells of St. Stephen's announced the freeing of the city. Again it was a European event when the Austrian armies of Prince Eugene drove the Turks out of Hungary and moved victoriously to the Balkans. As principal power of Europe, Vienna fought these battles— and as leader of Christian thought in Europe.

II

During the sixteenth and seventeenth centuries, European history was formed in Vienna. Another important European event was the battle of the Austrian princes for the reestablishment of the Catholic religion. In Austria, in Bohemia, and in Hungary, Protestantism had swept through the nobility and the bourgeoisie. Vienna itself had maintained a Protestant administration. In Upper Austria and in Styria, almost the whole country had become Protestant. In 1554, in Hungary, a Lutheran was elected imperial chief minister. With fire and sword, Rudolf II and the gloomy, Jesuit-educated Ferdinand II led the war on Protestantism. The Protestants were expelled from their positions and from their homes, and were tried before clerical courts. Two hundred Protestant nobles of Bohemia were beheaded on the market-place of Prague after the disastrous battle on the White Mountain. Catholic priests journeyed through the land. Education was handed over to the Jesuits. Jesuits taught at the universities of Prague and Vienna, and in 1585, the University of Graz was founded expressly for them. There were church processions in the streets. Emperor Rudolf himself, carrying a lighted candle, used to march in such processions, even in the cold of winter. In 1578, when after a long period, the first Mass was read at St. Stephen's, Emperor Ferdinand walked behind the tabernacle in the long train of priests and brothers.

In the smallest Austrian town, one can still see to-day the power of this fanatical faith movement. In almost every market-place stands a "Blessed Trinity Pillar," on which God is depicted wearing a long beard and sitting in the clouds, with Jesus, Holy Ghost and chubby-cheeked angels, as a memorial to the time of the Counter-Reformation. Naturally, the largest of these columns stands in Vienna. Emperor Leopold I had it erected on the Graben, not far from the Imperial Palace. It was designed by an Italian theatre architect, Burnacini. On it, too, the Trinity is enthroned in the clouds, and from the heights plunges an angel with shield and sword, and chases away the devil, who has the form of a shriveled old woman. The devil, of course, symbolizes Protestant Unbelief, and Emperor Leopold I, in full regalia, observes this edifying play, kneeling, his hands folded in prayer.

At this time, all Austria decked itself with new churches and in every town, even in the most remote alpine valley, a baroque church tower rose toward the sky. The great Benedictine and Augustine orders transformed their old monasteries into powerful baroque strongholds which, from their mountain heights, looked down over the land. In Vienna, between 1622 and 1627, almost every year a new monastery arose, and in some years, two.

Like the Emperor and the Archdukes, the Viennese nobility also exhibited the new Catholic piety of the Counter-Reformation period. Many princes, like the Esterhazys, were reconverted to Catholicism from Protestantism, and let themselves be bathed in the sun of the Emperor's favor. Prince Piccolomini, the imperial commander in the Thirty Years' War, had the Serviten Church, one of the largest in Vienna, built at his expense. Another nobleman, Prince Paul Esterhazy, in 1692, with the inhabitants of all his lands, in all, eleven thousand two hundred people, undertook a pilgrimage to Mariazell, to which point Emperor Franz Josef, and the nobility of his time later made pilgrimages. Countesses and princesses, citizens, musicians, priests and three hundred thousand eight hundred and sixty boys walked in the procession, singing. The coat-of-arms of the Esterhazy family was borne at the head of the procession. Thus they traveled six days on foot through the Styrian mountains where the famous church stood, at the edge of a forest. Five hundred and ten men stretched out their arms in the form of a cross. Prince Paul Esterhazy, the wealthiest and most powerful man in Hungary who, at coronations, placed the crown on the monarch's head, walked behind his musicians in the festive train. That was the pathos of the seventeenth century and the fanatical faith of the time.

Thus Vienna was great in the sixteenth and seventeenth centuries, and the leader in political and religious thought. Here one never felt in national terms. The idea of the empire was a universal one, as was the idea of Catholicism.

The ruler in Vienna who only in 1805 took the title "Emperor of Austria," was "Roman Emperor of the German Nation," and as such, the successor of the Roman Emperors and the crowned head of a universal monarchy, not a national state. As Roman Emperor, he also wielded the sword of the Catholic Church, which stood above all nations.

At this time, Italian music was not foreign music, but a universal language which was just as understandable in London and Paris, Madrid and St. Petersburg, as in Vienna. All modern forms of music were created in the sixteenth and seventeenth century Italy—opera, cantata, concert and symphony, chamber-music and oratorio. Italian music was simply music for all Europe. In this sense it was taken up in Vienna at that period. Italian music was international just as the Latin language was. To Mozart, Italian music meant just that. Musical beauty, musical brilliance in its greatest perfection was, in Mozart, Italian music.

In this spirit, Vienna became the musical city of the world in the seventeenth century. It was the representative of general European ideas and was so considered by everyone who assembled there at the time—by nobles and burghers, immigrants of all nationalities, the officials, the clergy, by Metastasio, the court poet, by Leibnitz, the philosopher, by the musicians, by the adventurers like Casanova and Da Ponte. In Vienna, the politics and business of all nations met.

Even in the age of the musical classicists, this state of thought was prevalent. Beethoven often said sharp words about the Vienna court and the Austrian state. Once he spoke of the "complete moral corruption of the Austrian state." Nevertheless, Beethoven did not designate himself as a

German musician but as an "Austrian musician" (Letter of January 8, 1812). And in 1809, one reads in Beethoven that he would never "cease counting himself among the Austrian artists." At this time, the Austrian Emperors were no longer German Emperors. But Austrian soil was always being considered universal by anyone who made his residence there.

This conception of Vienna and Austria rose, in the sixteenth and seventeenth centuries, to brilliant heights, and with it, the conception of a musical city whose task it was to cultivate music in the largest and most universal sense.

III

The highpoint of this development was achieved between 1640 and 1740. Music appeared in all phases of Viennese life.

Between 1640 and 1740, four Austrian Emperors were themselves composers, Ferdinand III (1637-1657), Leopold I (1658-1705), Joseph I (1705-1711) and Charles VI (1711-1740). The Thirty Years War, the Turkish Wars, the War of the Spanish Succession, did not hinder them from covering manuscript paper with notes. Leopold I left behind him sixty-seven church sonatas, one hundred and fifty-five opera arias, nine Theatrical Festivals, and seventeen collections of ballet music. When a member of the imperial house died, he would compose funeral music. Archdukes and Archduchesses were required to learn singing and dancing. Leopold's sisters, Marianne and Leonore, took part in the court cantata performances. In the city of the Music Emperor, musicians from everywhere had congregated. Browne, a traveler who journeyed through seventeenth century Europe, wrote in his account of Vienna that "there are so many musicians in Vienna" that "it would be difficult to meet more of them anywhere else."

The majority of these musicians were Italians. They were the court composers and conductors. The long line of these prominent court musicians begins with Giovanni Valentini (1629 or 1630), and progresses to Bertali (1605-1669), Johann F. Sances (1600-1697), Marcantonio Cesti (1666-1669), Antonio Draghi (1635-1700), P. A. Ziani (1706-1711), Antonio Caldara (1670-1736) and Francesco Conti (1682-1732). In addition, came Italians as court poets, among them the greatest Italian poet of his time, Pietro Metastasio; and the Burnacini family as theatre painters and festival designers. One understands how a biographer of Emperor Leopold I can say: "The German language is, in Austria, almost in a foreign country." Vienna where, under Leopold I, Spanish was spoken, was precisely more and something else than just a German city.

The whole glory of the court unfolded at opera performances. The number of opera and oratorio performances under Leopold I in the time between 1658 and 1705 was over four hundred. Twelve to fourteen new operas were performed between 1701 and 1711 under Joseph I. The scenery of these operas amazed the world. When Lady Montague visited Vienna, she wrote, on the opera, that never in all Europe had she seen anything which could compare with it in splendor and beauty. Opera performances were festival music at court christenings, engagements, weddings and birthdays. With their mixture of Greek mythology, arias, choruses and ballets, with scenic wonders, "flying machines" and numerous scene changes, with their homage to the Emperor, and their processions, they surely were colorful show-pieces, like the great ceiling paintings in the new Viennese palaces, where the heavens opened and all Olympus was visible.

The performance of Cesti's "Il Pomo Oro" (The Golden Apple) in 1666 was the wonder of all Europe. For this performance, a special theatre was built with three galleries, and with the portal of a Greek temple in front of the stage. On the canopy above the stage was the double-eagle of the Emperor with the sceptre and the imperial globe in his talons. In the orchestra sat Emperor Leopold, surrounded by halberd bearers, with his newly-married bride, the Spanish Infanta Margarita Teresa, and the entire court. In the opera's prelude, the might and brilliance of the court were celebrated. In the center of the stage stood an equestrian statue of the Emperor. On both sides, in pillared halls, were portraits of earlier Hapsburg rulers. In the clouds, "Austrian Fame" rode on Pegasus, accompanied by Amor and Hymen. On the stage, Austria's possessions—Austria, Hungary, Bohemia, Italy, Sardinia, Spain and America—sang. There was a festive atmosphere in the hall and on the stage. The opera formed a part of life, and was the jewel of a festive hour.

After the prelude, Burnacini's colored scenes unfolded: Earth, Heaven and the Underworld, temples, harbors, caves, woods and villas. In the sixty-seven scenes of the opera, there were always new wonders to be seen—lightning, rain, hail, the Furies fleeing in the Underworld, Neptune and Venus in their chariots, accompanied by Tritons and Nereids, the ship of Paris battling the sea-waves. At the end, all the members of the imperial house, past and present, appeared in the clouds and the chorus announced the great future of the children which would stem from this new marriage.

Music was entwined with all the events of court life. Ballets were introduced by opera scenes. Thus in 1681, on the Emperor's birthday, a "Baletto di Fate" (Ballet of Elves) was performed, and its introduction was a scene from Draghi's opera, "L'Albero del Ramo Oro" ("The Tree with the Golden Bough"). A year later, again on the Emperor's birthday, a ballet was performed, preceded by an opera scene, from "Li Tributi" (The Tributes) by Draghi. In 1685, there was still another birthday ballet for the Emperor. Vulcan, Peace and War sang their arias. There were similar operatic prologues and intermezzi in the Vienna court theatrical productions, and many of the opera scenes were sung by archdukes and archduchesses. When, in 1682, the ballet "Il Sogno delle Grazie" (The Dream of the Graces) was produced at the Castle of Laxenburg. Archduchess Marie Antonia and her ladies-in-waiting sang the arias and ensembles of the operatic introduction. Emperor Charles VI himself conducted opera performances at his court. A pompous man, he sat at the piano and directed the performance of Caldara's "Euristeo," in which archdukes danced in the ballet and nobles sang. The court poet, Zeno, paid the Emperor the compliment that he played like a professor, which pleased the Emperor far more than a victory on the battle-field.

The imperial summer palaces, too—the "Favorita" and Laxenburg—were the scenes of many opera, ballet and cantata performances. The last opera at "Favorita" was given in 1740. On that occasion, the opera "Zenobia" by the vice-conductor, Predieri, was performed. In the same year, Charles VI died, surrounded by music, in his summer palace. Wherever he traveled, his opera singers and orchestra accompanied him. In Linz, Prague, Wiener-Neustadt and in Oedenburg, there were court performances. When, in 1723, the imperial court journeyed to Prague for the Emperor's coronation, and, on the Empress's birthday, arrived at Znaim, a stage was erected on a wagon and Caldara's festival opera, "La Concordia dei Planeti" (The Concord of the Planets) was performed.

The imperial parks resounded with arias. In 1679, a Greek temple was built in the park of Schönbrunn, where Draghi's opera, "Il Tempio di Diana" (the Temple of Diana) was given for the Empress's birthday. Iphigenia sang her arias on the steps of the temple under the trees. In the same park, an opera by Draghi and Minato, "Il Trionfator di Centauri" was sung in 1674, and pixies, nymphs and centaurs danced under the trees. The sandstone statues which were erected later in the Park of Schönbrunn were all mythological opera figures. Similar statues, costumed as opera singers of the baroque period, stand on the walls of the Vienna nobles' palaces which were built during this period, as a reminder of the epoch where the atmosphere of every festive moment became music.

The great equestrian ballets did not lack music, arias and choruses. The most famous performance of this kind was "La Contesa di Aria e dell'Aqua" (The Contest of Air and Water) of 1667. The best theatre architect of Italy, Carlo Pasetti, was called to Vienna to stage the ballet. On the fortress square, he built a temple of Diana, made of marble, bronze and lapis lazuli, in which the chorus, hidden, sang. Court-conductor Bertali composed the music. The text of the operatic introduction was written by the court-poet, Francesco Sbarra. The performance began with an aria sung by "Fame," who, holding a golden trumpet, arrived on the festival square in the ship of the Argonauts, heralded by trumpet fanfares. Then came riders who performed jousts, and finally the Emperor himself as Roman Imperator, wearing a golden crown and gold breast-plates adorned with a rose formed of diamonds and topazes, carrying his gold sceptre. He rode a black horse whose bridle and saddle shimmered with precious stones. He was preceded by trumpeters, and behind him, the members of the Austrian nobility, whose robes were studded with jewels and whose horses were caparisoned with gold. They were followed by the sixty men of the Emperor's mounted body-guard, then a carriage drawn by eight white horses, and finally by four "Saltatori" (Dancers) whose horses walked in Spanish gait. The actual equestrian ballet commenced to the measures of the ballet-music which Heinrich Schmelzer had composed.

A few months later, a similar equestrian ballet was performed in the park of "Favorita." In this ballet, which had been composed by Cesti, the Emperor, with the Duke of Lorraine, also took part. Again the horses gleamed with gold and the riders with gems. On one of the carriages, "Germania" sat enthroned, the sceptre in her right hand, the globe in her left. On both sides of the goddess stood the Austrian provinces, with shield and sword. Germania sang an aria praising peace. Then followed the ballet of the Emperor, the Duke of Lorraine and the knights, and at the end, the

Emperor rode up to the Empress and paid her homage.

All these festivals and musical events were not entertainment or some special province parallel to existence, but life itself in its most festive hour. The Vienna Court Orchestra was the most famous in Europe. In the middle of the sixteenth century, it had thirty-six members; in 1705, one hundred and five; in 1723, one hundred and thirty-four. Emperor Leopold I allotted seven thousand more gulden to the orchestra than he did to the Imperial Privy Council—a total sum of thirty-six thousand gulden. Each day the orchestra played sonatas during meals in the palace, and on New Year's Day, when the court ate from golden dishes, special festive music was performed.

The last of the great musical emperors in Vienna was Joseph II. He had studied music with Gassmann and had Salieri as his adviser. Every day, according to schedule, he devoted an hour to music, and three times a week, opera excerpts were performed at which the Emperor accompanied on the piano and sang arias. Occasionally, he had music played in the Park of Schönbrunn where the people could listen. This was the Emperor who sat in the box of the National Theatre when Mozart played the piano there, and performed his "Marriage of Figaro" for the first time. Emperor Joseph's brother was the Archduke Maximilian who in 1785 was Elector of Cologne, and as such, was the Lord of young Beethoven. As member of this ruler's court orchestra, Beethoven wore its uniform—green frock coat, green breeches, white silk vest, shoes with black laces, and a sword. Like Haydn and Mozart, Beethoven, too, grew up in the baroque society which came to power in Vienna during the seventeenth century, and which transformed the imperial city into a musical city.

IV

There was a great deal of music, also, in the palaces of the nobility. After 1683, when the Turks had been expelled from Vienna, the aristocrats built, in the city and its environs, their large new palaces with Caryatides framing wide portals, and mythological gods on the roofs. Prince Eugene had three palaces built, Prince Esterhazy three, the Princes Liechtenstein, two. The Lobkowitzes, Morzins, Waldsteins and Kinskys built in Prague. In 1683, the Esterhazys began a great castle in Eisenstadt, before whose gates their own soldiers kept watch; and in 1766, they built another castle on the Neusiedler Lake which could only be compared with the Palace of Versailles. Its magnificent park had a theatre and a marionette theatre. Many of these palaces had their places in musical history. Gluck and Mozart conducted performances in the Auersperg Palace in Vienna. Haydn conducted in the Esterhazy Palace, and was resident conductor at Count Morzin's summer palace. As a young musician, Gluck was at home at the Lobkowitz Palace in Prague.

Even in Leopold I's time, there were aristocrats in Vienna who composed. Baron Storzenau composed ballet music for one of Draghi's operas (1699). Heinrich Gottfried von Kielmannseg wrote an overture for a Serenade which was held in 1681 at the "Favorita." Nobles and emperors were musicians. Where else in the world had there ever been anything like this?

In Moravia, Count Johann Adam von Questenberg built a castle in Jarschmeritz where he engaged instrumentalists for performing operas, whom he had ordered from Vienna, Venice, Rome and Parma. His conductor was his valet, Mitscha, who composed operas, congratulatory cantatas, ballets and church music. In 1728, the music-loving count ordered an opera by Court-Conductor Caldara for which the honorarium was two hundred and fifty gulden. Count Rottal of Holleschau, Moravia, also maintained an orchestra during Charles VI's reign. Holzbauer, the symphonist, was a member of this orchestra before he went to Mannheim and there became a predecessor of Haydn. Another Mannheim composer, Franz Xavier Richter, like Holzbauer, played in the Holleschau Orchestra before establishing himself in Mannheim. Each of these castles was a center of culture from which music poured forth.

Music spilled forth, too, over all the Austrian provinces, from the churches, monasteries and the ecclesiastically-directed cloister schools. The importance of the ecclesiastical school in the development of Vienna as a music city is still scarcely appreciated. One must only consider that in the seventeenth century in Austria, the teaching in high schools and universities lay entirely in the hands of the clergy, and that music there was a very important subject, to realize the meaning of these schools. All the aristocrats whom we have met as enthusiastic friends of music were educated in such schools.

In Vienna and Austria of the seventeenth century, ecclesiastical society developed side by side with the worldly. Like the worldly, ecclesiastical society was powerful, brilliant and wealthy. The old monastic buildings of the Danube valley and of the woodland valleys of the Austrian Alps were always rebuilt in the magnificent baroque style which, in Rome, had become the expression of a new and passionate Catholicism. At the beginning of the seventeenth century, new monasteries were built in Vienna. Ferdinand II, the fanatical general of the Counter-Reformation in Austria, endowed the building of the Capuchin Monastery where the Hapsburgs were laid to rest (1632) and the Carmelite Cloister in Vienna (1632). He had a great church and school building erected for the Jesuits (1628-1631), and a church and monastery for the Netherland Paulist monks. His successor, Ferdinand III, built the cloister of St. Anna, the Augustine monastery of St. Rochus and the new Dominican Church (1631). Leopold I had the Carmelite monastery of St. Joseph built. He had the old gothic church of the "Nine Angel Choirs" in Vienna rebuilt in baroque style, like the professed house of the Jesuits nearby. At that time, the pompous facade with its angel figures, which is one of the great monuments of the Counter-Reformation, was constructed. The same emperor built the monastery of the Black Spanish monks, the house where Beethoven died during a thunderstorm; the Barnabite monastery of the White Spanish monks, the monastery of the Spanish Piarists. The widow of Ferdinanl III had the Ursuline Convent built.

In 1739, the rebuilding of the Melk Monastery began. When one travels along the Danube toward Vienna, one can see this mighty monastery from far off, where the Danube bends toward the woods and vineyards of the Wachau. The great baroque terrace overlooks the Danube valley, and between the summer vestry, which had been decorated with light frescoes by the theatrical engineer of the court, Beduzzi, and the library, stood the Diezenhofer church. This monastery is like a fortress of baroque Catholicism, splendid and festive, like theatrical decoration.

Not far from this most beautiful of all monasteries is the monastery of St. Florian, which had been begun in 1686 by Carlone of Milan, with a wonderful stairway, marble pillars, Gobelins and frescoes, and with the beautiful church, and the organ under which, as he had wished, Anton Bruckner's coffin was laid to rest. From this his church stems the colored gleam of the Bruckner symphony since the Austrian baroque spirit had lasted into Franz Josef's time.

V

There was, of course, music in all these churches. It was the festive church music of the seventeenth century, with many choirs, brilliant orchestra and arias full of feeling. Music was zealously cultivated. In the Kremsmuenster Monastery, Italian operas were performed by students in the monastery theatre. From this period, 1651-1780, more than one hundred text-books of such opera performances have come down to us. Young monks were sent by the monastery to Italy for musical training. The same practice held true in the monasteries of Lambach and St. Florian. Leopold I attended an opera performance at St. Florian in 1680. In Salzburg, the Benedictine University was opened, and in 1636, the Archbishop presented it with a great hall and stage where ecclesiastical plays with music were produced. Another small theatre was opened at the university in 1657, a third large theater with twelve back-drops in 1662. Forty poet monks who wrote plays for this theatre are known to us, and thirty composers. All these theatrical pieces were operatic in character. Figures from Greek history and Roman sagas were the main personages involved. Genii came flying through the air and sang arias of homage to the Archbishop, who sat in the orchestra with the clergy. In one of these plays, which took place in the period of the Turkish Wars—"Corwin," produced in 1688—there are thirty-eight vocal roles which were sung by students and singers of the court. Mozart had seen such plays at the Salzburg University Theatre. When he later composed the "Magic Flute," he remembered this well, for his charming, fairy-tale opera originates in this type of ecclesiastical opera of the baroque time.

The most important clerical order of the seventeenth century was the Jesuit. Almost all Austrian teaching lay in the hands of this order which had placed all the modern means of the theatre and of opera in the service of educating the young. The most famous of the Jesuit schools in Rome— the "Collegium Germanicum," had its musical tradition. Carissimi had been active there as conductor. Ecclesiastical operas were splendidly produced there, and similar performances were given in all Jesuit schools, in order to win souls for Catholicism, or to reconvert them. In Vienna, the Jesuit performances comprised the second Court Opera Theatre. The Emperor was regularly present, and with him, the entire court. In 1620, the Jesuits built their own theatre in Vienna, and in 1650, a small practice-theatre for the students. Young Gluck received his first impressions of opera at a Jesuit school in Komotau, Bohemia.

During Leopold I's reign, in the Jesuit theatre in Vienna, the work, "Pietas Victrix" of the South Tyrolean Jesuit poet, Avancini, was given. This ecclesiastical festival opera dealt with the victory of Christianity over the Roman Emperor Constantine. It was a festival play, with opera music, dance and stage mechanics. One saw land and sea battles, flying angels, and heard the arias and choruses of the students. A prologue began the piece, and an allegoric intermezzo glorified the verity of Catholicism. The division of the place of action into a heavenly and earthly world, as was customary in Jesuit pieces, had its effect upon the Vienna folk theatre. One can still find this division in the fairy-plays of Raimund. Goethe, too, employs the device in "Faust." Thus lasting effects upon theatrical history have been produced by these Jesuit pieces.

The spiritual plays which were performed during Lent in the Vienna churches, and especially in the Court Chapel, also had operatic forms. In every Viennese church, a holy sepulchre was put up during Holy Week, before which the devout prayed. Behind the sepulchre a stage was erected, on which there was a cross; and beneath it Mary, the saints and allegoric characters sang of penance and redemption in opera arias. All the Italian court poets of Vienna, like Minato, Stampiglia and Pariati, made texts for these spiritual operas, and the court-composers wrote the music. Emperor Ferdinand III's widow, Eleanora, specially furthered these spiritual operas. She wrapped herself in a veil of gloomy piety and spent her last years in the cloister of the Ursulines. Holy services and pious meditation filled her life. The court-composer Draghi wrote ecclesiastical operas for her which were performed in the chapel during Easter Week. Even when she traveled, she never missed an opportunity of hearing religious operas. When she journeyed to Prague in 1680, her orchestra had to perform opera by Draghi and Minato on Holy Thursday. It was called "La Sacra Lancia" (The Holy Spear). The Catholic Church militant, Austria, Bohemia and allegorical figures like "Regret" and "Devotion" sang in this ecclesiastical opera, which was in costume. The scene must have looked like one of Guido Reni's pictures, with its saintly figures, come to life upon the opera stage.

Sometimes members of the nobility sang leading roles in these operas. In 1689, "Le Cinque Virgine" was performed at the monastery of St. Joseph in Vienna. The main roles were sung by the Countesses Czernin, Rappach, Fuersteinberg, Kinigl, and Opperdorf. In 1723, on the birthday of Charles VI, the "Melodrama di Sancto Wenzeslao" was given at the Jesuit monastery in Prague. The music was written by the Czech composer, J. D. Zelenka in which the Bohemian St. Wenceslaus sang Italian arias.

VI

The "people" of Vienna were separated from this courtly-aristocratic society. Only the music of the churches was equally accessible to both strata of Viennese society since, as in Italy, the church was the concert hall of the people.

Everywhere on Austrian soil during the seventeenth century, we encounter the music of the folk—or better, the music of the nations who were united in Austria. The ballet conductor of Emperor Leopold I, Heinrich Schmelzer, made use of much of this folk-music in his works. One time one finds an "Aria Viennese," another time "Hannakische Themen" (in the Kremsiere Suites); another time an "Aria Styriaca." In Hungarian manuscripts of the seventeenth century, one finds Hungarian dances, Slovakian songs and dances, and gypsy music; a Wallachian dance and several Polish dances. Naturally, the greater part of this folk-music was not written down. It was played at village inns, fairs and weddings by folk-musicians upon whom the art-musicians looked down. In 1839, Lanner, the originator of the Viennese waltz, was rejected by the Vienna Union of Musicians—the "Tonkunstlersocietat," because "he's in dance music." Only in Haydn does this folk-music flow out into symphonic form, and in Bruckner, who had played at peasant weddings in his youth— in the scherzi of his symphonies.

The Viennese folk sang the songs which the "Hanswurst" (Harlequin) sang in the folk theatres. In 1686, the first "Song Book" was printed in Vienna. In 1683, the melody of the "Prince Eugene Song" was known all over Vienna, and even in the pious pieces of the Jesuit theatre, songs in Viennese dialect were interpolated; and in 1685, Viennese market-scenes were performed with songs as "Intermezzi."

Thus Viennese music, even in the seventeenth century, had its foundation of folk-like quality. It had strong roots in the earth, in the fields and woods, and grew from here, a century later, into the music of Haydn, Mozart, Beethoven and Schubert. Only thus did music become a great whole. Only in this way did Vienna become a music city. Only thus did Haydn's symphonies, Mozart's "Entführung aus dem Serail" ("Abduction from the Seraglio")and "Magic Flute," Beethoven's dance themes, Schubert's "Heidenröslein," the waltzes of Lanner and the two Strausses come into being. The great, festive, brilliant style of the baroque which loses none of its strength in Bruckner, and the liveliness of the folk-music together left their marks on Vienna's music and music-making.

To the wealth and the originality of their folk-music, Vienna and Austria owes the fact that here alone, of all the other cities and lands of Europe, the great Italian period of the seventeenth century did not remain a passing episode. Classical music drew everything together on Viennese soil— great baroque music and folk-music. In works in a grand manner, Viennese classical music is always baroque, because all forms of baroque are employed in it. Though the religious atmosphere of baroque music changed into a philosophical, humanistic atmosphere, in the greatest works by classic masters, in the adagios of Haydn string quartets and symphonies, in Mozart's "Requiem" and "Magic Flute," in Beethoven's Ninth Symphony, in Hugo Wolf's "Ecclesiastical Songs" and "Michel Angelo's Songs," the full religious baroque atmosphere is still there. Baroque brilliance and feeling flows through all of Mozart's music and gives it its sunny brightness. Bruckner unconsciously returns to baroque style which had been imparted to him at the festival masses at Linz and St. Florian by the swelling organ sound and by his own strong Catholic faith. Vienna has always remained a baroque city. When one analyzes art, whether music—as it is here the case—or theatre, painting or architecture, one keeps encountering its baroque sources, just as one finds in the features of grandchildren the traits of their ancestors. Just as Viennese life and social order maintained their seventeenth century forms until 1918, these forms were preserved in music until the first World War, the social and political battles, the revolution of the world, and the great revolutionist, the Viennese Arnold Schönberg, destroyed the old order by force.

VII

We wished to recognize the law of life of the music city, and trusted ourselves to the direction of history. Now the time has come to draw conclusions. Before us as an entity lies the musical life of the great city. From the end of the sixteenth century on to the beginning of the twentieth, it is these same musical forces which were active in Vienna. Generations come and go. The law remains.

We call this law, too, the personality of a city. Cities are living beings—"Stamped from that living develops," as Goethe put it. We say the names: Rome, Naples, Florence, Athens, Paris, London—and the cities rise up in our minds. They have their distinguishing, outstanding features like impressive people who, upon entering a room, immediately attract attention to themselves. Such a city is musical Vienna. Even in the seventeenth century, its definite individuality could be noted when all Europe began to recognize it as a city which was destined to make music which belonged to the world.

There were three things which caused Vienna to appear, then, as the great music city. First, it was not a national city, and not the center of life of a single nation, but an international city. It was the cross-roads of Europe to which not only peoples and goods journeyed, but also ideas and artworks.

Second, Vienna connected music closely with life and drenched it with music. High society as well as common people adorned their whole lives with music. Vienna was unique in this connection of every-day life with music. The whole city was like a sounding-board and vibrated with music like an Italian violin.

Third, only in Vienna was the music of the folk the foundation of the great musical life. In Vienna, folk-music nourished opera, symphony, chamber-music and art songs. There is no city in Europe where the case has been similar.

From this, the following conclusions for the future of Vienna's music life may be drawn:

Of all the foundations on which musical life in Vienna has been developed for more than three centuries, one has been preserved unchanged: the folk-earth from which Vienna's music has grown. Vienna's old society has been destroyed. There is no Emperor, no court, no nobility, no feudal society. The baroque Vienna is only a memory, a closed chapter of history, of which only the old buildings, the palaces and churches remind us. After the upheavals of the great wars, in Vienna the society of the people will come to power and complete the rising which began about 1900. The character of the Viennese man of the people has not changed in the course of time. From the middle ages to the nineteenth century, it has kept its essential qualities and will also survive the great social revolutions of our time.

There are two more conditions which are demonstrated by Vienna's musical history. Vienna did not become a great musical town on a national basis, and it can only become a great musical town again on a super-national basis. Now, as before, the destiny of Vienna is pre-designed by its geographical situation on Europe's largest river which flows from west to east, and on whose banks various nations make their homes. Only as a European music town which absorbs and forwards all movements of European intellectuality can Vienna again become a music city which means something to everybody. Since the world in this age of telegraph, radio and airplanes, has become much smaller, this task is an easier one than it was in the past. Europe has become small and the countries on the other side of the ocean have moved much closer. This will enrich the spiritual life of Vienna. It will be able to remain a world town in the field of intellect if it preserves its talent of absorbing what new and great things are created in the world. And if, after the comparatively short period during which German Nationalism has oppressed Vienna, it again finds its unprejudiced sense for the characteristics of other nations, it will again discover its peaceful and human way of thinking.

The third condition for the re-emergence of Vienna as a music town is its capability of combining music with folk-society and daily life. Vienna had already proved after World War I that it possessed the will and ability to foster music as a public task. It was conscious of its mission and one can expect that the old city of world music will clearly recognize that it will have to assemble all its powers to make music for the world on its new social basis: the powers of the state, of the city and of the representatives of the people.

That is what history teaches. Out of war and devastation, need and social struggles, a new time is dawning, a new music and a new relationship between music and society. The old music city has become a legend which, like all legends, enchants us with its color and splendor. And if I told that legend, it was in order to show where the path to the future is leading. It would be bold to try to predict this future. We can only wish, hope and work. Vienna still stands as the old city, the same friendly landscape still surrounds it, the same people still live there, and the same river flows by. The same music is in the earth and in the air, in rustling leaves and rushing wind, in Beethoven's forests and in Schubert's vineyards, in Hugo Wolf's gardens and Anton Bruckner's churches. Great composers may hear this music and listen to the melodies. It is they who will add a new chapter to the glorious old book: "The Legend of a Musical City," the leaves of which the roaring storm of our time is turning up.